# CATFISH

A rookie detective murder mystery

# SADIE NORMAN

THE
BOOK
FOLKS

Published by The Book Folks

London, 2024

© Sadie Norman

ISBN  978-1-80462-229-2

www.thebookfolks.com

*CATFISH is the first book in a series of standalone mysteries by Sadie Norman.*

# Prologue

The very night held its breath in anticipation as she led the way through the empty park. Her hand was tangled in his. She felt giddy with a euphoric high she hadn't experienced since her days of youthful transgressions. How things had changed, how life had caught up with her, demanding so much and giving so little back. Tonight, she was willing to ignore the responsibilities and let loose.

Shadows watched them, the only two people for what felt like miles around. The park was untroubled, calm – its monuments and trees standing steadfast as the lovers hastened along the paths. Glimpses of the town rose over the treetops, serving as a reminder that this whirlwind of a romantic fantasy would be over at some point.

The man held his shoulders stiffly as she pulled him into the shadowy culvert of the medieval chapel sat in the middle of the park. It wasn't a bed, but it would do. She'd waited too long for this. He hadn't said much, but from his body language he was eager, ready to engage in whatever salacious ideas she put forward.

Falling back against the ancient bricks, she pulled him closer, kissing him whilst simultaneously hitching up her skirt. She hooked her leg round his hip. She felt something in his pocket, firm and metallic maybe, but it was of no consequence soon enough. They fell into a rushed rhythm. Either he was so keen he couldn't help himself or he had somewhere better to be. She didn't really care which it was.

When finished, he pressed her against the wall, catching his breath. Not great but better than her usual hook-ups. A bit more romance, a bit more effort, and she could almost convince herself that this was an actual relationship, rather than another bloke wanting to get his end over, which was all they ever wanted. Usually that worked to her advantage but sometimes, very occasionally, it started to get a bit lonely. She wasn't the wife or the real-life girlfriend. She never would be.

He fumbled in his pocket, pulling out the firm object. It was too dark to see what it was.

"You don't know how long I've waited for this," he whispered into her ear, still pressing her firm against the wall.

"For what?" she asked. It was done now. Any chance of an intimate dinner or moonlit walk was over. A tryst in the park was all she was worth.

Something glinted in the moonlight. Whatever he held in his hand was small and shiny. A lock knife?

At first it didn't even hurt, just the feeling of freezing ice spreading through her abdomen. Then there was another, and another. He kept going, until the iciness turned to warmth as liquid spilled down her front, trickling down her legs. Blood. Her blood.

"Wh–" Her words were stolen as she gazed at those haunted eyes. The millions of questions killed the excitement dead, and then the questions faded when her mouth betrayed her.

Why me? she thought. Why me?

The knife flashed once more in the light, slick with blood. It came to her chest, trailing along the exposed flesh.

Why me?

# Chapter One

Charlie Sweeney was the most boring person I'd ever met. He was boring when we were eighteen and I sat next to him in politics class at college, forced to do so by the ancient lecturer who still believed seating should go boy-girl-boy-girl. Now, eleven years later, he was still just as agonisingly dull as he was back then.

I swilled my glass of wine, watching the rosé swish in the bottom. I could easily go for another but given how expensive this bar was, I couldn't warrant it, even if Charlie did end up being the gentleman and picking up the tab at the end of this excruciating date. Surely, he could afford it – he'd already told me all about his equally boring job. Insurance accountant... No, insolvency accountant. Either way, he earned more than I did, so I just nodded and sipped from my glass, as Charlie finally finished off his decade-old story of his gap year in Uganda.

"Am I boring you, Anna?" he asked, catching me yawn. "You've been yawning for the last half-hour."

I hastily shut my mouth. "No, sorry. It's... well, I haven't stayed out this late in a while."

Actually, I hadn't been *out* in a while.

Charlie eyed me, his expression turning sickeningly pitiful as he met my gaze. Up until now he'd been the talker, not able to look at me without his pasty white skin blushing with such intensity that I wondered if he would catch fire. He'd filled the awkward silences with inane chatter, but now, he waited. He was really going to make me say it.

"I haven't been out much since... you know. The incident." I rubbed a spot on my shoulder, which began burning at the words. My cheeks glowed as embarrassment seeped in, which was ridiculous, as I had nothing to be embarrassed about.

Charlie pouted. "Yeah, my mum told me about it. Nasty business. Did they ever catch the guy?"

I shook my head and downed the last of my drink. There was no way I would get out of this date without having to talk about the shit turn my life had taken.

"Shame," he said, which was a mild way of putting it. "Mum said you were working on a big case at the time."

"Yep." It was actually the big case that caused the incident; a spate of random attacks on young women. I was one of a handful of detectives drafted to help the Serious Crimes team with the case.

"When will you be going back to work?" Charlie asked.

"My bosses say the position is still there for me when I return. I just need to…"

The words trailed away. There were a lot of things I needed to do. Firstly, I needed to recover – the wounds were gone but the niggling pain remained. The dent to my confidence was worse. I had a long way to go before I could consider attempting the evaluations needed to get back on the ground and return to work in the police.

"What station were you based at?" At least Charlie didn't press the subject.

"Here, in King's Lynn. At the Investigation Centre outside of town."

With a nod, I poured the last drop of wine onto my tongue and ached for more. I glanced through the wide, tinted windows of the bar, where the Saturday night revellers were starting to pour out into the street, and I felt an uncomfortable pang of sorrow.

I missed it. I missed my old days on the beat, patrolling the streets and responding to calls. Telling the same old drunks to go home and telling them again twenty minutes later, until finally one of us relented and either they left or I arrested them. I missed my career, indefinitely stalled while I was finding my niche as a detective.

I wished I was back out there, breaking up a drunken fight outside the pub rather than on a date with Charlie Sweeney.

Charlie was a sweet guy, really, and I had nothing against that. He'd plucked up the courage to ask me out after months of badgering from his mother Marie, who was close friends with my own mum, Susan. With their precious children approaching thirty and still single, the pair of them were getting antsy for grandbabies. Sometimes I wished I had siblings, so that they could share in my misery as well.

With the wine all gone and the bar emptying out, I was anxious to make a move. The night had drawn in hours ago, the rustic mood-lighting of the trendy wine bar only succeeding in making me strain my eyes and feel even more dozy. Charlie made no move, not even a shuffle in his seat. He wasn't ready to end this nightmare yet.

"Excuse me," I said as I got up from the tacky table. Why were tables in bars always sticky? "I'll be right back."

Snatching up my first-date handbag, I turned for the toilets, passing the barman who gave me a sympathetic smile, and the hostess, glowering at me for still taking up a table. Inside the restroom, luminous lighting shocked me awake. I ignored the temptation to check myself in the mirror – I had made minimal effort for this date – and instead checked my phone.

Nope. Nothing. Of course not.

I slipped my phone into my bag and sighed. This was pointless. I should have been honest with Charlie and told him I wasn't interested. The spark wasn't there, blah blah blah. It was clichéd but it was true, although also a little disappointing. Looking for love wasn't on my agenda when the rest of my life was in tatters, but something had to go right for me at some point.

I shook away the self-pity from my mind. It was so easy to let it set in and sink its claws into me and not let go. I'd battled it for ten months now and was afraid it was winning. It was the owner of the little voice in the back of my mind, telling me I wasn't good enough – smart enough, fast enough, careful enough – to return to work, and I never would be. It was the constant ache in my shoulder, piercing from back to front, following the line of the knife. I could shake it away but it would come creeping back eventually.

This was no good. I could be miserable here, or be miserable at home, where at least I didn't have to listen to Charlie's stories or face the judgemental looks of people I didn't know. I needed to get out of here. I needed some fresh night air and my own company.

Back in the bar, Charlie's eye lit up as I approached, but his smile dropped as I picked up my jacket and folded it over my arm.

"Time to call it a night," I said. The words brought with them a relief I hadn't expected. No more pressure to socialise, to pretend I liked him or enjoyed his company.

"Oh." He rose to his feet, hastily finishing his glass of red wine. "Can I walk you to your car?"

"There's no need," I said with a shake of my head, making sure his impression of me was set. I was not a damsel in distress, scared of the night and the things hidden within it. I'd faced worse than he could imagine. If anything, he needed me to walk *him*.

With a hasty, awkward goodbye, and a promise to text him when I made it home, I left the bar and headed out onto Norfolk Street. Even though the street was alive with revellers, I turned my back on it all and strode on, keen to get away. A midnight walk might clear my mind enough to dismiss the cloud of melancholy.

It was worth a try, so I made my way through town, ducking my head as I passed two patrolling officers who would probably recognise me, and headed for the darkest, gloomiest place I could think of.

Twenty minutes later, I was finally alone in the still night, the sounds of revelry now in the distance. The street lights on the main promenade of The Walks sparkled like lanterns in a mine, guiding my way through the urban park. They looked like old-fashioned gas lamps, making me wonder if I'd somehow stepped back in time. The odd star poked through the cloudy night and light pollution. I felt lighter away from the bar.

I didn't know this place well, even less under the cover of night, and my hasty walk brought back memories of policing the town Bonfire Night celebrations in the park several years before. The event was a pickpocket's wet dream, but I hadn't taken in the scenery as I chased the miscreants through The Walks. Tonight, it was serene, not even a tree branch swaying. I passed a manicured garden, with a water fountain in the centre turned off for the night. It was calm; a bit too calm for my liking, reminding me of a horror movie before the killer attacks. But at least the calm night was less stifling than the bar and the pressures of forced socialisation.

At the end of the illuminated path, I came upon an ancient stone gateway, a piece of history almost lost to the ages. Beyond, more parkland lay in the shadows, trees lining the way like giants watching over the town.

I stopped and listened. There was nothing; no rustle of people, no quiet whispers. I was alone at last.

To my left, the path extended round to a deeper shadow that sat on the crest of a slight hill, sucking in all light that touched it like a black hole. I approached it, conscious that the only sound was the scuff of my feet on the gravel path. It was the Red Mount – an octagonal medieval chapel, sitting squat on its post like a guardsman overlooking the park, untouched by the moonlight. Something prickled my senses, urging me to approach with caution. Was there someone there? There couldn't be, the night was still and I was completely alone, but I could still feel something. A glint caught my eye.

The path veered off, leading up to the door of the chapel, but another sat below it, buried into the ground.

An entrance to a cellar perhaps, I didn't know. The monument watched me, leaning over like a god from above.

At the foot of the chapel, buried into the hill, a figure was slumped against the door. So, I wasn't alone.

It was a woman with fiery hair and bright-red lips. Her pale skin was almost translucent in the moonlight. She wore a purple miniskirt and black strappy top, but both of those were hard to distinguish under the blood that covered her torso and limbs and seeped into the gravel. Blood oozed from her wounds but she was statue-still, dead under the stars. Against my instincts, I crept forwards, taking her cold hand to feel for a pulse but coming away with only slick blood on my fingertips. She'd been butchered and abandoned, repeatedly stabbed and left to die.

Only her white face was free from the carnage, lips parted as though in protest as she stared wide-eyed at the sky, ready to argue with the night.

## Chapter Two

Rhythmic, repetitive flashes of cold blue light pierced through The Walks, casting long, engulfing shadows along the ground. With nothing else to do other than sit on a cold bench and observe, I watched the well-oiled machine of the local police as it sprang into action.

Within half an hour of my call, at least six police cars and forensic vans lined the pedestrian paths. A rather large response for a small, unexciting town. Scene cordons were set up around me, by the ancient gateway and each entrance to the park. Scene-of-crime officers donned their white suits and headed off for the darkened corner of the chapel where the woman lay.

"Anna?" someone asked. A police officer sat down next to me and removed her bowler hat. It was Maddie, one of my old shift colleagues. She peered at me through the dark and rested her hands in her stab vest. "What are you doing here?"

I used to enjoy working with Maddie. She was one of the more sensible officers around; happy to keep her head down and not partake in the usual pissing competitions some others did. However, her penchant for keeping her head down meant she didn't usually like to work with me.

"Hey, Maddie. Sorry for dragging you out here on a Saturday night." My breath drifted off on the night air.

"*You* found the body?" Maddie asked, a sceptical look crossing her face and making her thoughts as obvious as reading a book. Out of all the people in the world, it would be me.

I nodded. I still couldn't shake the shock I felt from finding the poor woman. All I had wanted was a walk to clear my mind, maybe dismiss my depression, but instead I found myself faced with someone whose life had been ripped away in the most violent way possible.

"I would ask you what happened," said Maddie, rolling her big brown eyes, framed by thick, unnatural lashes, "but I think you know this is a bad one. Serious Crimes will be dealing with it. You can give your statement to them."

I knew the Serious Crimes team. I'd worked with them on attachment and even hoped to join their unit one day; before my career took a nosedive, that was.

"Great," I said, not quite meaning it.

Maddie gave me a look. "How have you been?"

"Fine," I replied quickly. "Getting there."

"And the injury?"

I rolled my shoulder, where my stab wound pinged with pain. "Yeah, getting there."

"Think you'll be back soon?" She didn't sound hopeful. Maybe she didn't want me back on the force, dragging everyone along into my chaos.

I shrugged. "Hopefully."

Obligatory conversation out of the way, Maddie relaxed next to me and I followed her gaze to the SOCOs beside the chapel, luminated like ghosts in a haunted forest. They were working slowly; Maddie was right, this was a bad one. They would comb over every inch of this park to tease out any clues to help solve such a brutal murder.

"You're looking quite dressed up. Where have you been?" Maddie asked.

As innocent as she tried to sound, an involuntary shiver ran through me. The bloody station gossip vines were merciless and there was no privacy in this job. I supposed, since I'd been absent for several months now on sick leave, the gossipmongers were thirsty for news on me. And since Charlie was my alibi for the night, news about him would get out eventually.

"On a date," I replied.

"I knew it." Maddie's resting frown vanished with a look of triumph.

"How did you know?"

Her lips tightened, as though I was challenging her. "Well, there's the get-up for a start." She waved a hand at my outfit and make-up. "Then there's the fact you're here in town in the middle of the night. Come on then, tell us. Who with?"

"I think you're wasted here," I said to her, getting up to walk away before she tried to glean any more information out of me about the most boring date of my life. "You should take your detectives' exam, join Serious Crimes and give DCI Burns a run for his money."

"Oh, you haven't heard?" Maddie followed me, keen to not let me get too far ahead. We reached the end of the crime-scene cordon, where another officer guarded the entrance to the park. "He's not on Serious Crimes anymore."

I paused, mid-step. "He's not?"

Just as Maddie shook her head, ready to explain, a commotion from the roadside made her turn. At the entrance to the path, where the scene cordon blocked the rest of the world out, two people were making their way inside. I recognised them both.

Detective Inspector Chris Hamill was a grizzled detective, not through hard living or hitting the bottle, but through the sheer number of years he had been doing the job. He'd been on the Serious Crimes team as long as I could remember. Retirement was often whispered on the breeze as he passed, but I had a solid feeling that he would retire when he was dead and not a moment before. His dark eyes, so brown they were almost black, widened a little as he recognised me.

"Oh hell," he grumbled to his colleague. "This one will be trouble."

Next to him, Detective Sergeant Jay Fitzgerald rolled his eyes. The prodigy of the team, I always got the impression Jay fancied himself as a rock star. He had the good looks to go with it, with his coifed black hair and keen smile.

"Oh great. If Crazy McArthur is here, then this one's going to be a mess."

"I can hear you, you know," I said as the two stopped in front of us. What once would have been considered playful banter – an unimaginative nickname I'd earned over the years and failed to shift – was now less endearing. I would have happily given up the unwanted reputation if I had half a chance.

"Uh, *you* found the body?" Chris asked as he pulled a notebook and pen from his pocket.

"Yes." I ignored the inflections in his voice. Before I knew it, I fell straight back into the old pattern. "The victim is female. I'd say around thirty years old. Red hair, pale skin, no obvious distinguishing features. Death wasn't long ago, the blood is still wet, but it's hard to tell in the dark. There's a lot of blood, I mean a lot. No signs of a weapon or the perpetrator when I got here."

Three sets of bewildered gazes stared back at me, like I'd suddenly grown a second head. Of course, I cursed myself, I wasn't here as a police officer. I was the witness.

"Thanks for the update," said Chris, not looking thankful in the slightest. He put his notebook away. "What were you doing out here anyway?"

"Having a walk," I replied. "I'd just been on – or rather escaped from – a really boring date. I've been in The Lounge on Norfolk Street all night."

"And your date will back that up?"

"Of course." As if they actually believed I'd had anything to do with this death. I was supposedly 'crazy', not a murderer.

"What's someone doing out here in the park in the dead of night?" Jay asked, humming thoughtfully as he watched the SOCOs at work. "Homeless person?"

"Doubt it," I replied. "She didn't look much like a rough sleeper and the night shelter is just down the road."

"A mugging turned nasty?" Maddie suggested.

"We won't know more until the crime scene is swept and we find out who this woman is." Chris exchanged a look with Jay, making the latter nod in understanding. Then he faced me. "Thanks, Anna. You can go."

"Go?" I asked, the word sounding hollow in the night air. There were hours of work to do here at this scene.

Chris gave a curt nod, already turning away. "We'll call you in the morning for your statement."

"But I can help."

As the words left my mouth, I realised how ridiculous I sounded. I wasn't sure how I could help, not that I was even allowed to. I'd had the same conversation with my senior officers dozens of times over the last few months. I kept telling them I was fine, and I would slide right back into work without any problems. They didn't believe me. The only way I could prove myself to them was to complete an evaluation of my mental health. And there was no way I was passing that with this black cloud constantly hanging over my head.

"You can't," Chris said flatly, as though he expected my protests. "You're on leave."

"*Indefinite* leave," Maddie added.

"As I said, we'll call you in the morning."

And just like that, I found myself dismissed, ushered to the nearest exit of the park and swept under the crime-scene tape without another word.

With the town in front of me and the disturbed park behind me, I drew in a stiff breath of air. My shoulder niggled once again. I wondered how long I would have to put up with the twinges, the constant reminders of the incident which ruined my life. I was stuck in limbo; too well to sit by and do nothing, too unwell to return to work. Feeling the air held tightly in my lungs burning away, I headed home. As much as I longed to be reinstated, it wasn't that simple. I had a lot to prove and a reputation to overcome.

And now, a red-haired, red-lipped woman to haunt my dreams.

* * *

There was nothing else I could do. I declined the offer by Maddie to drive me home – in her words, to 'make sure I got home safe after the shock', but I suspected it was more to shoehorn some more gossip from me than actual concern for my well-being.

It was the early hours of the morning when I arrived home and let myself into the flat, flicking the light switch on. Nothing happened. I flicked it a few more times, just to be sure. In the darkness, I heard the cat rouse awake at my intrusion.

"Fuck's sake," I mumbled to myself, slipping my jacket and shoes off and heading into the dark. I meant to top up the electric meter while I was out – the ancient, warped plastic key was waiting in my handbag. I'd forgotten. I wondered who on Earth trusted me to be a functioning adult sometimes, when I couldn't even trust myself to keep the lights on.

I collapsed into bed, with mental images of the flame-haired woman to keep me company, only to be woken by my mobile phone beeping impatiently with three successive calls. Daylight now peeped around the edge of the curtains; I must've fallen asleep after all. I answered the last call on the last ring. There was only one person who would call me so relentlessly.

"What?"

"Don't *what* me," my mother said down the line. "Why weren't you answering?"

"I was asleep."

As if my groggy voice wasn't evidence enough, I groaned as I rolled over. The blouse I'd borrowed from her was wrinkled since I went straight to bed without undressing.

In my dreary state, I'd forgotten to shut the cat out of the bedroom. Poppy stirred as I accidentally kicked her and reared her calico head to glare at me. Poppy the cat wasn't my cat, but rather the flat's cat – she was a part of the tenancy agreement. Look after Poppy or find somewhere else to live. When she decided I wasn't feeding or pampering her enough, she would disappear for a few days to the downstairs neighbours, but she always found her way back into my home, regardless how many windows and doors I locked shut.

Sunlight streamed through the window of my flat as I threw open the curtains and blinked away the streaks in my vision. The flat was on the second floor of an old shop overlooking a quiet side street – the curtains were superfluous as there was little chance anyone could look in. Downham Market was a retirement town, quiet even at its busiest times, but that also meant the rent was dead cheap.

Poppy followed me to the kitchen, weaving herself round my legs, trying to murder me. She stopped when I placed half a can of cat food into her bowl on the kitchen floor.

"How did it go?" Mum asked me down the line, not bothering to hide the eagerness in her voice. "Did you have a late night?"

"Yes, but I probably ruined the mood when I ditched Charlie."

"Oh, Anna!"

"What? I can't help it; it was a work thing." I could already imagine my mum's face if I told her the full story about finding a dead body. According to her, it was my fault she had wrinkles.

"That job isn't the be-all and end-all. You need to start thinking of your future."

"I've had the last ten months to think about my future," I muttered back. And I didn't want it to be with Charlie.

"Life doesn't revolve around work," she chastised down the line. "When I was your age, I was already married and had you. You can't sit around, waiting for happiness to come to you. What work thing was it anyway? You're on sick leave. Oh, was it something to do with that body found next to the Red Mount Chapel?"

I frowned, not that Mum could see me. "How do you know about that?"

"Marie told me."

Of course, someone in my mother's gossip cartel would already have the scoop on the dead woman in the park. I waited for her to elaborate.

"Everyone's talking about it, The Walks is still closed. Anyway, you can tell me all about it later. Lunch is at one."

And before I had a chance to protest – which she knew I would – Mum hung up.

Now that the pesky Poppy was off my back, I jumped in the shower, letting the fresh water wake me up. I dressed, but dived deeper into my wardrobe for some actual clothes, rather than the joggers and hoodies I'd been living in for almost a year. Jeans and a cardigan. That would do.

I flicked the kettle on and found my favourite mug from the cupboard – a huge thing I'd been given as a Secret Santa present a few years before. But as I waited for the water to boil, I remembered – no electricity.

"For fuc–" My mobile phone pinged in the bedroom. I'd put it back on charge after talking to Mum, not that it would've charged at all with no electricity. I found the device, still clinging to life with 20% left, and a text from a number I hadn't bothered to save.

*Hi. Thanks for a super time last night. We should do it again. Free next weekend? Lemme know xx*

Charlie. I wrinkled my nose at the screen, unable to think of a suitable reply. Still in my hands, the phone pinged again with another message.

*You need to come in and give a statement. 10 a.m.*

Ah, short and simple and direct. That text definitely came from a colleague of mine. Only a police officer would lack the time to be polite or just miss off greetings altogether.

I pocketed the phone, found my keys and headed downstairs to my car. With each step a new anticipation grew, the same feeling I'd felt the night before as I watched my colleagues get to work. It was familiar and comforting, like putting the final piece into a puzzle and stepping back to see the finished article. I was heading to the police station, and for the first time in several months, I felt like I was heading home.

# Chapter Three

There were several routes to the King's Lynn Police Investigation Centre, but the shortest was along a series of potholed roads through endless fields. Bright-yellow rapeseed flowers shined in the golden summer sun on either side. As the fields ended and the town of King's Lynn came into view – a slight rise of urbanisation among the flat landscape – so did the steel, pointed angles of the modern police station. It stuck out like a sore thumb in the farmland surrounding it, a modern fortress overlooking the edge of the historic Fens. Factories and industrial units hid behind it, kicking out fumes that rose to meet the solitary clouds drifting by.

After a quick stop at one of the village shops on the way, to top up the meter key, I parked up and walked into the main entrance of the station. A tingle travelled down my neck as I crossed the threshold and found the sender of the text message waiting by the front desk. DCI Aaron Burns leaned against the desk with a mug of coffee in each hand, and a schooled expression on his face as he listened to the front-desk officer babble away. I took a moment to survey him before he realised that I was there. He looked no different to the last time I'd seen him, ten months before. Broad-shouldered and what I was sure was once firm muscle, now softened after several years working behind a desk. Fair hair was whitening around the edges of his clean-shaven face, where the odd wrinkle was starting to show as middle age hit.

He spotted me and straightened up.

"Well, if it isn't Calamity Jane." He held out a mug for me and I took it, grateful as the aroma of strong coffee hit me before suspicion started to creep in.

"I thought my nickname was Crazy McArthur."

"Oh, it is," Aaron replied. "But I thought we only called you that behind your back. Come on, let's get this over and done with."

He motioned for me to follow him and led the way into the inner sanctum of the station. We passed a large board, mugshots and grainy CCTV images staring back, reminding everyone of the area's most wanted. It was the usual mix of thugs responsible for the Saturday night assaults and a few higher-profile targets; human traffickers, county-lines operatives and such. I felt their beady eyes following me along the corridor, judging me like I was a criminal too.

An interview room was already prepared, the door propped open and waiting, and I dutifully filed inside. Aaron closed the door behind him and motioned for me to sit down. A few things had changed since I was last present; insignificant things that only highlighted how long I'd been away. New posters lined the walls. There were new chairs, these ones bolted to the floor.

Aaron sat down opposite me, taking a fraction of a second to watch me. "How have you been?"

"Fine," I said automatically. "Getting there."

Aaron didn't look at me with the same pity that others usually did. In fact, his expression was hard to read at all, barely changing from one emotion to the next. He rarely gave anything away and, despite the years we'd worked alongside each other on this small force, the only emotion I could ever be certain of from him was when he was well and truly furious.

"Do you miss work?"

"Of course." I had a pretty good poker face, but I was nothing compared to Aaron and I was certain he could see right through me. I didn't just miss work, I longed for it. The only thing holding me back was myself.

"Odd that you were the one to find the body then, out of all the people in town that night. Miss work so much you decided to make your own crime?"

"Are you kidding me?" I snapped. I set my mug down a little too hard on the table, creating an echoed clang and spilling the contents over the side. "Is that why I'm here, you think I killed that woman?"

Across the table, Aaron sniggered at me. "No. Come on, Anna, I'm winding you up. One of the first things we did was establish your whereabouts for the night. Jay checked the CCTV of the bar you were at, but you know that I'm still going to need the details of your date, so the team can follow it up and check."

I gritted my teeth; I missed work but I didn't miss the relentless wind-ups. Pulling my phone from my pocket, now hovering at 11%, I thrust it across the table at Aaron. "Here. Charlie Sweeney, there's his number. He texted me this morning to say what a good time he had. You can check right now if you want."

"All right." Aaron jotted down the number in his notebook, scanning my text messages as he went. "The guys will call him, but don't worry, you're not a suspect. I'm sure this Charlie will back that up."

"Yeah well… don't mess with me like that. I've had enough of my motives being scrutinised."

"All right, sorry." He didn't look sorry though.

A prickly silence fell over the room as Aaron continued to scroll through my messages with Charlie. I fought against the uncomfortable feeling that came with the invasion of my privacy.

"Was it a good date?" he asked.

"Huh?"

"Well, you haven't texted him back yet."

"It was fine," I said, snatching the phone back. "Not that it's any of your business."

"So, what were you doing in The Walks?"

"Walking."

"On your own?" Aaron raised his eyebrows and the self-consciousness started to creep up my back. "How did you find the victim?"

"I was just… walking. I saw a glint of light on the ground. She had a watch on, didn't she? It was reflecting the light from the street lights. I approached the mount, saw her, established she was dead, then retreated and called it in. I touched her to find a pulse but nothing else."

Aaron hummed at my story, but after a quick jot in his notebook, he closed it and I guessed he believed me.

"Is that all?" I asked when he didn't speak. "Can I go now?"

"Go? What's the hurry?" He narrowed his gaze at me. "You've been on leave for months, Anna. We haven't seen you. Tell me how things are."

"I told you, they're fine—"

"No." Aaron cut me off with a sharp look. "Don't bullshit me. Tell me the truth. Because I know you, and I know ten months off work has probably been torture. So, tell me really, how have things been? What's holding you back from returning?"

I stiffened under his gaze. Maybe it was the room; the atmosphere was meant to be thick and uncomfortable, after all. The walls, marked and battered, felt like they were closing around me. And the worst part was that there was no escape. The door was closed and Aaron's gaze was unwavering. There was no way I was getting out of answering that question.

"Things are…" I licked my lips, but it made no difference to my dry mouth. "The same. Everything is healed, but it still aches." I rolled my shoulder and the pain twanged all the way up my neck. "Other than that, it's fine. As soon as I'm signed off for active duty, I'll be back."

"Well, you won't get signed off for active duty if you don't take your psych eval," said Aaron. "You've missed the last two appointments. Why are you delaying it?"

"I don't know," I mumbled back. "Something's in my mind, telling me I'm not ready. Physically, I'm all healed, but mentally…"

As the sentence drifted away, lost to the consuming silence of the room, I realised that was probably the first time I had admitted that out loud.

"You know," said Aaron, his calm voice filling the void, "a lot has changed around here in ten months."

"Like what? There's still a job for me, right?"

"Of course," Aaron said hastily. "In fact, we need you now more than ever. I don't know if anyone told you, but Superintendent Russell retired six months ago."

"He did?" Something Maddie said the day before popped back into my mind: *Oh, you haven't heard? He's not on Serious Crimes anymore.* "You got promoted to superintendent?"

But Aaron grimaced. "Not exactly. I'm still detective chief inspector but now station lead. And that leaves Serious Crimes a person short and, to be honest, they're drowning under the workload. I'm worried this stabbing in the park might tip them over the edge. They need some help."

He looked at me expectantly, as if I could read his thoughts. I frowned back.

"You want me to help them?"

Aaron nodded. "Your investigative skills are good and your attachment to the team during the Ali Burgess case gave you enough experience of how they work. You'd be an asset, Anna."

"But I haven't passed my psych evaluation."

My shoulder twinged. Aaron watched me as I rubbed it, but he didn't look sly, like this was another crap joke at my expense. That gave me a bit of hope. Maybe he really did think I could be an asset.

"That's something we can keep quiet for now. Working this case will be off the record but it'll be helpful all round. It'll relieve the pressure off Chris and Jay, and who knows, maybe it will help a bit with your confidence. You're a good copper, Anna. Crazy but good. This force needs you as much as you need it."

For the first time in as long as I could remember, I smiled. The action felt strange but natural at the same time. Someone out there thought I wasn't a complete walking disaster, that I could actually be useful.

"But," Aaron continued, "if you ever do anything like you did during the Ali Burgess case again, I'll kill you myself. Got it?"

My smile fell and I nodded. Yeah, I got it. The back of my shoulder niggled away, a constant reminder that what I did during the Ali Burgess case was an idiotic move. But the small seed of self-confidence remained. I gripped tightly to it, desperate for any hope that somehow, deep down, I was still a good police officer. And now Aaron was giving me the chance to prove it.

"Good." He rose to his feet, satisfied that I was serious.

I stood up too and as Aaron opened the door, the noise of the station filled the silence, a shrill phone ringing and muffled shouts coming from the cells. The whole building operated like a machine with hundreds of different parts, and I was finally about to reclaim my small piece.

Aaron paused at the door and held out his hand, as if to shake my hand and thank me for my time. He quickly changed his mind and dropped it down, but I saw the small hints of a grin on his face, his eyes crinkling at the corners.

"I'm glad you're back, Anna."

"Me too," I replied as I banished the doubt starting to creep back in. "Me too."

# Chapter Four

We didn't get far into the station before we ran into the Serious Crimes team, all two of them. DI Chris Hamill looked no more impressed to see me than he did the night before, whilst DS Jay Fitzgerald flashed me a grin and looked expectantly at Aaron.

"Hey, Anna," he said. "Well, what's the verdict?"

"She'll help," Aaron replied. "Just confirm her alibi with her date and then set her to work."

He handed a scrap from his notebook to Jay, who gave a curt nod before hurrying off to call Charlie. He left behind an awkward silence, repelling the bustle of the station like we were in a bubble.

Chris glowered at Aaron, his glare speaking volumes. "A word." He motioned with a jerk of his head before stalking away.

With a slight roll of his eyes, Aaron sighed and followed.

Left in the middle of the station corridor, I strained to hear what was being said about me. Snippets drifted by, Chris snapping phrases like 'liability' and 'Burgess case'. To my surprise, Aaron's response was calmer and louder, as though he wanted it to reach me.

"I hear your concerns, but Anna's a good officer. Under your supervision, she'll be fine."

My heart swelled as they departed. When Chris made his way back over, I avoided his unimpressed gaze and pretended I hadn't heard a thing. Aaron headed off into the station.

Jay appeared at my side, bouncing with newfound energy. "All right. She's good. Let's get to work."

I blinked at him. They wanted me to get stuck in right away?

"Hold up." Chris held his hand out. "Before you go running off to the morgue, it's worth mentioning the elephant in the room."

Uh. I hated elephants.

He turned to me, trapping me under his surly gaze with no room to wriggle. "We're all sticking our necks out here, you're not on active duty yet. That means you do what we say, when we say. Understood?"

"Yes, sir." I dipped my head.

Chris wrinkled his nose. "And if you ever pull a stunt like you did during the Burgess case—"

"Yes, yes, I know," I said, waving my hand. "Aaron already gave me a talking to. I won't be so reckless again. I won't ignore orders. I've learnt my lesson."

He didn't look convinced.

"Give her a break," said Jay. "No one blames her for what happened during the Ali Burgess case. It was just unlucky." He clapped his hands together, as if that would distract from what he said being blatantly untrue. "Can we go now? Fancy a trip to the morgue, Anna?"

"Sure." What better way to spend a Sunday morning.

We left Chris behind, glowering with such intensity, he could probably melt ice if the weather permitted. Jay was more jovial and he bounded to the car park with strides of determined energy. He stopped by a sleek orange BMW and waited for me to catch up.

"Come on, hurry up. Pete sounded excited, and exciting stuff never happens in the morgue."

I hadn't ever been to the morgue before. I wasn't even aware King's Lynn had one. Bewildered, but not enough to question him, I got into Jay's car. It was customary for the junior detective to drive, but I knew full well he wanted to drive just to avoid being in my old banger. He set off, heading for the main road and taking the bypass round the side of town.

"Why are they excited at the morgue?" I asked.

Jay peered at the road ahead, flicking a floppy piece of black hair from his eyes. "I don't know exactly. Pete said he'd found something during the preliminary examination of the victim. Said we should come and look in person."

"Were they starting the post-mortem?"

Jay gave a sniggering laugh. "Nah, that won't be done today. No one works on a Sunday."

"Except you."

"Except us. Although to be fair, it's been a while since we've had a murder like this. Not since…" He trailed off and, in my head, I finished the sentence for him – *not since the Burgess case.* "Of course, things would liven up again as soon as Crazy McArthur was back."

There it was again, that bloody nickname of mine. Ten months off on sick leave and I still hadn't shaken it. I was beginning to think it would haunt me forever. Keen not to let the memories of the Burgess case slip in again, I found myself recollecting the night before. That poor woman's face, stark and unmoving as she stared at her sky. Her blood over the gravel.

"Does the victim have a name yet?" I asked.

Jay's hands flexed on the steering wheel as he navigated onto a busy roundabout. "Not yet, she's still a Jane Doe. Hopefully that's why they've called us in. Maybe she had her name tattooed across her navel or something."

Jay slowed the car as we reached a queue of traffic, presumably all heading for the coast. One sunny day and the roads around Lynn became gridlocked, full of tourists heading for the seaside resorts along the Norfolk coast.

"Damn it," he muttered under his breath. "Should've gone the other way. Sorry, by the way."

"For what?"

"For Chris. He's a miserable bastard at the best of times."

I felt a hot flash under my collar. "It's all right, I deserve it. I didn't exactly prove myself on the last case I was on."

Eventually, we turned from the long queues and pulled into the hospital complex. I almost kicked myself for not realising sooner – of course, the morgue would be in the local hospital. Jay bypassed the main car park and headed around the back of the boxy, concrete building, parking by a nondescript door. He led the way inside, taking us through brightly lit corridors until we reached a door labelled *Morgue*, his vigour not fading a bit. I think he liked taking the lead.

Inside was very light for a morgue, with bountiful air-conditioning and off-white tiles from floor to ceiling. I would have found it creepy if it wasn't for the 1980s soft rock blaring away from a radio in the corner of the room. A middle-aged man with a grey combover, slid across the slippery floor in a shuffling dance.

"Morning, Jay," he greeted us. "Who's your new pal?"

"Morning, Pete. This is DC Anna McArthur. Anna, this is Pete Kerry, the pathologist's assistant. We're just trying to ease her in, Pete. It's her first case in a while. And her first time in the morgue, judging by how quiet she's gone."

"Oh." Pete wrinkled his nose at me with pity. "First body?"

"Unfortunately, no," I replied. I'd attended enough road traffic accidents and welfare checks over the years to see my fair share of dead bodies. I just didn't usually see them at this stage of the post-death journey.

"Well, your unknown female is over here." Pete motioned to a steel table, where the telltale figure of a body lay under a white sheet. "I thought you guys better see this yourselves, because even if I sent over pictures, you wouldn't believe it. This young lady had no sort of identification on her; no tattoos, no birthmarks, no distinguishing features. Well, none that she had prior to her death."

He whipped back the sheet to reveal the top half of our victim. Her copper hair looked more orangey in this light, fanned out around her like a halo of innocence. Her eyes were closed, peaceful and serene. The blood was all gone from her face and body. It didn't take a detective to work out the cause of death; her abdomen was a maze of stab marks. I counted ten. That wasn't an accident, that was a very resolute way of killing someone. But the most notable thing was the series of scratches across her chest, spanning across the top of each breast.

"Did…" Jay lost his words for a moment, gulping hard. "Did someone do that to her?"

Pete nodded as he ran a hand over his chin. "Yep. I'm not a detective but I would guess it was the killer."

"What's it meant to be?"

The scratches were purposeful, some short, some longer. Some were deeper than others.

"It's a word," I replied. The penmanship was sloppy, but it was definitely meant to be a word carved into the flesh of our victim.

"I've been staring at it for a while," said Pete. "My best guess is that it says *catfish*."

"Catfish?" Jay asked.

I squinted at the scratch marks. I could make out a *C*, *T, F, I, H*. The rest was just a muddle, but then I supposed it probably wasn't as easy to write into human flesh as you would imagine it to be. Especially not letters with curves.

"What's a catfish?" Jay asked.

"A fish," said Pete.

"Apart from the obvious, I mean."

"It's a fraudster," I said. "Means someone who creates an online persona to deceive others into a relationship."

"So, it's an online dating thing?" Jay furrowed his brow. "I don't do online dating."

"It's a slang word. Someone who lies about who they are, uses different profile pictures, that sort of thing. Do you think our victim was a catfish?"

He hummed back, giving it some thought. "Possibly. Look at her, though. She's not exactly someone who needs to fake her appearance to lure someone in."

I gazed over the Catfish Girl. With her eyes closed and her clean hair fanned around her, she looked angelic. She was attractive but crinkled lines around her eyes gave away her age; she was possibly heading towards forty. Her fingers and arms were thin and gangly, the type of thin that made me wonder what she was hiding; drug use, eating disorder, stress? Not many people hit middle age and maintained that level of spindliness.

What else was she hiding? There was more to Catfish Girl's death than just a misadventure in the park. Someone had carved that word into her skin for a reason.

Pete handed me a manilla file. "I took her fingerprints for you. Bagged all the evidence; it's gone to the lab. Sorry, I can't do much more until the chief coroner gets here from Norwich tomorrow morning, but if you need an estimate of cause of death, I'd say it was the multiple stab wounds."

"No shit, Sherlock." Jay took the manilla file from my grasp and headed back to the door. "Thanks, Pete. Let me know when the post-mortem is done."

* * *

During the Burgess case, the Serious Crimes team had set up an incident room downstairs in the police station. When we got back from the morgue and I followed Jay upstairs to the actual Serious Crimes office, I realised why they'd needed the extra space.

The office was little more than a walk-in cupboard, with three desks facing each other. One was empty, save for a computer and printer; I guessed that was Aaron's old desk. He must have moved into Superintendent Russell's office down the corridor. A square window let in a perfect parcel of light, which bounced off a whiteboard attached to one wall, where someone had pinned details of the case at hand. A photo of the Catfish Girl from the scene stared at me as I entered, her lithe body sticky with the blood I'd found her covered in the night before.

Chris glanced at us as we entered. Jay waved his hand at me and nodded over to the empty desk with an absent, "Make yourself at home." I fired up the computer and was pleasantly surprised to find my old passwords still worked.

"What did Pete want then?" Chris asked. He sounded no happier than he had when we'd left the station.

Rather than answer him, Jay pulled out his mobile phone and showed Chris the photos he'd taken of the victim's wounds. The DI scrutinised them, holding the phone at arm's length as he squinted.

"Catfish," he said and gave the phone back. "What does that mean?"

As Jay filled in Chris, I set to work by running our victim's fingerprints through the national database. Grunt work for the grunt worker, but it came to me easily. It felt unexpectedly good to have a purpose again.

"So, a catfish is like a Nigerian prince? A scammer?" concluded Chris.

"Kind of. But more romance scams, rather than blind emails."

"I don't understand what that has to do with fish."

The fingerprints returned no matches, but that wasn't a complete surprise; the national database was far from national. If the victim had never been processed by the police before, then her prints wouldn't be on file, same for any DNA samples taken.

"Any luck?" Jay asked me, having given up explaining online dating scams.

"None," I replied. "There's nothing on file that matches the description of Catfish Girl."

"Catfish Girl. I like that," he said, throwing a glance at Chris. The DI scowled back. "What should we do next? Obviously step one is to identify her."

He looked to Chris, who repelled Jay's fresh enthusiasm like he held a shield of jadedness. After a pause, a grouchy reply came back.

"Keep an eye on the social media feeds and missing-person reports, someone might identify this victim before we're able to. I've got the local press on my back, so I'll sort a statement with the media team. Canvassing of the local area has been lacklustre, so sort out some extra help to go round town tomorrow. There must've been someone who heard something or saw our victim at some point during the evening. She didn't just appear in the park."

"And me?" I asked, sitting upright so my head was above the parapet of computer screens.

Chris faltered, as if he'd forgotten I was there again.

"You can make a round of coffee. Then help Jay."

I nodded. "On it." But before I ducked my head back down, I spotted the look Chris shot at Jay, one of distrust and annoyance.

Without another word, Chris scooped up a file from his desk and mumbled something to Jay, before exiting the room. Jay settled at his desk, avoiding my eye contact until my gaze bore into him enough that he had to look. He offered me a sheepish smile.

"Don't take it personally."

"He really doesn't want me here, does he?"

"He does," he replied hastily. "It's not that. He's been like this ever since Aaron left the team and he had to take over. Trust takes a while to build up with him. You'll get there."

As sincere as Jay was being, I couldn't help but feel he was downplaying Chris's disappointment and poor opinion of me. If it took a while to build trust ordinarily, then I was already at a disadvantage. The reputation of Crazy McArthur was enough to set me back a few steps off the post.

"He's just feeling the pressure," Jay continued, fixing his gaze on his computer screen. "We all are. We need to make some progress with this case or the bigwigs from headquarters will come and snatch it from us. They love a good murder."

"But it's our case."

"And I'd like to keep it that way. I don't know if Aaron told you, but ever since the Ali Burgess case went sideways, headquarters have been on his back. They want to merge our team with Serious Crimes in Norwich. We need a win – it's long overdue."

# Chapter Five

"I've saved your lunch, it's in the fridge," my mother called as I opened the front door.

It was late afternoon when I let myself into my parents' house, not surprised that Mum had saved me some food. Ever since I was a teenager, I often wondered if my mum was somehow psychic. She knew things about me that I'd never told her, even knew what I would do or say before I had thought it myself. I was greeted by the lingering smell of Sunday roast dinner and the dull drone of football commentary on the TV. After reheating the roast, I joined my parents in the sitting room, where they cuddled together on the big sofa. Thirty years of marriage and they were still lovebirds. Sometimes it was enough to make you sick.

"Where have you been?" Mum asked, scowling at me for daring to eat off my lap.

I ignored her indignation. "I got called into work, to help out."

Dad tore his gaze from the screen. "Help out?"

I nodded back through a mouthful. Glazed parsnips. My favourite. "Short-staffed."

"But you're on sick leave," Mum said.

Her hazel eyes sparkled with intrigue, ready for gossip and details. In every conceivable way, Mum was just an older version of me; same blonde hair, same short stature, same smile according to Dad. At least I knew what I'd look like in thirty years' time.

"It's just a little help with a big case. Office work, searching the databases, things like that. It will help prepare me for going back."

But Mum's lips tightened together. "*You're* working on that murder case, aren't you? The body found in The Walks. Gosh, Anna, what a case to go back to, a gruesome death like that. Have they caught the guy yet? I can't bear the thought of you getting back out there with a killer on the loose. Was it a random attack?"

"Don't start," I replied, waving my fork at Mum. "You know I can't tell you anything. Don't ask me. It's an active investigation."

There wasn't anything to tell anyway, other than what my mother had probably already heard on the grapevine. Tomorrow's headline in the local newspaper was easy to work out; *young woman found stabbed to death in park*. The lack of progress made a small knot form in my stomach – a niggle reminding me that I should get moving and *work*.

Mum pouted at me like a spoilt child. "Oh, come on, Anna. Random murders like that don't often happen around here. This is a nice, quiet area. Marie has already been on the phone, she's ever so worried. Apparently, the victim looks like someone Charlie went to school with, Jessie Harrow."

"Mum, you're forgetting I spent my Saturday evening being bored to death by Charlie and his stories. He told me Jessie Harrow now lives in Australia and that he went to visit her last summer. It wasn't her."

Dad snorted a laugh, but after a dagger-like glare from Mum, he returned his attention back to the football. Gossip spread far and fast around here, especially with people like my mother at the helm. It was possible that the rumour mill would ID the Catfish Girl before we could.

She leaned over to me. "You owe Charlie an apology for skipping out on him like that. I don't care if work got in the way. He's a nice boy."

"He's nearly thirty and still living at home with his parents," I said, sounding a little snootier than I intended.

"He just got back from Uganda."

"Eight years ago, Mum! I know you and Marie would love us to couple up so you can share grandchildren, but it's not going to happen. At least, not with Charlie Sweeney."

Mum huffed, folding her arms across her chest as she settled down. "Well, you'll need to explain that to Marie on Tuesday then, because I'm not telling her you said her son was boring."

"What's happening Tuesday?" I asked.

"Our dinner party." Mum patted Dad's arm and he huffed back at her, although he managed to make it look like he was huffing at the TV.

I frowned as I munched on a forkful of carrots. "I didn't think I was invited. I thought you said it was couples only. Why would you want me there anyway? I don't exactly fit in with your friends. I won't be able to help you win this little dinner party competition you have going on with them."

"You're coming, we have an extra place to fill now," she said, turning her nose up at my expression. "Can't have an odd number of people."

"Who's coming?"

"Marie and Jack, of course. Sally and Peter from over the road. Liz too."

"What about Daniel?"

She sniffed dramatically. "I already told you, they broke up. Liz could do with the company."

"So, I have to be company for Liz from next door so she can drown her sorrows and bitch about Daniel?"

Mum nodded and gave me a patronising pat on the head. "That'd be great, honey. Don't worry, I'll get plenty of wine in. Liz will brighten up after a few bottles."

"Don't call me honey," I said.

I could feel a headache coming on. I was not a socialiser, like she was. An evening with her middle-class friends was an evening of torture to me. But, as always, I reminded myself that I loved my mum, and life was easier when I just swam with the current rather than against it. I could pretend to be cheerful and happy for one evening, for her.

\* \* \*

Three lanes of traffic flew past me as I trudged through the fine rain the following day, managing to avoid the largest puddles in the uneven paving stones. Maddie stomped along next to me, huffing every time a gust of wind threatened to take her bowler hat. By this point in our door-to-door canvas of the closest streets to The Walks, rain was dripping from our noses.

Our first stop had been to the short terrace of houses that lined the edge of the park, then over to the row of Georgian town houses on Blackfriars Road. None of the neighbours had heard or seen anything, which wasn't impossible; the Red Mount Chapel stood in the middle of the park, blocked from sight by the trees.

Whilst we were stuck out in the rain, Chris was over at the town council offices, reviewing the CCTV footage from the night of the murder. Jay was back at the station, doing exactly what, I wasn't sure, but it was probably just an excuse to keep him from getting wet and ruining his hair.

"This is crap," Maddie said, as we made our way up the stoop of the last house on the street. "Fucking June, my arse. It's freezing."

"It was lovely Saturday night. At least it wasn't like this when you were on scene guard," I replied.

"Give me a summer night shift over a day shift in the rain any day."

The porch of the last town house offered us a little shelter and Maddie huddled in next to me, a bit too close for someone who didn't even like me. I rang the doorbell, the shrill chimes echoing throughout the house. Even if no one was home, moving on from the cover of the porch wasn't very appealing.

The door to the house opened and an elderly man appeared, but he was thoroughly confused about the crime that had occurred nearby, and after a few minutes of attempted conversation, I realised he was profoundly deaf. There was nothing forthcoming from him, but I left him a contact card anyway and, with despondent sighs, Maddie and I headed back out into the rain.

We made for the park and paused under a leafy horse chestnut tree as the red-bricked chapel came into view. All signs of our police cordon were gone; the scene was wrapped up the day before, just in time for the rain to hit and wash away any evidence of it ever being there. I spied a few gawkers pausing by the chapel, peering round, probably trying to find the infamous site of the rumoured murder they had read about in that morning's paper. The fine but persistent rain made them move on quickly.

Maddie watched me, giving a thoughtful hum as I gazed over the scene.

"You know, legend says there's tunnels under the Red Mount, leading to all sorts of places."

"Like where?" I asked.

"It varies," she said, making the grass squelch beneath her feet as she shuffled from side to side. "Some say to Greyfriars Tower. Some say all the way to Castle Rising. And some say a tunnel leads to the pub."

"Is that true?" I was unable to tell if she was pulling my leg or not. She wasn't usually one to joke.

She scoffed at me. "Of course. This area is full of history, there was the old hospital, the old workhouse.

That bit over there used to be a cemetery." She pointed behind us to an area of the park filled with raised flower beds. "And that indentation in the grass on that side is where a bomb fell during the war."

"I didn't know you were such a local-history guru." I gave her a grin, but Maddie stiffened up with a prickle of her back, as though I'd insulted her.

"Got to pass the time doing scene guard somehow," she said. She pressed on through the park, heading for the other side of the grass expanse past the chapel, where more properties waited for us to knock on their doors.

"Do you think our killer could've used the tunnels?" I asked.

Maddie thought this over for a moment before shaking her head. "I doubt it. It's locked up. They only open the Red Mount on those historical days when all the old places are open to the public."

"Are you sure?"

She stopped dead in her tracks and motioned at the little octagonal structure. "Go see yourself."

So I did, whilst Maddie waited in the drizzle and watched me with an irritated stare. Sure enough, the door at the top of the chapel was padlocked shut. I made my way to the lower door, standing in the exact place where I had found the poor woman, imagining that the shadows I saw on the flagstone floor were there from old age and not from her blood. The lower door was locked too, with a shiny and very robust padlock. When I rejoined Maddie, her irritation gave way to a small amount of smugness, gone just as fast as the rain dripped down the rim of her hat.

"Anyway, now that you're on Serious Crimes, you can tell me," she said, as we carried on through the park, "is progress usually this slow? This woman died two days ago, and no one seems to know who she is."

"I know." I tried my best to not let the despondency from Maddie's attitude and the God-awful weather seep into my veins, but she was right. Two days after her death and still no one had come forward to claim to know our victim yet. No one missed her.

"I suppose she was just one of these people that prefer to be alone," I replied.

Maddie raised a perfectly manicured eyebrow at me.

"A loner," I reiterated. "Some people don't have a lot of friends or family around them. If anyone is going to understand it, it would be us. Odd shift patterns, unpopular job. You know what I mean."

However, Maddie was still giving me a questioning look. "Yeah but, she was someone's neighbour. A daughter, wife, work colleague. You would think *someone* would have noticed her absence by now and called it in."

"Not necessarily," I said and a sad realisation came to my mind. "The only person who would notice I was gone would be the cat. Or my mum when I missed Sunday lunch. It would be at least a few days before anyone else came looking for me. If I was murdered on a Monday, it'd be nearly a week."

"Jeez. That sounds lonely, Anna."

I bristled, her words making my face flush hot. "No. I'm not lonely. I have plenty of people."

"Really?"

"I do! Anyway, there's nothing wrong with being alone," I said. "And even if I had someone in my life, I'm not about to tell you. You're the biggest gossip in the station."

Maddie gave a sly grin. "Yep, that's me."

"So then, what's the latest? I don't suppose me finding a body is the only interesting thing to happen around here in the last few months. What have I missed?"

"Hmm, let's see. Pres made sergeant. Frenchy's wife left him. And the latest gossip on the vines is how Aaron has slung his new girlfriend."

"What? Not another one."

Maddie nodded knowingly. "Yeah, he mentioned something about not seeing it going anywhere. We both know that's bullshit though, a week ago it was going well. He probably did his usual trick, and freaked out and ended it at the first sign of it getting serious."

I almost felt sorry for Aaron, what with the demise of his latest relationship being the juicy gossip of the week. But there was no harm in swapping a few rumours now and then, especially when the day job involved so much death, violence, abuse and murder.

"I suppose it's better that way."

"Why do you say that?" Maddie asked, pinning me with a narrow stare.

"No reason, I just mean it proves my point. Some people prefer to be alone, there's nothing wrong with that. Maybe our victim was a loner."

"And are you one of those people?"

I ignored the question.

Our inquiries a bust, Maddie and I headed back to the station to report on our lack of findings. The thought of telling Chris we had no leads gave me a sour taste in the mouth. I'd been out of the game for so long that maybe I wouldn't be able to find my place again, reclaim my cog in the machine. Aaron had called me an asset, but what if I couldn't be helpful?

The nick was busy as I made my way inside but then it was Monday, and Mondays were always hectic. People wanting to report crimes over the weekend, those with a conscience wanting to hand themselves in. We followed a group of people inside, hurrying in from the rain, but I paused at the threshold.

Maddie turned back a few steps ahead of me. "You all right?"

I considered sharing my misgivings with her, but then I didn't fancy my tentative mental health being the newest gossip in the air. So, I just wiped some rain from my forehead and nodded back.

"Yeah, fine."

She didn't look convinced, but she never did.

Inside the front foyer of the police station, a large desk occupied most of the space, a solitary officer working flat out behind it. To the right were the secure access doors leading to the rest of the station, including the stairs and interview rooms. To the left were a line of seats for people waiting. The custody cells had their own entrance further along the building, but on the odd day, the commotion coming from their end was loud enough to be heard from here. Today, however, the commotion was right in front of us.

A young man stood by the front desk, tugging ferociously at an older woman who had an iron grip on his forearm. The desk officer was trying to calm them both down, but the man was keen to get away, ripping his arm from her grip and almost sending her flying. When he turned for the exit, I got a good look at his face, thick eyebrows and squinty eyes. I knew him.

The bloke thrust his hands into his pockets and ducked his head as he tried to dodge around me, but I stuck my foot out. He fell flat on his face.

"What the fu—" he called out, but before he could climb to his feet, I pushed him back down. "Get the fuck off me!"

His protest was loud enough to gather a swathe of attention, led by the desk officer with handcuffs already out. The older woman followed him as well as several people from the waiting area, keen to see what had happened.

"See, I told you, it's better to hand yourself in!" screeched the woman, who had the furious look about her of a stubborn mother, aggrieved by her son.

"Get off me!"

I helped to wrestle the bloke to a better position and the handcuffs were slapped on. The desk officer started the spiel.

"Richard Tate, I'm arresting you on suspicion of grievous bodily harm and assault, for which a warrant has been issued for your arrest. You do not have to say anything, but it may harm your defence if you do not mention when questioned something which you later rely on in court."

Maddie appeared behind my shoulder, gently pushing me aside to help the officer pull the man to his feet. His slew of swearing continued, but he was dragged away with the woman in tow, heading for the custody cells. One last disdainful glare was thrown at me. As fast as the disorder had occurred, it was gone again, and the station returned to its usual steady pace.

As the rabble dispersed, I peeled my wet jacket from my arms and felt a tingle on the back of my neck, as though I was being watched. There was one person standing by the stairs who hadn't moved. Aaron watched me with an unusually suspicious look in his eyes, which didn't relent as I dusted myself down and headed for the Serious Crimes office as casually as I could. Aaron's footsteps echoed more than mine as he followed me up the stairs.

"What happened there?" he pressed, easily keeping up with my pace as I attempted to get away. "How did you know who that was?"

I frowned, feigning ignorance. "Huh? Good morning to you too, boss."

"Don't call me boss, the distraction won't work. You heard me."

I gave an apathetic shrug, not too sure how to explain that it had all been a split-second decision, too fast for me to properly articulate. The man trying to get away, his familiar face. My instincts kicked into play, and thankfully, I'd been right.

"I saw his mugshot on the noticeboard when you took me in for the interview. He was wanted for assault last week, wasn't he?"

I paused as I reached the top of the stairs, almost causing Aaron to bump into me. I glanced around. It was mercifully quieter upstairs than downstairs. The only sounds were the muffled workings from behind office doors. Smells of unnaturally strong coffee wafted through the air. It was always either coffee or cake in this police station, two smells I'd missed intensely.

"I suppose I should expect odd things again now that Crazy McArthur is back," he said.

"Don't say that," I groaned. "I was just in the right place at the right time."

I hoped Aaron would do his usual thing and give up quickly. To my surprise, he was smiling at me. He didn't often smile.

"See, I was right, you're an asset to the team. You've always had good instincts." His grin faded away as quickly as it came. "And you've never let a silly nickname bother you before. How is it?"

"How is what?"

"Getting back to work."

"Fine," I answered quickly, although I wondered how convincing that was with damp hair and rain dripping from my sleeves.

If Aaron felt any sympathy for me, he didn't show it as he merely pointed to the Serious Crimes office and started to walk to his own. "Good. You better get back in there. There's a mountain of CCTV footage to get through and I can hear Chris complaining about it from down the corridor."

Ah, great, hours of CCTV footage to trawl through. Almost as much fun as going door-to-door in the rain. I wasn't going to complain though. At least this way I stayed dry and got a chance to prove my worth to Chris and the rest of the team.

# Chapter Six

As I was contemplating heading home that evening, tiredness edging its way in and dismissing the frustration that had steadily built all day, Jay slapped his hands on his desk. I wasn't sure if it was to instil us with confidence or to invigorate us. It did neither of those things. But I played along with his brainstorming session regardless, because I wasn't going to be the first one to admit defeat and leave for the day.

"So, what do we know so far?"

Chris leaned back in his chair, a resting frown on his face. "Fuck all."

"Our victim is a female, mostly likely in her mid-thirties," I recited, glancing at the case file on my desk. The post-mortem results had arrived but were less than illuminating. "She was stabbed ten times in the abdomen, sometime between the hours of nine and eleven on Saturday night, in The Walks part of King's Lynn town centre. No identity so far and no reports of missing people matching her description. And no witnesses."

"It's coming up to forty-eight hours," Jay said. "How has no one realised she's missing?"

Chris turned to me. "You searched all missing-person reports in the region?"

"Of course," I replied. "I even went back a few years. There's nothing that matches her description. She hasn't been reported missing by anyone."

"Maybe she's a night-shift worker," said Chris. "When I worked shifts, I could go a week without seeing the missus. We were like ships passing in the night."

I flicked through the report again, hoping I'd overlooked something vital or enlightening. "The post-mortem report says the coroner is quite certain of time of death, so if she was a shift worker, wouldn't she be getting ready for work at that time?"

"Could have been her day off," Jay suggested. It was clear he still clung on to the hope that hard work and perseverance would prevail.

Chris sneered back; his enthusiasm had disappeared years ago.

"This is a lot of speculation for someone we can't even identify," I pointed out.

The desk chair squeaked loudly as Chris leaned back in it. "Anna's right. We won't figure out why our victim was in The Walks at that time of the night and who she was with, until we find out her identity. What else do we know about her death?"

Jay eyed the case file again. "According to the post-mortem report, there's a high likelihood our victim had sexual intercourse shortly before her murder. DNA was recovered, but it's still with the lab."

"A promising lead, but we'll have to wait for the lab to hurry up. And if there's no match, we're back to square one. What else?"

"You mean apart from the obvious?" I asked.

All three of us flicked our eyes to the whiteboard behind Jay's desk, where a new set of gruesome photos had been staring at us all day. Dead centre was the raw, scratched markings on our victim's chest: *CATFISH*.

"We're still working on the theory that she was a catfish and was killed by someone she conned." Jay thumbed through a stack of papers as he spoke. "Maybe one of her victims tracked her down and got their revenge. I've checked all the local users on the common dating apps like Tinder this afternoon."

"What on earth is a tinder?" Chris asked.

"It's too late in the day for me to explain this to you, old man," said Jay as he pinched the bridge of his nose.

"Just trust me when I say I set up a profile and tried to find our victim on there."

"So, that was why you were taking selfies," I said.

He glared across the desks. "Whatever I tried, I had no luck," he concluded.

Chris hummed, the tone the same as his usual despondent groan. "So, the post-mortem didn't shed any light on the killer and neither did canvasses of the neighbourhood. No sign of a murder weapon. What about the CCTV from the town council?"

I shook my head as I slumped further into my chair. "I've gone through every camera angled to the park. No sign of our victim in town, but there are multiple entrances; it's possible she entered through one that doesn't have a camera. I've still got some traffic cameras left to check."

"Gosh." Chris ran a hand over his face. The longer the day dragged on, the more he slouched and his frustration grew. "It's been a long time since we had a case with this little progress. We need to identify the victim. We could wait for the DNA to come back, but even that might not lead anywhere."

"What do you suggest?" Jay asked him. Usually chirpy, it seemed Chris's despondency started to weigh Jay down as well now.

"We'll have to appeal to the public for information," Chris decided as he pointed at Jay. "You can get the media team on it; the local news is always happy to run a story like this if it'll scare more people into watching. I'll continue coordinating the neighbourhood canvasses and online searches. Anna can wade through the responses to the public appeal."

I wrinkled my nose. It was the most time-consuming and mundane job of the lot. But then, if just one report paid off and we were able to identify our victim, it would be worth it.

As Jay left the office, mumbling something about getting more coffee, I shuffled in my desk chair and stretched my neck. My shoulder ached in protest at not going home yet, but there was still work to be done. I couldn't surrender. Sooner or later, our hard work would have to pay off because the only other option was unthinkable. I wouldn't let a killer go free on my first case back. I couldn't.

* * *

By late afternoon the following day, I was slouched over my desk, third coffee in hand and waiting for the day to end so I could retreat back home to a scalding-hot bath and a cool glass of wine. My shoulder ached more than ever.

The team worked in the office in an amicable silence, which I was happy to join in with. I liked their tendency to work quietly and not bother each other. I worked my way through the flood of information from the public appeal since that morning; social media posts, radio news bulletins, segments on breakfast news. The inbox was full of anonymous tip-offs. Any likely leads, I gave to Chris and Jay to follow up, but they were few and far between.

My phone beeped next to my computer mouse, and I glanced to see a text from my mother.

*Don't forget dinner tonight. Love, Mum xx*

Damn. There went my plans for a relaxing bath and too much wine. Now I had to endure an evening of polite conversation with my mother's stuffy friends. The things I did to keep the woman off my back.

She followed up with:

*And don't come empty-handed xx*

So not only was I being forced to attend the pompous dinner party, I had to bring my own wine too? She had some serious making-up to do for this. I knew when it came to my mother, everything boiled down to perception. If I appeared straight from work, bottle in hand, then she could show off to her friends how successful her daughter was – Anna the professional, the organised detective. She might have hated my work, but she loved to flaunt my status.

I thrust my phone aside and focused back on my computer screen. I couldn't give up yet, there was still so much work to do. At some point, we needed a breakthrough and if I was the one to find it, then that would prove to Chris, Jay, Aaron and Maddie, and anyone else doubting my return, that I was ready to be back. Someone needed to help the Catfish Girl.

I was vaguely aware of Chris leaving the room at one point and Jay held his head in his hands, still trawling through the responses to the appeal for information. The minimal noise of the office seemed to grow with each tick of the clock on the wall. After a moment, I realised even the ticking had stopped, leaving nothing but the pounding of blood rushing through my ears like a pulsating river. But the second hand kept moving.

"Are you all right?"

Jay was watching me, wondering why I was sitting upright like a meerkat on guard. With a slight shake of my head, my hearing returned to normal, along with the irritating ticking of the clock.

"Fine," I said, slumping back down.

"Because it's okay if you're not," he continued. He glanced at the door, still closed from when Chris had left the room. "I mean, just say if you need a break or anything. You were off work a long time. It must be hard coming back to this."

"Really, I'm fine." I followed his gaze. "Although I don't feel like I'm being much help. We've made no progress finding this woman's killer."

Jay snorted at his computer screen. "We've made more progress than if you weren't here."

"We still don't know who she is. Doesn't that bother you?"

"Of course it does," he replied, "but I'm not going to work myself to death just to figure it out. Why don't you call it a day and get yourself home? We can pick this up tomorrow."

I scowled, not quite able to meet Jay's gaze, but luckily, he was as embarrassed to meet mine. Was that really what people thought of me? That I was fragile and needed mollycoddling after the incident? I had to nip that perception in the bud very quickly.

"I'm not burning out," I said, the words stiff. "I'm managing fine."

"You've snapped that pen in two." He motioned to an old biro I had been fiddling with all day. The tip had broken off after being stabbed at my notepad one too many times.

Jay grimaced at me. "Look. I haven't had a junior rank on this team before, and if I want to make inspector one day, then I need to practice my line-managing skills. You're my guinea pig. Go home, Anna. That's an order."

I wasn't great at obeying orders, however, this time, with a relentless pain in my shoulder and a headache from staring at a screen for too long, I wasn't in the mood to argue with Jay. I rankled a little at giving in but placated myself by deciding that as soon as I was done with Mum's snooty dinner, I would get to bed and be in early the next day. I would squash any ideas he had that I was too fragile for this assignment.

# Chapter Seven

I joined the slow crawl of traffic leaving the industrial estate, heading for the main road and the fastest route home. I wondered how many of them were going to the nearest supermarket to stock up on alcohol too, in order to get through an evening with their mother. I wondered how many of them knew the Catfish Girl, if any. Maybe one of them was zooming by in their car now, wondering why she hadn't returned their call or why she had missed lunch with them that day.

A stone's throw from the station, the A47 dual carriageway curved its way around the southside of King's Lynn, laid through the countryside like a snake slithering through grass. The villages and settlements it cut through had tried to reclaim their way with bridges over the highway, but they were only like matchsticks trying to hold up a dam. One such overpass separated me from the town and closest shops. The road headed to Norwich and beyond to the east, and all the way to Birmingham to the west, the main artery through Norfolk. As I drew nearer, I heard the traffic as it roared along its carriageways with haste, sounding just like the blood rushing through my ears as I waited to join the flow.

In front of me, a black Audi was also heading up, over the overpass. I followed it until it came to a stop in the middle of the road at the centre of the bridge. A very inconvenient place to stop. I was just about to sound my horn when the car door opened and I realised the driver's attention was focused on something up ahead. He was a young man, his shirt sleeves rolled up to his elbows and his mobile phone in hand. I followed his gaze.

"What are you doing, mate?" I heard him ask.

I jumped out of my own car, able to hear my own heartbeat as loud as the lorries rattling along the main road beneath me. The wind hit me like a cold slap in the face. Coming up behind Audi man, I tapped him on the shoulder, stopping him mid-sentence.

"Is everything okay?"

The Audi man glanced at me, but he couldn't tear his gaze away from what was up ahead. "He's going to jump – call the police!"

A few metres in front of us, the grey railings of the overpass peaked in the middle of the carriageway. Straddling the bars, an older, heavyset man clung on with white knuckles and trembling fingers. The wind whipped his suit jacket around him and lifted what was left of his floppy white hair. He kept his gaze on the rushing cars below, ignoring the pleas from the Audi driver. Either he couldn't hear him, or he didn't want to.

Desperation coursed through me, raw and overpowering. The man intended to jump. I had two choices; call the police as the Audi driver said or stop the jumper. I had no time for both. No time to think. I couldn't let him jump.

"Hey!" I said, loud enough to be heard over the wind as I stepped towards the man at the edge.

He glanced round, wild panicked eyes spotting me before he quickly turned away.

"Don't!" His voice cracked under the pressure of sobs. "Don't come any closer."

"Hey," I said again, now closer enough to reach out. "Hey, just wait a minute, okay? I'm Anna. What's your name?"

Behind me, I heard the Audi man using his phone to call for help. His babbling fell away into the wind.

The man on the edge glanced at me again, his eyes bloodshot and wide. "J-Justin. Carter."

"Hi, Justin." My voice was level and gentle. I was good at appearing calm in a crisis, even if my heart was racing as fast as the traffic on the carriageway below. "Justin, I don't think it's a good idea to be up here. How about you come back over the railings?"

He shook his head furiously. "No. No, I can't go on anymore. I've lost it all."

"Lost what?"

"Just leave me alone."

"I'm not leaving, Justin," I replied. "I'd like to help you. It must have been something terrible to drive you up here. What have you lost?"

He was talking, responsive. Maybe this wasn't an attempt but rather a cry for help. I hoped it was the latter.

"Everything." He sniffed, wiping his nose on his sleeve jacket without letting go of the railings. "My business, my house, my girlfriend. I've lost everything."

I nodded. "Everything. That's a lot to go through. What business did you have?"

Justin watched the speeding cars underneath his feet. "Coach company. It all went wrong so quickly. I kept telling myself it was just a spell of bad luck, that it would pass. But then more and more things kept piling up until in the end I had to declare bankruptcy and then it was all gone. The vehicles, the workshop, everything."

"And your girlfriend?"

"Disappeared as soon as the money did."

An artic lorry thundered past, shaking the ground. For the people below, they had no chance to slow down before spotting Justin up on the ledge. It could be catastrophic for many people if he were to jump.

Behind me, I could hear Audi man reciting our location. He spoke with frantic urgency, which made Justin sound all the more despondent. It would only be a matter of minutes until emergency help would reach us, but those minutes might not be enough. He had made up his mind.

"Justin? All that stuff that happened to you – you know, this isn't the answer."

His hands tightened around the railing and his bottom lip trembled.

I edged forwards, the wild wind whipping my hair around my face. "There are people and organisations out there that can help. People you can talk to. I can help. You don't have to face this difficult time alone."

"There's nothing for me on that side."

"I think there is. You just need to give it a chance."

I touched his hand. After a pause, Justin's grip loosened and his fingers found their way to mine. He held on as though he had never held hands with another person before.

"Come back this side. We can get you the help you need."

The wind howled around us like a screaming banshee. It carried with it the sound of sirens and I noticed that the traffic was beginning to thin. Within seconds, traffic on the carriageways below had stopped. Blue lights gleamed in the distance as the rolling roadblock approached; police cars travelling slowly to draw the traffic flow to a halt.

Justin nodded at my words whilst his grip tightened around my hand. For a moment, I wondered what he was nodding for; agreement with me or a final self-assertion. His whole body shook as though chilled in ice, and I held his hand with a firm grip, as if that would help if he decided to let go.

To my relief, Justin spun around on the narrow ledge and faced me. He nodded once more. He was ready to come back over. I inched away, reluctant to let him go, but as Justin raised his leg to climb back, a gust of wind rushed down the carriageway. It thrust him away from the railings like some invisible force had given him a shove. His foot slipped and, our hands still clutching one another, he fell from the ledge.

The force smacked me into the side, the railing digging deep into my ribs with blinding pain. My legs caught in the rails. Justin dangled, his legs flailing in the air. He let out a cry.

A stark voice berated me inside my own head. *What the hell was I thinking?* I was far too small to pull this man up, this would end in only one of two ways; either he would drop, or we both would. Justin's free hand clawed at mine, desperate to hold on. I couldn't let him go, but I couldn't take the crushing of my chest against the bridge much longer.

As the pain in my ribs threatened to make me pass out, I felt a hand on my shoulder. The Audi driver was at my side, his large hands gripped around my arm, attempting to drag me away from the railings. Other hands appeared, more onlookers joining in and grabbing Justin. Together, they managed to pull him up enough to gain a footing on the ledge. The hands didn't let go. They pulled and dragged until, with a final heave, Justin was over, and we both collapsed to the ground.

Through bleary eyes, I saw the small crowd of bystanders assembled around us. They sighed with relief as the screaming sirens halted, signalling their arrival. My trembling fingers felt the solid, unmoving ground. I closed my eyes, wincing from the pain just as I heard Justin descend into gut-wrenching sobs.

\* \* \*

"It's always you!"

The scene around me was a blur through my streaming eyes but I could tell what was going on. I saw a familiar silver SUV arrive at the police cordon, stopping rather than turning around and heading away like the rest of the traffic. The aftermath was causing traffic chaos and there had been plenty of irate shouting in the interim, but this voice was horribly familiar. I watched the occupant get out and noticed the other police officers stiffen a little at the new arrival. He ignored them and stalked over to me.

An ambulance was parked up at the side of the overpass, the paramedics dealing with Justin. His howls had subsided, but he was still in a bad way emotionally. Several police officers took the statements of the heroic group of bystanders who stepped in to save a man's life and my own. The Audi driver was just a few feet away, unsure if he should talk to me and still shaken from the whole ordeal.

And I still sat on the ground, attempting to catch my breath and ignore the furious voice aimed at me.

"It's always you!" Aaron growled as he appeared in my view and crouched down next to me. "Whenever the hell anything happens, I find you in the middle of it. Three days, Anna. You've been back at work for only three days!"

"Don't," I said with a groan. My breaths were short and sharp but at least now the world had stopped spinning. My ribs ached like I had been punched in the gut. I was in no mood for a telling-off. Aaron could reprimand me tomorrow if he still felt the need to, but right now, I just needed to catch my breath.

I forced my head up to meet his gaze. His expression surprised me; his face redder and his eyes wilder with fury than I had ever seen before. He glared at me as though the moment he took his eyes off me, I might run right back to the bridge. This was no ordinary telling-off.

"Don't what? Tell you how stupid you are?"

"I saved that guy's life," I managed to say.

"And nearly killed yourself doing it. Stand up."

With tremendous effort, I climbed to my feet. Aaron surveyed me. I held one arm across my chest, holding together my ribs which felt like they were smashed into a million pieces, but I stood up straight, ignoring the pain. I was not going to let him see how right he was.

"Look at you," he said, throwing a hand in the air. "You're hurt."

"It's just a bruised rib."

"You better hope that's all it is. You shouldn't have been here, Anna. You shouldn't have done this by yourself – you should have called for backup, waited for help to arrive, someone specially trained who could get that guy down without anyone getting hurt."

"There wasn't time!" I bit back. "If I had waited, there wouldn't have been time and he would've jumped."

"This is always your problem, Anna. You don't think!" Aaron huffed as he folded his arms. I could tell there was more fight in him, more words desperate to point out how reckless I had been. But he held them back, instead taking a deep breath before muttering, "Go see the paramedics."

"I'm fine," I said. "Just bruised."

"I'm not asking you," he said firmly.

"The paramedics are busy with Justin. He needs help more than I do."

He knew I was right but answering back earned me another intense glare. Aaron looked me over again, deciding his next move.

"Where are your keys?"

"In my car." I pointed to my abandoned vehicle, looking like a pile of scrap behind the deserted black Audi.

Aaron caught the nearest officer by the arm and leaned in close. "Pres, take Crazy McArthur's car back to the station for me, please. She's in no fit state to drive."

"I'm fine!"

"You're shaking like a leaf. Get in my car, Anna. I'll take you home."

I was about to protest again until I caught sight of my own hands. I did indeed have a bad case of the adrenalin shakes. The shock would pass quickly but the shakes would come and go over the next few hours. I couldn't drive, even if I wanted to.

"Actually, I should really get to my parents' house," I said, even my voice feeling weak. "My mum will have a fit if I don't make it to her dinner party."

With a hefty sigh, he growled once more. "Just get in the car, Anna."

Not waiting for another word, Aaron stalked off, heading for his car whilst muttering under his breath, "It's always you. Always bloody you."

Without a protest, I followed him, doing my best to hide the pain that radiated through me with every step. Aaron wasted no time in buckling up, and soon we were traversing our way around the police cordon and onto the dual carriageway. The tension in the car was enough to suffocate, tightening my chest almost as much as the spasms in my ribcage. Aaron still seethed, throwing the car around corners as though he was a rally driver. I could feel the words unspoken between us; he wanted to yell at me some more but was holding back. Maybe deep down, he knew I was right and I had just saved Justin's life.

Still fifteen minutes from home, the atmosphere was too uncomfortable for me to handle, and I broke the silence.

"Why are you so mad at me?"

"Huh?" Aaron blinked, pulled from his thoughts. "The usual reason, your total lack of awareness for your own safety. Should've known something crazy like this would happen with you around again. No one else gets themselves into this many situations."

"You didn't have any attempted suicides while I was on sick leave?"

"We did, we just didn't have anyone stupid enough to nearly fall over the bridge with them. Most officers remember their training and don't get close enough to be pulled over."

Aaron swerved the car, avoiding a pothole at the last moment. I gripped my torso, hoping no important organs were switching places.

"At least it will give the station something else to talk about," I offered with a weak smile.

"What, in addition to you finding a body? And Frenchy's wife leaving him and Pres's promotion."

"And you breaking up with your latest girlfriend."

The car hit a hole with a thud, and I gasped as my lungs recoiled from the pain. I wasn't sure if he'd done that on purpose.

"Don't engage with Maddie and the other gossips," Aaron said through gritted teeth. "We're all entitled to personal lives."

I noted how he didn't confirm or deny it, so it was probably true. However, I chose to keep my mouth shut as this journey was going to take even longer if every pothole winded me and Aaron threatened to bite my head off every time I spoke.

As we reached Downham Market, the evening sky turning blossom pink above us, Aaron followed my directions to our destination without another word. He pulled the car up outside my parents' house and turned the engine off.

"Are you coming in?" I frowned at him as he unbuckled his seat belt.

He shot me a withering look. "Are you able to get out of this car unaided?"

I didn't quite understand what he meant until I turned round to give the large car door a shove open. Pain exploded under my breasts, making me suck in air like a rare commodity. I could feel the bruises forming, burning my skin with their tenderness. I was going to be a mess tomorrow. If I could just make it through this dinner, then I could collapse in bed and recover. I hoped I had enough painkillers stashed at home to see me through the night.

With an undeserved roll of his eyes and a noise that sounded suspiciously like a chuckle, Aaron leaned across me to the glovebox and produced a box of paracetamol. I gratefully downed two and looked forward to chasing it with a large glass of wine. He watched me, monitoring how tenderly I held my ribs.

"How are you going to explain this?" he asked, genuinely interested. "Are you going to tell your folks you almost ended up as a pancake on the road?"

I shrugged, but even doing that hurt. "If my mother sees you helping me get out of the car, I won't need to explain my injuries. She'll be too excited thinking I've brought a guy home for dinner."

Aaron sneered, all traces of his anger finally fading away. "Really?"

"Yep. The station rumour mill has nothing on her and her friends."

"Then perhaps I should just let you fend for yourself," he said, but as he spoke, he was already climbing out of the car. With careful manoeuvring, Aaron helped me out of the SUV until my feet touched the ground and a new wave of pain reverberated through my back and ribs. The journey had left me stiff and crippled over. Aaron took hold of my waist and I leaned on his shoulder, and together we made it to the front door.

Mum threw the door open before I could even reach for the doorknob. "Anna! What on earth have you done now?"

"Would you believe I pulled a muscle?" I replied.

Behind Mum, Dad appeared, peering over her shoulder as they both took in the sight of their daughter rosy-cheeked from pain, exhaustion and regret. From their blunt expressions, they didn't believe me.

"And you are?" Mum's gaze fell on Aaron, lingering far too long to be considered polite.

Aaron wasn't fazed and I shifted my weight away from him, allowing him to hold his free hand out for my parents to shake.

"DCI Aaron Burns."

"You're Anna's boss?"

"Kind of," he said. "I oversee her team. Not that she ever listens to me."

"Welcome to our world," Dad mumbled back.

"What were you even doing?" Mum continued to me. "You shouldn't even be at work, you're still off from the *last* incident. What happened?" She not only glared at me but also flashed an accusing look at Aaron.

"Mum, don't."

"To be fair to Anna," Aaron said, "this wasn't work-related. This was just a case of–"

"Being in the right place at the right time," I finished, and gave my parents my best innocent smile.

I must have passed some imaginary test as suddenly, my parents moved aside and let me enter with Aaron's help. I gave a half-hearted wave to the dining room, where the dinner guests were staring bewildered as I shuffled my way in and collapsed in a free chair. A bottle of wine, almost full, sat in front of me. That was me sorted for the rest of the evening.

Behind me, I heard Mum turn on Aaron. If he was hoping for a quick escape, he was going to be disappointed. She launched into a barrage of questions, not giving the man long enough to think of an answer before moving on to the next one. It was an interview technique worthy of the finest investigator. In less than five minutes, the guests were well enough acquainted with Aaron for conversation to start to flow again and, as I poured myself a hefty glass of wine, Mum introduced Aaron to her lovely, newly single friend Liz and set him a place at the table.

## Chapter Eight

The next morning, two separate pains vied for first place in my list of problems; the constricting ache around my ribs and the rumbling headache that came with too much wine. When the alarm went off, I pulled myself up and put on my big-girl pants, working through the stinging of the bruises.

But it was only when I left my flat and tenderly made it downstairs to my car, that I realised I had no means of transport. Of course, how could I forget? My car was at the station.

As if on cue, a patrol car pulled up outside the building and slowed down to a stop a few feet ahead of me. The passenger window rolled down and the driver gave me a sly smile.

"Word on the street is that you need a ride this morning."

I scowled at Maddie. "How did you know?"

She surveyed me, taking in the damage herself. "Pres told me. He got lumbered with driving that piece of shit you call a car back to the station yesterday." She reached over and opened the passenger door. "Come on, hop in."

But I stood firm and raised my eyebrows at her. "Really?"

I found it hard to believe that any of my colleagues cared enough about me to organise a lift.

Under my scrutiny, she relented quickly. "Okay, okay, I was tasked with making sure you go to the hospital for a check-up. Chief's orders."

I gave a sigh but climbed in the car no less, making sure to hide the twang of pain from my face. "That's a bit outside your remit, isn't it? If DCI Burns wants me to go for a check-up, he should take me himself."

Maddie shrugged. "He knows what you're like and that you'd refuse. He said to get you there whether you want to go or not, and I'm not going to argue with Aaron when he asks for a favour. I've seen him when he's angry. And so have you, from what Pres was saying. Did you really stop that jumper on the A47 yesterday?"

As the car accelerated off, I positioned myself so that my bones didn't rattle too much inside my chest.

"Yep," I said, stiffly. "And Aaron was not happy about it."

Maddie laughed. It was a rare, hearty sound. I wasn't sure I'd ever heard her laugh before.

"Ah, just like the good old days then. You're such a liability."

"Well, I didn't go in expecting to be nearly pulled over the edge of the bridge."

"No one does."

Sitting in a car with Maddie once again reminded me of the shifts we used to share when working on the same team. We were friendly, bantering and such, but there was always a slight frostiness to her. A condescension in her tone that I could never be sure was aimed at me or just her natural way of speaking. Here, I could hear it again. I liked Maddie, but it was hard to tell if she actually liked me.

Sensing my discomfort, Maddie filled the rest of the journey with babbles about her evening with her partner. They had done normal couple things like walk the dogs and wash the car. Mundane stuff that I had no doubt was a hundred times better when with someone you adored.

When we arrived at the hospital, Maddie stopped the car in front of the main entrance.

"Call me when you're done, and I'll get you picked up."

I thanked her for the ride and headed inside the Accident and Emergency department. Ordinarily, I would have fought tooth and nail to avoid the hospital. Any injury, no matter how minor, needed checking out before I could return to work – a process I loathed. But – and this was a very hard thing to admit – this time I needed to go. A beautiful mosaic of deep burgundy and rich purple crossed my chest, lining a ridge underneath my breasts to the base of my ribs. Breathing was manageable but not the easiest. Moving triggered an uncomfortable pain I could do without.

So, I rationalised as I checked in and settled into the thankfully quiet waiting room, it was probably best to get looked over. At least then, I would have the peace of mind that I was fit enough for this case… well, physically fit enough.

I checked my emails as I waited. Jay and Chris must have heard of my predicament as there was an email detailing several promising leads that had come in from the public appeal. They were following them up. As I typed out a reply, a sparsely worded email landed in my inbox.

> *Don't dare walk into this station without the all-clear from hosp.*
> *Aaron*
> *DCI Aaron Burns – Station Lead, King's Lynn Police*

He followed it up with a text to the same tune.

Before I could come up with a sarcastic enough reply, a door across the waiting room opened and a handsome doctor stepped over the threshold. He scanned a paper file in his hands and opened his mouth.

"Anna McArth… Oh, it's you."

I smiled sweetly at the doctor and followed him through the door.

"My favourite patient," he said, the sentiment not quite matching his tone of voice as he ushered me into a bay and threw the curtain around to block out the rest of the A & E department.

"My favourite doctor," I said back. "Have you missed me?"

"Like a hole in the head… Please, tell me you haven't been stabbed again."

"Not this time."

Dr Leonard Walker had a good reputation around the hospital, which may have been partly due to his loveable charm, dimples in his cheeks or floppy mousey hair. He was young and a breath of fresh air compared to the other stuffy doctors that usually stalked the halls. And I was ashamed to admit that I had fallen for that cheeky smile from the first time I met him.

"Possible broken ribs," Dr Walker read from his file. "How did you manage that, Detective McArthur?"

"It involved a bridge, it's a long story." I felt my face flush as I realised that he was going to need to inspect my bruises. "I just need the all-clear from you, and the paperwork, so I can return to work."

Dr Walker tutted, pulling his stethoscope from round his neck. "That's all you ever want me for, McArthur, my paperwork."

"And your flawless medical mind."

With a roll of his sparkly blue eyes, Dr Walker indicated for me to raise my blouse and he set about inspecting my wounds. After a moment, I felt myself return to normal temperature. There weren't many people who could just look at me and make me quiver like that, but Walker was one of them. His was the first face I'd seen when I regained my senses after the incident, and found myself in the hospital's A & E department, dripping blood all over their tiled floor. I remembered that moment like a TV show I'd watched a thousand times, like I was an observer rather than actually there, watching his frazzled face break into a smile as I came to.

But then I also remembered that Dr Walker was a married man, with two gorgeous children who shared his dimples. Ah well.

"You'll need an X-ray," Dr Walker decided, "but your breathing sounds good. You did this on a bridge, you say? It wasn't anything to do with that jumper last night, was it?"

"Yeah," I replied. "Did you hear about that?"

He nodded. "I was here when they brought him in, I was working a double shift. He was in a bad way."

"Is he still here?" I had spent all night wondering about Justin, but closure was not something I ever expected. Me and my actions were just a small part of the process needed to help Justin get better. Whether he made it down that road or not, I would probably never know.

"Yeah, I think so." Dr Walker crossed the bay to a computer terminal and tapped in a few keys. "Looks like he's still admitted. He's on Terrington Ward."

* * *

I held my all-cleared-for-duty notice tightly. Shame it didn't cover psychological evaluations as well. *Moderate bruising, recommended for 1 week of light duties*; 'recommended' being the key word. Dr Walker knew full well that I wouldn't take his recommendation.

Outside of the A & E department, I found a car waiting for me in the drop-off zone, one I recognised well. Burnt orange, sleek and sporty. It had to be Jay. Sure enough, as I approached, he got out.

"Got the all-clear?" he asked, eager and a little bit in awe. I wondered if he was on his way somewhere.

I waved the form in my hand. "All clear. Just some bruising."

"Good," he said. "I can't believe you tried to stop a jumper. What was going through your mind?"

I didn't bother to ask how he knew. With Maddie in the loop, I was sure everyone knew by now.

He hummed when I didn't reply. "No, that was the wrong question. I mean, what can we learn from this experience?"

"Are you still trying to line-manage me?"

"Trying," he confirmed with a nod. "What have you learnt?"

"That metal railings can hurt."

"Is that it?" He tutted. "I'm sure I can come up with a better lesson for you to learn, like don't try act as an anchor for middle-aged men trying to commit suicide. Never mind. Get in, we've got work to do. I need you back to filter through the crap for some actual leads."

"I just wanted to pop to one more place before we go. Upstairs," I said, pointing to the main entrance and giving

Jay my best pleading look. "The guy I stopped is still an inpatient. I was hoping to check he's okay."

Jay chewed this over for a moment, scrutinising me as though he was trying to imagine what sort of predicament this could lead to. He locked the car and walked around it to me. "Yeah, all right. I'm coming with you, though. There's never a dull moment with you around."

We followed the signs for Terrington Ward through the hospital corridors. I was slow on my feet compared to the hospital staff that rushed around me with their squeaky shoes. A nurse directed me to Justin's bed and I peeked around the curtain at the far end of the bay. Justin was staring wistfully out of the window to his prime view of the smoking shelter outside.

"Justin?"

He jumped at my voice, spinning round with a flicker of an irritated scowl. But his expression softened as he recognised me.

"You," he said. His voice had the hoarseness of someone who had been hysterical and I spied scratches and bruises on his forearms. Despite this, Justin appeared relaxed and calm, a far cry from the day before.

"Anna," I reminded him, not that I expected him to remember my name given the circumstances under which we first met.

Justin nodded and motioned for me to take a seat at his bedside. He gave Jay a wary glance.

"This is my colleague, Jay. We both work for the police, but we're not here because of that. I just wanted to see how you are."

"Better," Justin replied but an undertone of uncertainty ran through his words. "I'm so glad to see you, I wanted to say sorry for… all that I put you through."

I held up my hands. "It's okay, really. I'm just pleased to hear you're feeling better. Have you been able to access help in here?"

He gave a small nod. "There's a psychiatrist who's treating me. She says I can go home in a few days."

"Well, that's good. Do you have any family who can stay with you a few days?"

"No."

"What about your girlfriend?" I asked. "I know you said she left you but I'm sure she'd want to know you're here."

Justin looked back out the window, avoiding my gaze. "She, um… she wasn't really my girlfriend."

I waited a moment for him to elaborate. His face flushed bright pink when he glanced back at me. I slouched down in the chair, no other position comfortable enough to maintain for more than a minute, but I worried it gave Justin the impression that I didn't care. I did care; in fact, my stomach was churning into a knot of latent anxiety because I could already sense where this conversation was going.

"She was online," he said in a mutter. "I never actually met her. We connected on a dating website, but she lived at the other end of the country. We hadn't got around to meeting, there was always something that got in the way."

"So how long were you in a relationship for?"

"A few months, maybe six. I realise how stupid it is now – probably nothing about her was true." Justin shivered, as though he was cold. I could tell he wanted nothing more than to abandon this conversation, but the detective in me pushed on with the line of questioning.

"What was her name?"

"Callie," he answered. "She's gorgeous. We would Skype once a week. I should have known she wouldn't really want me when I had no money left."

The anxiety grew, turning from a stubborn knot into a definite feeling of dread deep in my gut. I needed to find out more about this woman.

"So, you never met her at all?"

"No."

"What about gifts? Did you ever exchange gifts?"

Justin shuffled in his bed. "I sent her loads of things; a watch, nice clothes. She never gave me anything, said she was too skint."

"Did you ever loan her money?"

At this point, Justin cottoned on to what I was thinking. He stared at me for a moment, opening and closing his mouth as words popped into his mind and back out again. I felt a prickle of guilt for assuming the worst when he was already in a fragile state. Jay stayed silent behind me, but there was a frown set on his face, showing he was thinking the same thing I was; this so-called girlfriend was bad news.

"I paid her rent a few times. Put it straight into her bank account."

"How much?" Jay asked.

"She *is* real, you know! She wasn't some fat bald guy pretending to be a beautiful, young lass. She was real, I saw her."

"I know, you said you video-called her," I said hastily. His anger reminded me that I wasn't here as a detective. "I believe you, Justin. We just want to know if she took anything from you. Did she ever pay you back?"

"No."

"How much?" Jay asked again.

"About four thousand pounds."

My stomach tightened at the amount. No wonder this guy had gone bankrupt if he was giving it away to some stranger on the internet. I'd studied a few cases of besotted people sending swindlers on the internet thousands of pounds – it was fraud by misrepresentation. But those really good at it were nearly impossible to track down.

"She's real," Justin maintained. "Look, I have a picture." He grabbed his mobile phone from the side and jabbed at it a few times with a shaky finger. "Look, this is her."

He turned his phone to me and showed me a selfie photo of his girlfriend. She pouted at the camera, flame-red hair falling in waves around her face and shoulders.

Catfish Girl.

## Chapter Nine

The dilemma I faced only gave me seconds to decide. This was her, our victim, the Catfish Girl. That meant Justin was the only person so far who knew her, in any way, shape or form. He could have been a victim of hers, if she truly was a catfish, a scammer. Or he could have killed her.

But then, from the way he spoke, I wasn't convinced he even knew she was dead. I could tell him the ugly truth and get all the information out of him for the investigation, but that might hurt his already-damaged mental health even more.

I glanced at Jay, but his expression had turned blank, impossible for me to read. One day down the line, I hoped to know what his stoic look meant, but now it meant nothing other than it was up to me to break the news to Justin.

I couldn't tell him.

Instead, I asked Justin to write down the name and login details of the dating website he used, and his permission for me to access it. I simply said I was going to see if I could find Callie for him. I didn't tell him 'Callie' was in the same hospital as him, in the morgue.

Back at the office, Chris was waiting for us, ready to chastise me for my lateness and general absence for the whole morning. I ignored him and sat down at my desk, firing up my computer.

"We've found her," I said. I found the website Justin had used to meet Callie and logged in using his details. The profile loaded straight away, a sad little blue banner telling me there was no new notifications.

"Found who?" Chris asked.

"The Catfish Girl, our victim," Jay replied, just as excited as I was.

As I scoured the computer, Jay updated Chris on our conversation with Justin and his connection to Catfish Girl. When he finished, I turned my screen and together the three of us pored over the profile of Callie Whitton.

The more I read, the more I became convinced that she was lying with every word. Her profile said she was five foot four – definitely not true, it was more like five foot eight – and a size 8 – more like a very curvy 14. She lived in Blackpool and worked in a bingo hall. Easily the biggest lie was that she was twenty-three years old.

Over my right shoulder, Chris snorted. "She was twenty-three all right, about fifteen years ago."

"This is her, though," I said, barely containing myself. "Look at the picture, this is definitely her. We've finally found her."

"It could be," said Jay. "The photo is our victim but that doesn't mean this profile is her. It could be a…"

"A catfish?"

Jay nodded. "This site doesn't look like one of the more reputable ones out there. I doubt they have verified her identity in any way."

"Then how do we find out if this Callie online is the same woman as our victim?" I asked.

"We will need to obtain her IP address from the website and see if we can locate the profile owner that way." Jay gave a grimace. "That means filing for a court order, as I doubt that they would hand over that information willingly."

"It's worth a try," said Chris. "And I'll contact Lancashire Constabulary, see if they have any missing-person reports from the Blackpool area matching our victim."

"What should I do?" I asked. This was the best lead we'd had since the beginning of the case and I didn't want to get left behind. I hoped my little stunt hadn't persuaded Chris that I was more trouble than I was worth. Even the best horse riders slipped once in a while when getting back on the saddle. But he took a second too long to answer.

The guys both gave me a sly smile.

"You can read through Callie's messages to Justin," said Chris. "See what their relationship was really about."

* * *

I spent the rest of the day reading the growingly explicit messages between Justin and Callie. I felt like I was intruding on someone's personal fantasies, the type of stuff you keep in your head and never reveal to another living soul. After an hour of reading, as the pair began to act out those fantasies, my skin began to crawl.

The girl was good – she was vague enough to make fervently tracking her down hard but open enough to let Justin trust her. Their relationship had begun at the beginning of the year, and from what I could see, it was just a simple match on the website findtherightoneforyou.co.uk based on the fact they both liked the Rolling Stones. If only true love was as decisive as music taste.

On the other hand, Justin was an open book with Callie. He played down his company's cash flow problems whilst showering her with gifts like flowers, jewellery and clothes. All gifts were collected by courier as Callie claimed her neighbours had been stealing her deliveries. They video-chatted about once a week, still through the website, which held records of all interactions they had together. I made a mental note to never go on a dating website – the lack of privacy was worrying.

It didn't take long for their relationship to turn sexual – well, virtually sexual. Callie was willing to try anything. It had come to an abrupt stop the week before our victim died, right after Justin's last message where he told her his company had folded. He'd pestered her to reply ever since, even as recently as that morning, but no response was forthcoming.

I shared all my findings with Jay and Chris as the end of the day approached. Their silence told me they too were thinking the same thing I was. Our victim's post-mortem report showed she'd had sexual relations prior to death. And here was evidence of Justin having an online explicit relationship with the victim right up until her death. Her body was found in the local area not far from where he lived. It didn't take a detective to work out things didn't look good for Justin.

As we discussed our findings, Aaron checked in to see our progress. He pulled up a chair next to Chris at his desk, being careful to avoid eye contact with me.

"Ah," he said as he reached the same conclusion at the end of our briefing. "I think it's fair to say that Justin is now a person of interest. We should get an interview set up."

"I don't think he knows she's even dead," I said. I looked to Jay, hoping he'd agree with me. "From the way he was speaking, it hadn't crossed his mind. He just assumed Callie had dropped him after he went bankrupt. I'm not convinced he knows she was even in the area."

"Your impression is noted," Chris said stiffly. "Either way, we need to get his statement and find out where he was when the victim was killed. Let's gather as much information about Callie as we can, and Anna can go back to Justin tomorrow. One of us will go with her."

I was just about to protest about being babysat when Jay hummed loudly, musing as he gazed at the whiteboard. Now we had a few more documents pinned to it, including Catfish Girl's dating profile picture, duck face pout and all.

"I don't think her name is even Callie."

"I agree," I replied. "She lied about nearly everything else. It's no big stretch to think she lied about her name as well."

"What if she had other pseudonyms?" An excited glint crossed Jay's eyes. "Other profiles on other dating websites that she was using to con more men."

"You think Justin wasn't the only man she did this to?" Aaron gave him a quizzical look. To con one person convincingly was hard enough; to do it to multiple people was almost an art form.

"Look at her death," Jay said, with a wave of his hand at the whiteboard. "This was a crime of hate, nothing accidental about it. Whoever killed this woman was angry at her and wanted to hurt her. They left the carving on her chest as a way of highlighting what she had done, how she had wronged them. I think we're looking for one of her victims. Not necessarily Justin," he added with a glance at me.

"Have Lancashire police got back to you yet?" I asked Chris.

Chris grimaced. "Yeah, they say they have no missing-person reports matching our victim's description and no known people by that name and description. As we know though, she lied about her age and height. She was probably lying about her location too."

"So it's possible she wasn't even from Blackpool?" asked Jay.

"It's possible," said Chris. "To find out for certain, we need the data from that dating website. That's where we'll start tomorrow. We'll verify her location and identity. Jay, try tracking down Callie Whitton on the national databases and social media. I'll look into Justin, see what background can be dug up on him."

"And me?" I asked hopefully. I couldn't take another day of reading Justin and Callie's conversations.

"You can find out if our Catfish Girl was on any other dating sites." If the task was meant to be a punishment or a wild goose chase, Chris didn't let on.

Jay yawned, stretching his arms towards the ceiling. "Tomorrow, right? Because I have a tikka masala at home that's been calling my name all day." And not even waiting for an answer, he started to pack away and gather his belongings.

Giving us a nod, Aaron disappeared back to his own office down the hall now we were finally making some progress. I knew full well I would have to come grovelling to him to get my car keys before I could go home. Leaving them on my desk would have been the easy thing to do.

As Jay bid us goodbye and left, the day outside was turning into a glorious summer evening and the sunlight reflected on the office walls as the door swung shut again. I contemplated following his lead and what I would do with my evening. Go for a walk, see my parents. Maybe a nice hot bath. Who was I kidding? I knew I would spend my evening fishing around on various dating websites, looking for the Catfish Girl. Saving Justin had opened a door to a new line of inquiry but there was still so much to do.

As I prepared to head home, I realised Chris was standing in my way.

"What?" I asked, feeling flushed under a sudden wave of self-consciousness from his unwavering expression.

He looked down on me, like I was a delinquent teen who'd stayed out one too many times. "I thought I'd made myself clear," he said. His tone was flat and gravelly; no nonsense, no excuses. "No going off-task. I heard you were always landing yourself in trouble, but this is Serious Crimes. It's all hands on deck here. I can't afford to have Jay babysit you all the time."

"I don't need babysitting," I said back. I held a lungful of air in my chest.

"I don't want another repeat of the Burgess case."

A shiver ran up my neck, starting at my shoulder. I didn't want that either. But if I let him, or any of them, see that the Burgess case still got to me, that my injury and dented pride still made me doubt myself, my time helping out would end. I'd be packed off back home to languish my days with daytime TV and aimless walks around town. I couldn't let that happen. I couldn't go back to that now, not after having a taste of the role in Serious Crimes.

"Okay, I'm sorry," I said. "What happened could've been an unfortunate event, but it got us the best lead we've had on our victim since she died."

"It was a fluke," said Chris, not holding back the bite in his tone. "A coincidence and a lead that we would have reached ourselves eventually. This is a quiet area, lots of small communities. Someone would have come forward soon enough."

"Then I saved us some time," I replied with a huff.

Chris shuffled on the spot. For a moment, I thought he might give up and move out of my way, but he didn't. Instead, he crossed his arms and slowly shook his head from side to side.

"I knew having you back was a mistake."

A sharp pain ran through my shoulder, shooting up my neck and making me flinch.

Chris continued. "I tried telling Aaron, he wouldn't listen. Just said that you could help. The thing is that once you gain a reputation, Anna, you never really lose it."

"I'm not…" The words died on their way out. I was about to say that I wasn't Crazy McArthur, but I think I had already proved I still was. I would never shake the reputation, but I wasn't sure that I could change who I really was. If I hadn't approached that bridge and tried to save Justin, then he would've jumped. I wouldn't have found Callie.

There was no happy medium. Either I acted or I didn't. Either I followed my instincts or I ignored them.

"If you feel that way, then why not take me off the team?" I asked.

"It wasn't my decision to have you here," said Chris. "And if you want to stand any chance of working within this team in the future, then you'll get one thing into your head; you're not indestructible. Most young officers grow out of this phase after a few years on the job and they realise that there's someone at home who will miss them if they were gone. At the end of the day, it's not only you who might get hurt, but also everyone else. Your team, your cases, your loved ones."

I opened my mouth to argue back – I still had plenty more to say. But something stopped me. It was the niggling in the back of my mind I had been battling since I'd received a knife in the shoulder all those months ago. The niggling that told me that Chris was right, I wasn't indestructible. What if I had fallen from that bridge?

Chris shuffled once again, pulling me from my thoughts. His voice mellowed and filled with an even-tempered wisdom I'd never heard before from him. "Don't let that crazy streak overrule your head, Anna. It's hard work and perseverance that solves a case like this, not sheer dumb luck."

## Chapter Ten

When I knocked on the door to Aaron's office and let myself in at his beckoning, I adverted my gaze. After my confrontation with Chris, I now felt even more like a scolded schoolchild. I took in the bright office instead, where everything was in its place. Wide windows that faced out over a scene of flat rapeseed fields and specks of dust danced in the evening's dying sunlight. The station stood like a gatehouse, separating the bustling town from the subdued countryside.

"I just need my keys," I said. I heard a jingle and glanced up to see Aaron holding them out to me. "Is that it?" I asked, tentatively taking them. "No more telling off?"

"I'm pretty sure Chris has already given you a piece of his mind," Aaron said with a hint of amusement, not even looking up from his computer screen.

"He wants me off the team."

"He says that but he doesn't really mean it. He's just not used to you."

"Used to me?"

Aaron glanced my way, his face set with the usual indifference that told me nothing about how he was feeling.

A memory popped into my mind, of an evening like this one, with bright sunlight pouring through those windows and heating my face. It was the first time I had ever set foot in this office. The building had only just opened and the furniture was still being moved from the old station in the town centre. It was also the first time I ever considered becoming a detective.

"Remember that time you collared those machinery thieves?" Aaron asked. I smiled to myself; he was thinking of the same memory I was. "Remember what I said to you?"

"That I was an absolute idiot?"

Well, it had been true. I had single-handedly arrested the prime suspects in a spate of farm burglaries after spotting their car whilst out on patrol. It was only after dodging a clumsy right hook from one that I realised how short-sighted I'd been. The two guys were known for violence and outnumbered me. Luckily, I'd diffused the situation by the time backup arrived and was able to arrest them, much to the amazement of my colleagues.

"No, what else did I say?"

"You said…" I pursed my lips, trying to remember how the conversation had gone.

"You said, had I considered moving from uniformed policing to CID? That I'd be good at it once I adapted to the different pace."

"And I was right," said Aaron as he smiled to himself. "You have what it takes to solve this case. You're just out of practice. This… attachment, shall we call it, wasn't just to help the team out. It was to get you back on your feet too, but that won't happen overnight."

His words, however kind, didn't quite squash the feelings of frustration left behind by Chris. If Aaron believed I was good enough for this team and this case, then why hadn't we solved it yet? Why was the killer still walking free?

Why was no one mourning the Catfish Girl?

"Call in here tomorrow," Aaron said, his tone shifting away from wistfulness and letting me know it was time to move this conversation along. "I'll come with you to interview Justin at the hospital. My meeting at Norwich got cancelled, I have some time."

"I don't need babysitting," I said, once again feeling a flush of anger across my cheeks.

"I wasn't asking."

Although I still felt unsettled by the frustration bubbling away under my skin, I rose to my feet and made for the door. I still had a long way to go, and a lot to prove to everyone. Even to him.

* * *

I wasn't surprised to find an extra place had been set for me at my parents' dining table that night. Mum dished me up a plate of spag bol and watched me curiously as I descended on the food.

"How do you feel today?"

"Fine."

"How is your case going?"

"Getting there," I said. Vague answers was all they would get from me, especially with delicious home-cooked food on offer. Mum had tried numerous times to teach me how to cook from scratch. I just didn't have the patience.

"And how did you get on at the hospital?"

"All good, just a few bruises. I saw Dr Walker." I felt myself turn red just saying his name.

"Oh, I like him," Mum said with a prim smile. "He was so kind to your dad when he sprained his knee."

"I tore a ligament, Susan," Dad protested through a mouthful of garlic bread. "It was more than just a sprained knee."

"Serves you right. You shouldn't have been up that ladder on your own."

With a ding of her cutlery, Mum picked up her empty plate and handed it to Dad. He didn't need any other signals, the hint was clear enough, and he cleared his own plate before retreating to the kitchen to wash up. It was like a choreographed dance, an exchange the two of them had perfected over thirty years together. My parents were two flawless halves making a whole.

With a wistful smile on her face, Mum turned her attention back to me. "I liked your boss. He was nice. Liz was quite smitten with him by the end of the evening. Do you think he'll call her? She gave him her number."

"I doubt it," I said, mumbling through a mouthful.

"Why not?"

"He doesn't do relationships."

Not even Aaron deserved to be a target in my mother's matchmaking missions. I'd warn him off Liz if I had to, although I thought he'd given the distinct impression he wasn't interested at the dinner party. Politeness didn't necessarily mean attraction.

"What's wrong, Anna? You're very quiet."

I shrugged back, ignoring the prickle on the back of my neck as Mum surveyed me. "Nothing. It's just been a long day."

When I glanced up from my plate, I found my mum giving me a hard stare. It was a look that could – and had – made grown men shake with fear; a look I knew well. I was not getting away with wishy-washy answers.

"There's something wrong. What is it?"

"What if..." The issue was on the tip of my tongue, hard to enunciate. What if I wasn't good enough to help solve this case? What if the Catfish Girl, Callie or whatever her name really was, remained anonymous forever, unknown and unloved? I wanted so badly to share it all with Mum, to tell her every gory detail of the case, but I knew she wouldn't like that. She preferred to live in a lovely bubble, where crime and murder didn't touch her world and were only things that happened elsewhere. She would only chastise me for having these thoughts in the first place, proving that I wasn't ready to be back at work and that I needed more time off.

So, I let the question die away. Mum wouldn't understand. I only let her into one part of my life and protected her from the rest, same with my dad. They didn't need to know the details of the woman's red hair, her glazed eyes, her sticky blood that popped back into my mind every so often, reminding me that while I wasted away the evening with my parents, her killer was still walking free.

"You're getting frustrated," Mum said knowingly as she watched me carefully. "Maybe you weren't ready to go back yet."

"Progress is slow, that's why I'm frustrated," I replied, minding my words.

"So what does every other police officer do when the case is going too slowly for their liking?" She picked up my plate with a tut at the rest that I had left, unable to stomach it. "They *investigate*. They plug away until a breakthrough suddenly blows the case wide open."

I opened my mouth to tell her that policing was definitely not like she'd seen on the TV, but I knew she had a point. All I had to do was continue to investigate the case of the Catfish Girl and find her killer, and the frustration would go away. Easy, right?

Of course, it wasn't so bloody easy. And there was no way I would be able to do it on my own, out of practice and off-duty. But that still didn't stop me from going home, pouring myself a hefty glass of wine and firing up my laptop, where I proceeded to spend the rest of my evening wading through the dark, unappealing corners of the internet to find our Catfish Girl's other alter egos.

# Chapter Eleven

She was Jessica from London. Bethany from Derby. Aimee from Poole, Hannah from Coventry, Lacey from Dundee, Tara from Glasgow, Emmy from Hull.

The list was endless. By the next morning, I was poring over my findings in the Serious Crimes office, letting the early sunlight shine off the whiteboard where I had printed and pinned up a profile for each of our Catfish Girl's identities. There was almost a dozen of them so far.

Our victim had been prolific over the last two years. A few of her pseudonyms were inactive; it had been several months since she had last updated them. Others were more recent, and one even as new as last month. All shared an image of our pouting Catfish Girl, meant to entice in some poor lonely singleton, with exposed cleavage or seductive poses. So many websites. I marvelled as I imagined if she had managed to con someone from every profile, someone like Justin who was willing to send her gifts and money in return for the illusion of a relationship.

I turned as I heard the office door open, where Jay and Chris stopped dead in their tracks, taking in my new display.

"You found all these?" Jay asked incredulously.

I nodded as I finished tacking the last profile to the board. "This is just what I found from searching the most prominent dating websites. I mean the first few pages of Google. I dread to think what we could find if we dived a little deeper."

"This is almost too many leads," said Chris. "Have you found out if she had online relationships using any of these profiles?"

I grabbed a pile of papers from my desk and waved it at him. "All information requisition forms are ready for you to sign. Hopefully at least a few of the sites will be cooperative."

Chris looked impressed with my progress. Well, I guessed impressed, given that he signed the forms with no further word – it was really quite hard to tell with him. My gut feeling was that I still had a long way to go to win him over, but maybe I could get there.

Jay watched me scan the forms on our office printer, which took up half of my desk, as he and Chris settled in for the day. He had a devious look in his eyes as he lounged back in his chair.

"You know what tomorrow is?"

"Friday," I answered slowly. Was this a trick question?

"Shut up," Chris snapped from his side of the room.

Jay ignored him, his face fixed with a cunning grin. "Friday is old man Hamill's fiftieth birthday. We're off down the pub after work for a good old-fashioned knees-up. Are you coming?"

"Don't," Chris warned him. "Stop encouraging people. I told you, no one needs to know it's my birthday."

"Too late now, everyone knows." Jay smirked back. "So, come on, Anna, are you in?"

"Of course."

For a group of people meant to be upholding the law, there really wasn't a worse gang to go out drinking than a load of police officers. And as a police officer, I knew that a pint was the answer to most problems. Bad day – pint.

Good day – pint. Promotion – pint. Bollocking – pint. Celebration – pint. There weren't many reasons to not go for a pint. Of course, I preferred wine, but my colleagues weren't too fussed what was drunk as long as a suitable amount of it was consumed.

"Who else is coming?" I asked.

"Half the fucking force at this rate," Chris mumbled back.

"Hey, it's not every day one of us hits the big fifty," said Jay. He reached over to give Chris a slap on the back, earning an unimpressed glare. "You need to see out your forties in style."

"It's been ages since I last went to the pub. I wouldn't miss this for the world." I gave them both a grin, with varying responses back.

Jay rubbed his hands together with glee. "I'm going to get you so drunk you'll forget your own name, old man."

Chris merely glared back.

The door to the office opened and Aaron entered, casting an eye over our jolliness. My laughter stuttered out, like a flame starved of oxygen, as I remembered I had an important task today, one that instantly killed my mood.

I needed to see Justin.

* * *

I'd never been to the hospital as much as I had in the last week, and I hoped to never set foot in there again when this was over. At least, Aaron seemed in a better mood with me today, chatting about a collar the Rural Crimes team had made over the weekend that involved an immense amount of paperwork. I guessed that was what he was trying to avoid with this little outing.

We entered the hospital, its corridors moving like a busy motorway, and made our way to Terrington Ward. Just inside the door, a grumpy-looking matron and plain-clothed doctor accosted us before we could get any closer.

"You're here to see Justin?" the sister asked, folding her arms.

Despite being even shorter than me, her formidable expression made me pause. Both women scrutinised us, their gazes flitting over me and lingering on Aaron. I coughed to draw their attention back to me and fished my warrant card from my back pocket. I shouldn't have been carrying it given that I was still on indefinite leave, but since I shouldn't have been working on this case either, I figured why not go all out when breaking rules.

"Yes. I'm Detective Constable Anna McArthur." I showed the ladies my ID, but their gazes drifted to Aaron again. "This is DCI Aaron Burns. We're here... Well, I'm the one who stopped Justin on the overpass."

The doctor, Allegra Birney according to the ID swinging from her breast pocket, wrinkled her nose at me. "We know. You visited yesterday. Justin has been quite jittery ever since."

"We need to talk to him," I said. "It's about a matter he asked me to look into."

"Is he in trouble? Is he under arrest?" Dr Birney asked. She looked to Aaron and her cheeks flushed a little as her hostility faded.

I cleared my throat. This was getting embarrassing.

"No. But we do need to speak with him."

"You can't. He's an inpatient under the Mental Health Act, you're not allowed."

"Look," I said, holding my hands up in surrender. "We're not here to cause any distress. But someone Justin knows has died and we need to ask him a few questions about them."

"And besides," Aaron chipped in, speaking for the first time as Dr Birney swooned so hard, she dropped the pen from behind her ear, "the Mental Health Act only covers sectioning for the first twenty-four hours. After that, Justin is a voluntary inpatient and can discharge himself at any time."

The doctor and the matron shared a glance with each other, an almost impermissible look of guilt. They weren't banking on us knowing the details of the law, which was, well, foolish.

"Does Justin know he can discharge himself at any time?" I asked them.

Neither replied, but I didn't need them to speak to know the answer. They had neglected to tell him he could leave whenever he wanted now.

"Is he still a danger to himself?" Aaron asked, his tone flat and unimpressed.

"No," Dr Birney said carefully. "Nor to others. But I wouldn't feel comfortable with him leaving with anyone other than a family member or friend who can look after him right now. He's still in a fragile state."

"Then wouldn't it be best if we spoke with him now? Whilst he's in a safe environment? We just have some questions, we won't be hauling him down to the station," I assured them. Well, I hoped that wouldn't be the case.

The matron glared at Aaron and me, a deathly glare that I was sure was the reason many of the patients stayed put in their beds and didn't leave. But next to her, Dr Birney huffed.

"Fine." She relented, once again blushing as she met Aaron's gaze. "You can have five minutes. No more."

With reluctance, they both stood aside and let me pass, with Aaron a step behind me. I led the way through the ward, heading to the far end to the bay where Justin was.

"What a pair of battle-axes," I mumbled under my breath as the matron stalked several feet behind us.

"I'm sure they only had their patient's best interests and health in mind," said Aaron.

"I think the doctor liked you."

He didn't reply but I caught him smile out the corner of my eye. I wondered how hard this visit to see Justin might have been if I had been on my own, but I turned my mind back to the task at hand as we reached Justin's bed.

On our arrival, Justin jumped, and a pleased smile erupted on his face for seeing me again so soon. He gave Aaron a wary stare as I greeted him, just as he had done with Jay. I introduced Aaron and we both sat down.

"I'm going home tomorrow," Justin said, almost tripping over the words.

"That's good news." I smiled back, his joy contagious. His excitement was palpable, such a turnaround from the day before. A bit of good news could do wonders to lift spirits. "Is there anyone at home or someone you can stay with for a few weeks?"

"Yeah, I've already sorted it. I had an apprentice at the coach company, a young lad named Gregory. He was a star, more like a son to me. He said I can stay with him."

"Can I have his address so I can contact you still? That's great news, Justin. I'm glad to hear that."

Aaron nodded too, but he kept his mouth shut under Justin's nervous glances. Justin obliged and scribbled down the details on a scrap of a newspaper discarded at the foot of his bed. I folded the paper and slipped it into my notebook, where I knew it would be safe.

"Justin," I said carefully, weighing up my words. I felt bad I was about to destroy the happiness that plastered his face. "I need to ask you a few questions about Callie."

"Callie? Did you find her?"

Oh boy, I hated situations like this.

"I did. But I don't think her name was Callie."

I watched Justin process this for a moment. He seemed shocked but I think a part of him had suspected it all along. His bloodshot eyes searched the ward, keen not to meet mine, but he settled when he spotted the matron, watching us intently from across the bay.

"How do you know?"

"We've been checking online. We've found multiple other accounts all run by the same person, all pretending to be in relationships with people like you to extort money."

"You found all that just based off what I told you?"

"Not exactly," I said. I took a deep breath. I could feel Aaron watching me, which somehow made it worse. I'd given bad news plenty of times, but his presence made me stumble. It was like he was evaluating me, which I guessed in some ways he was.

"We… we found the body of a person who matches the photo of Callie that you gave me. We believe it's her."

"A body…" Justin's breath left his lungs and for a frightfully long moment, I wasn't sure if he would take another breath. I expected him to cry, sob or even lash out, but he didn't do any of this. He just stared at me.

"Yes," I said, hoping my words would distract him a little. "Justin, we need to ask you a few more questions. Did Callie ever give you her address?"

He shook his head. His mouth floundered, no words coming.

"Justin, where were you last Saturday night, between the hours of nine and eleven?"

"What?" Justin's eyes flicked over to Aaron, but he remained as expressionless as always. His bottom lip trembled. "I-I was at home. Why?"

"Can anyone confirm that?"

"My neighbours probably can, they have cameras everywhere. Why? Anna, why?"

"Callie was murdered."

He shook his head. All traces of his jubilance were gone and now his eyes darted around and his breath rattled in and out of his mouth. I felt a groan deep inside my chest, my own pain at causing his. I could have tipped him back over the edge.

"By whom?" Justin demanded, but he continued before I could speak. "I was at home, all Saturday, you can check the cameras. I couldn't have gone to Blackpool. It wasn't me."

"Callie wasn't in Blackpool. She was found in King's Lynn."

"I didn't do it!"

Justin thrashed his arms at his sides, either trying to get up or simply unable to control his limbs. I jumped up and held his arms, stopping the waving around almost in its tracks before he hit me or himself. His panicked eyes watched me like prey caught under the gaze of a predator.

"Justin, listen to me. We are still investigating. When you're feeling better, I'm going to need you to come to the station to give me a statement."

Justin shook his head, "No, I don't want to."

"Not right now. Your doctor will tell me when you're ready. In the meantime, I want you to focus on getting better."

He threw his head from side to side and as tears began to form, he turned away. I had seen this man break down before. At least I knew he was safe here. He shook his head again and turned his whole body away from us. He stabbed the nurse call button repeatedly, and before I knew it, the matron appeared and ushered Aaron and me straight from the ward.

Back out in the corridor, the foot traffic swept us along, leaving the commotion of the ward behind us. Aaron headed for the hospital exit and I followed, my legs slower than his, my determination fleeting with every step. My mind reeled. This was one part of the job I hated, destroying someone. Justin was fragile and all I wanted to do was help him; this wasn't helping him.

"You have Justin's home address?" I heard Aaron ask me, before he turned round and noticed I was several steps behind now.

"Huh?"

"Do you have his address so you can follow up his alibi? Check if his neighbours can confirm he was home all evening."

I nodded, an odd hollow pit forming in my stomach. "I'll do it as soon as we get back."

"Do you think he's involved?" Aaron asked.

No. Deep in my gut, I knew he wasn't at fault for Callie's death. His reaction was one of pure shock. But my gut wasn't the decider here, only evidence could prove Justin innocent.

"Do you?" I asked.

Aaron gave nothing away in his expression. "I'll guess we'll find out."

## Chapter Twelve

My first port of call was to Justin's neighbours in Walsoken, a village by the town of Wisbech on the Norfolk–Cambridgeshire border. Unsurprisingly, his alibi checked out. His nosy neighbours had their security cameras at just the right angle to see Justin's house opposite. Justin's silhouette was clear through the glowing front window, curtains wide open all night and TV flashing away.

For the rest of the day, the team and I dived deeper into each of the Catfish Girl's aliases. Every account was perfectly crafted to reel in a sucker like Justin. She oozed sex appeal in her photos, but was down to earth and humorous in her descriptions. She loved quiet nights curled up with a book, or going out on the town with her friends. She was an avid skier, a former dancer, a marathon runner. She worked disadvantaged jobs like primary school teacher, where she did the work for the children, not the money.

We had to assume it was all lies. So, who was this girl really?

It concerned me that someone could exist in the world and not be missed when they were gone. Catfish Girl had all these likes and comments on her profiles, yet no one in her real life knew she was dead.

As the day ticked by, my tenuous determination waned with each passing minute. For the first time, I felt we were making progress, but something still didn't sit right in my gut. We were finally a step closer to discovering who she was. Thanks to me, we now knew of multiple victims of her fraud. Soon, we would be closer to finding out who had taken her life and bringing them to justice.

So why wasn't I pleased about it?

The day was lost to the futile efforts of trying to find the Catfish Girl's victims, and then the next day too. Before I knew it, Friday afternoon arrived and Jay was urging me to switch off and join them at the pub for what he was calling "a night to remember". I let him drag me away from my desk, because if I didn't, I would sit there all weekend and obsess.

As we entered the pub, cheers erupted at Chris's arrival. The guys headed straight for the bar and I followed. I spied a quiet corner I could hide away in. I hadn't seen most of these people in months and I couldn't bear an entire evening answering the same questions: *How have you been, feeling better?* I was fine, I was getting there. I might as well write those words on my forehead and save myself the trouble.

Jay shot a jibe at me, an attempt to draw me out from my melancholy thoughts. "Come on, liven up. Where's Crazy McArthur when we need her?"

"I'll need a few drinks in me first," I warned him.

It was a half-hearted attempt at banter, even he could see that. As Chris joined the queue at the bar, Jay leaned in close, forcing my attention on him. The pub was filling up, an eager cry of merriment rising through the air as more and more people arrived.

"What's up?" he asked, a serious glint in his eyes as he bent his head low, blocking out the surroundings. I could see he longed to join in with the well-wishers, happily tormenting Chris with their jokes about old age and retirement.

"Nothing," I said, but it wasn't convincing. Jay gave me a look which I returned with a stern gaze. "Nothing. This case is getting me down. It's nothing a few drinks won't solve."

"Why is it getting you down?"

"I'm not here to analyse my subconscious. I'm fine."

Jay blinked, surprised at my tone. I immediately regretted it. Jay, in an unusual show of compassion, was only trying to look out for me. He didn't deserve my frustration. After a moment, he sighed and gave me an empathetic smile.

"I get it," he said. "This job is the most infuriating and rewarding job in the world, and this is a heavy case for your first one back. When you figure it out, just know there's plenty of us who understand. It helps to talk."

"Thanks, but I don't need to talk."

Jay cast an eye over me and gave another shrug, before heading off to the bar. The celebrations filled the air, plenty of drinks flowing as a steady trickle of colleagues arrived from their shifts. Before long, the entire pub was just a collection of people more than happy to drown their sorrows and hard days in the alcohol and good company.

* * *

I found myself drinking alone in a corner, nursing my third or fourth glass of wine. Around me, the merry festivities were turning more into rowdy games. I knew how this night would end – Aaron had arrived an hour before and put money behind the bar, which meant the drinks would keep going until just after midnight. By then, everyone would be suitably smashed and ready to call it a night. In my time away from the old routine, nothing had really changed.

I was just thinking of ways to sneak out unnoticed when a figure landed in the wooden chair next to me with a hefty thump. I almost didn't recognise her for a moment – a petite woman with flowing brown hair and sweet-pink lipstick. After a second glance, I realised it was Maddie.

"You look different out of uniform," I said to her.

She swayed in her seat. Absolutely hammered.

"I know what's wrong with you." She sang the words, sipping from her glass with a straw.

"What?"

"I know why you're so miserable." She waggled her eyebrows. "I know why you're moping in the corner rather than joining in. I knew it when we were canvassing the other day and I know it now."

Intrigued to hear the musings of Maddie when drunk, I said, "Go on then."

"You *are* lonely!"

"I'm what?"

"Admit it," she said. "Ever since the Burgess case, you've realised how short life can be. It's no fun being alone. If you're that desperate, Cass has a brother. I could introduce you. He's bit of a twat but not bad really. Good for a shag, at least."

"No!" I pushed myself away from the table. "I'm not lonely, Maddie. That's not what's wrong with me."

"You are! Admit it."

"And how did you come to that conclusion?"

"Easy," she said with a slight slur to the word. "When we were talking the other day, you said there's nothing wrong with being alone. But look at the victim." She waved a hand in the air, very close to hitting herself in the head. "Whoever she was, she kept everyone away, so much so that no one's noticed she's dead! You're like her."

My heart stuttered inside my chest, and I prayed that my face hadn't betrayed how close to home Maddie's words had hit. I was disappointed that no one missed our Catfish Girl in her real life. I was bothered that Justin didn't even know the real Callie. Just how close was I to ending up like her?

"No way." I pushed all those thoughts away and downed the last of my drink. "I'm not lonely."

"You brought it on yourself," she sang.

"How?"

"You pushed us all away," she said with a fair amount of accusation. "When the whole… incident happened." She indicated to my shoulder. "Me, Pres, Aaron, all of us, we tried to reach out to you. You pushed us all away. You made yourself lonely, Anna, there's no point in denying it anymore. I can see through you."

"You barely know me, Maddie," I replied with a huff. That certainly wasn't the way I remembered it. Yes, my colleagues had reached out, but I was unwell. I was recovering.

She snorted back and leaned in close. "I know you better than you think."

I rolled my eyes at her. Maddie always prided herself on knowing everyone's business. This was probably just her way of trying to engineer a juicy rumour, to prompt me into doing something ill-thought-out so they could all proclaim that Crazy McArthur was back in action. Whether that was get fall-down drunk to drown my feelings or run into the arms of someone else, she didn't really care so long as everyone had something to talk about tomorrow.

"See," she said, smirking at how she'd made my mind spin. "You need a shag. I'm just trying to help you, Anna."

Well, at least that confirmed my theory.

With that, she shoved herself away from the table, giving a dramatic huff as the rickety chair scraped across the floor. She reached across me for an unused bar mat and scribbled down a number.

"That's Cass's brother, Kyle. Give him a call. Unless you find a better offer."

I pushed it back across the table to her. "I'm not lonely, Maddie."

"Come on, it'll make you feel better."

"Why are you doing this?" I asked. I felt several pairs of eyes on me as I stood up too, moving towards Maddie before she could stagger away. I didn't want the whole pub watching me, waiting to see what nonsense I got myself into next. And I didn't want to give Maddie the satisfaction of getting to me.

She cocked her head to the side, genuinely confused. "Doing what?"

"This," I said, pointing to the beer mat. "Trying to entice me into something. Pretending you care. You don't even like me."

"Huh…" Maddie surveyed me for a moment, keeping her gaze surprisingly steady for how drunk she was. She licked her lips. "I know I'm not the friendliest person, but I've never disliked you, Anna. I'm just trying to be a friend."

And with a swish of her thick hair around her shoulders, she swaggered away, usual frown set on her face.

## Chapter Thirteen

Since drinks were free for the time being and sick-leave pay was barely enough to pay the bills and keep a roof overhead, I made the most of the booze, until a subtle pressure in my head was telling me I had reached my limit. Leaving the merriment of the pub behind, I went outside for some sobering night air.

The pub sat on the corner of a historic square in the centre of town, the Tuesday Market Place. Surrounded by other establishments all housed inside the grand eighteenth-century buildings, music floated across the marketplace, creating a lulling sensation as the noises blended together. A few people staggered from pub to pub or headed off down the High Street in search of fast food.

I heard the pub door creak open and close again as someone joined me outside. I had to think of a way to get home before I was stuck in another conversation with someone I didn't want to talk to. Taxi? Brave an SOS call to Mum and Dad? Or walk it to the train station, if the trains were even still running at this time of the night?

The weather had changed since the last time I was out in the middle of the night, nearly a week before, looking over a blood-covered body in the shadows of an old chapel. Now, the crescent moon shone brightly overhead, and the cool air threatened to whisk my breath away. Better weather was coming but some nights still held a chill, and I shivered as someone joined me where I leaned against the wall of the pub.

"What are you doing out here?" Aaron asked, frowning as he settled beside me. Without a second look, he took off his jacket and placed it round my shoulders.

I smiled, but it didn't fool Aaron.

"What's wrong?" he asked quietly.

He pulled out a pack of cigarettes, offering one to me. I shook my head. Smoking was a habit I'd tried, but it just wasn't worth the grief my mother gave me when she smelled it.

"You want to start psychoanalysing me too? Jay reckons I need to talk. Maddie reckons I'm lonely and need a shag. What's your expert opinion?"

"Well, I don't know. I only came out here for a fag." Aaron looked taken aback by my outburst. He took a long drag and exhaled deeply. "What do *you* think is wrong?"

What was wrong was that they were both right.

"I guess…" My words fell away on the stale night air. I admired my shadow on the pavement, stretching in front of me like a perfect mirage of myself. The shadow didn't have issues or worries; it didn't have anything to prove. "I guess, I'm worried I'm going to end up just like her."

"Who?"

"The Catfish Girl," I said. "She's been dead for nearly a week and no one has noticed. No one has come forward. All she had was a string of desperate men on the internet, none of which knew the real her, not even her real name. Even we don't know her real name! She had no friends who are missing her, no loved ones, no partner or family. No one knows she's even gone."

Aaron blinked at me. He blanked his face, not reacting to my words, but I noticed a subtle clench in his jawline.

"You're nothing like her."

"I'm not far off. No friends, no boyfriend. All I have is work and for the last few months, I haven't even had that. I pushed everyone away and I didn't even notice." I sighed, watching my breath break through the puff of smoke hovering in front of me.

"You still have plenty of people around you, Anna. Plenty of people who would miss you if you were gone."

"I guess." I laughed, the sound hollow and not at all like me, but my mind was clearer after my confession.

Aaron leaned heavily on the wall next to me, his face was ruddy in the bleary orange light. I had no doubt his head was pounding as much as mine now with the added depression brought on by my self-pitying.

"Actually, it's a good thing you are thinking this," he continued.

"Oh yeah?"

"Yeah." He nodded definitely, the motion getting carried away. "Now you know what you are missing, what you want from life. When you say it out loud, you realise just how ridiculous it is to whine over something only you can change. And Jay's right, it does help to talk."

"I don't want to talk to anyone."

"You're talking to me now."

"I suppose." He had me there.

"And Maddie was right too."

I scoffed. "That I need a shag?"

"I meant the other thing. We all get lonely sometimes."

Aaron finished his fag and dropped it to the ground, clumsily stepping on the butt. He heaved a deep sigh into the night, as if happy for the silence, before looking at me to see if I was still paying attention. I looked away before those light-blue eyes could gaze too deep. Something quivered inside me. Must have been the drink.

"How are you getting home?"

"Well, I can't drive in this state, I'll have to get a taxi," I replied. "Do you get lonely then?"

"Of course," he said, a little briskly at the personal intrusion.

I snorted at his response. "Ridiculous. How can *you* be lonely? I'm not stupid, I see the looks you get, the way women fawn over you."

He didn't reply. Only shrugged.

I stopped myself laughing before I looked rude. It took a lot for me to admit what was bothering me and it probably took just as much for Aaron to admit he was lonely too. Rather than ridicule or tease him, I let the alcohol-induced confidence take the lead and tried a different approach.

I reached across and took his hand.

His skin was firm and cool from the night air, but warmth ran underneath. For a moment, he didn't react, but then suddenly, he laced his fingers between mine.

"Want to be lonely together?" I asked.

He smiled. In my drunken, uninhibited state, I couldn't recall ever seeing him smile like that. Something quivered inside of me again, like a shiver from the cold but deep enough to make me wonder what it really was.

"I'm glad you're back. It wasn't the same without you around," Aaron said, so quiet that the night air threatened to take his words before I heard them. I had heard them though.

"You mean without me causing trouble?"

"Well, yeah. The Burgess case did go cold after your little run-in with the perp. But I'd rather have a cold case and you back on the force than a killer behind bars and you…"

His words drifted away. A trickle of shame ran down my neck, settling on my shoulders at the mention of the Ali Burgess case. It had been a night not dissimilar to this one; moon high in the sky, unseasonal chill in the air. I quickly pushed away any thoughts of that night, because if I started down that line of thinking, I'd be lost even more into my spiral of self-pity. Instead, I looked up at Aaron, meeting his slow-blinking gaze only inches from my own. He drew in a stiff, uneven breath.

"Do you... do you want to come back to mine?" he asked.

The question threw me. By the look on Aaron's face, it surprised him too.

"Yours?" I repeated.

He nodded quickly. "Uh-huh."

I waited for him to retract it, but he didn't.

"Say yes before we both realise what an awful idea it is."

"Okay."

\* \* \*

Aaron lived down an unassuming side street just outside of the town centre, called Extons Road, made up of old-fashioned terraced houses. We walked there in a little under half an hour, barely passing a soul on our way. Neither of us spoke for most of the journey. We didn't dare curse whatever uninhibited impulses were carrying us this way.

He finally released my hand when we reached a darkened front porch to open the door and show me in. Despite the shadows, I could make out a narrow hallway with grey panelling and a striped staircase. Understated and functional, just like Aaron.

Aaron locked the door behind us, and we both found ourselves at a loss, standing in the hallway just staring at each other. Who would make the first move? A dim light from the kitchen illuminated his face, showing me conflict and confusion under his normally passive expression. Now that we were here, he was floundering.

I guessed the first move was mine.

I took a step closer, shrugging off his jacket from around my shoulders and reaching up to touch his face. His skin was burning compared to my icy hands. He didn't move away, but instead trailed his fingers along my arms, his touch light, almost non-existent.

"Anna," he said with a deep sigh. On his breath I smelled the remnants of the cigarette and the whisky he'd downed at the bar with Chris. "This is—"

I silenced him with a finger to his mouth. If he said any more, he would jinx it. It was a terrible idea, I knew that. In fact, in the corner of my mind, sober-Anna was screaming at me that this was the stupidest thing I could have done, and I'd done some very stupid things in my time. I should have just called Maddie's brother-in-law if I was lonely in that way, if I wanted someone to satisfy the quivering inside. But the rest of my mind squashed those thoughts like a drunken giant stepping on a bug.

When I released him, Aaron continued, "A bad idea."

"You want to stop?" I asked. My hands had a mind of their own as they played with a button of his shirt.

"God, no."

"Then don't jinx it."

We met in the middle, both of us swooping in for a kiss before we sobered up and changed our minds. It clouded my thoughts, silencing anything that wasn't the feel of him or the flutter growing inside me. I wanted more. I needed more. I pressed deeper, letting the kiss turn hungrier and my hands insatiable. I fumbled at his shirt, desperate to feel him closer, to feel anything other than my self-induced frustration.

There was a thud and a rattle as Aaron guided me back, pressing me into the wall and knocking his keys from the side table. Nothing broke his stride though, as his hands pulled at me, tangling my hair, touching every inch as though he had never seen me before.

After a moment, we broke for air. Aaron's hands paused and I caught sight of his flushed and eager face.

"This is such a bad idea," he said again but excitement swelled with his heaving chest.

"You'll jinx it," I replied.

He leaned in close, running his lips over mine. "Then we better make the most of this night."


## Chapter Fourteen


Something was wrong. Through my closed eyelids, bright sunlight was intruding, attempting to rip me from my peaceful, dreamless slumber. Which was weird because if I was laying on my left, the sunlight was coming from the wrong direction.

Before opening my eyes, I reached out a hand and tentatively felt around the bedsheets. I encountered something firm, unmoving and warm. I blinked away the sleepiness to confirm my suspicions. This wasn't my bedroom. And I wasn't alone.

Memories of the night before flooded back like an unrelenting tsunami, bringing along with them a dry mouth and thick headache. My legs ached, but in a good way. A way they hadn't ached in quite a while.

I risked a glance at my bed companion but found him still fast asleep.

God… I had really slept with Aaron.

As silently as I had ever moved in my life, I crept up, finding items of clothing scattered around and gathering them as I left the room. Downstairs I found my keys and mobile phone, the screen of which told me it was still quite early in the morning. The house was still, apart for the chorus of birdsong floating in from the back garden. Taking a quick shower downstairs, I let the warm water quell whatever small panic I'd woken up with and got dressed. I helped myself to a glass of water in an attempt to combat the stifling headache numbing every thought, and I sat down to contemplate my next move.

I couldn't just leave. I wasn't that sort of person and even then, this wasn't some random one-night stand. This was Aaron.

But then I also didn't want to wake him, and risk reminding him of what had happened the night before. He might reach the conclusion that it was a terrible drunken mistake. It didn't feel like a terrible drunken mistake to me, but as always, it took two to tango.

The indecision tore at my mind, like ripping sheets of paper into small confetti. I wasn't well-practiced in the etiquette of the morning after the night before. What was I meant to do?

I debated with myself until my phone sprang to life in my hand. I recognised the number as the control room. For a moment, I wondered why the station was calling me but I answered before the shrill tones woke up Aaron.

"McArthur," I said in a hushed voice.

"Sorry for the wake-up call, McArthur," replied a monotoned drawl of a nameless control room operator, who was definitely not sorry. "PC Dave Harris is requesting a member of Serious Crimes attend a welfare check he's conducted. He thinks he's found information relating to a case of yours."

That sounded promising.

"Have you told DI Hamill or DS Fitzgerald?" I wasn't sure I was even meant to be taking these types of calls; I was working off the record, after all. I was under strict instructions to follow their lead and not go off plan, like they worried I would.

"Yeah," the operator replied, short on patience, "and they told me to call you, so I am. Are you going to respond or what?"

"Sure. Send me the address, please. Tell Harris I'm on my way now."

My phone pinged to signal the arrival of the address. Aaron was still asleep. I didn't want to leave without an explanation, but I couldn't possibly ignore the lead. This was exactly what I was hoping would happen, that we'd be able to find the Catfish Girl and finally find someone who was missing her.

The possible fallout with Aaron would have to wait. Perhaps I was taking the easy option but I was also taking the one that would lead me to solving this case. And after all, wasn't that what I wanted most?

\* \* \*

North Lynn had a reputation, perhaps a bit unfair in my opinion. Every town had its rough areas, its less affluent and run-down areas. North Lynn had something that always surprised me when I visited the estate – an incredibly nosy community. If the police were outside one house for any reason, then the rest of the neighbourhood would be sure to gather round like a hoard of spectating seagulls waiting for some scraps. As I pulled up outside a set of miserable concrete flats four storeys high, it didn't surprise me one bit that some spectators had already gathered, trying to figure out what the police were up to. Harris, an older cop with not a lot of hair left, was waiting by his patrol car.

"Looks like we have an audience," I said, motioning to the group of teens on bikes and a couple in their front garden in dressing gowns. It was still a bit too early for a full audience.

"Bloody vultures." Harris rolled his eyes. "I heard you were back at work."

"Yeah well, good news travels fast," I said with a grimace. "What did you want me for?"

With a nod of his head, Harris headed inside the building and made his way up the first flight of stairs to Flat B. The door was already open. I said a thankful prayer in my head that the thing I needed to look at wasn't in the urine-stinking, dilapidated stairwell that linked all four flats. The lock on the door was broken, I noted as I entered, but that could have been by Harris.

As we entered the flat, I took in the surroundings. It was a homely place. Like my own flat, everything was a little dated; the kitchen units were a hideous brown, the carpets worn and stained. But the rest was clean and tidy with an off-white and bronze-coloured theme running through. The flat was pokey, again just like mine, but it suited one person, maybe two at a push. Cute cushions lay scattered on the sofa, high-heeled shoes discarded by the door and a pile of laundry sat in a basket on the kitchen counter, waiting patiently to be put away.

"We received a call from the manager of the big supermarket outside of town. One of their night-shift workers failed to attend their second shift in a row," Harris explained. "She wasn't answering her phone and when they called by here, there was no answer, so they called it in and asked for a welfare check."

"So, you broke in?" I asked.

Harris gave me a defensive glare. "I asked the neighbours first, they confirmed no one had seen the occupant in days. I thought it best to be proactive."

"And what did you find?"

"Nothing," said Harris. He earned a quizzical look from me. "There's no one home. No signs of any foul play or anything of concern. Until I found this."

Putting on a pair of gloves, he handed me a wallet from the kitchen counter, with a pink card poking out of the top. A driver's licence. A small photograph stared back at me, glazed-over eyes staring straight at the camera, and waves of hair framing a thin, expressionless face.

Catfish Girl.

According to the licence, her name was Miranda Alder. She was thirty-eight, a UK citizen, home address the same as the very flat I stood in. It was really her.

As my mind reeled from the revelation, my subconscious was already getting into gear. A set of car keys lay on the kitchen counter too. I handed them to Harris.

"See if her car is nearby. Looks like a Vauxhall. If it is, search it. There must be some clue somewhere about who she was with and how she ended up in that park."

"So, it is her? The victim from The Walks?"

I nodded. "But if her keys are here then she was picked up and taken there. You say she worked at the big supermarket?"

Harris jingled the keys in his hand. "Yep, night-shift cashier. The control room have the details of the manager who notified them and asked for a welfare check."

"Great, I'll get his details."

As Harris left to look for the car, I pulled out my phone. There was so much I had to do now, I needed to get my head in the game. It took a moment for me to remember, fighting against months of inaction and a hangover that continued to niggle away.

But the night with Aaron pushed itself to the front of my mind and overshadowed any relief at finally finding our victim. Memories flooded back, determined to pull me under; the perfect night, something I never expected, and a million different ways that dealing with the aftermath might evolve into.

I couldn't let myself hang onto the turmoil. I had a job to do and in order to do it well, I couldn't waste time analysing my feelings for Aaron. Were there even feelings? He was a senior officer, a good guy and a helpful friend. Nothing more. Right?

No, there was definitely something deep inside, churning with annoyance at being relegated to the back of my mind. The night before had awakened emotions I didn't even know existed, but I couldn't allow myself to get caught up in trying to figure out what they were. Right now, I had work to do.

# Chapter Fifteen

Mid-morning glowed over the tops of the nearby flats and shined in through the kitchen window, highlighting the thin layer of dust that covered the victim's home. I spent hours poring over the belongings of Miranda Alder, speculating over her final hours of life and hunting clues. Hours thrusting myself into her life and ignoring the imminent problem I had in my own.

Miranda was neat and tidy, everything in its place. I left her laptop untouched, set up in a corner of her bedroom next to a case of expensive make-up and a large lighted mirror. Rather than dive into the online life of Catfish Girl and her alter egos, it would be easier to leave that to the tech experts, who would be able to decipher if she was the same person as Callie, Jessica, Bethany, Tara and so on.

Harris stayed with me, keeping watch over the scene and abating any nosy neighbours desperate for a look. More officers and SOCOs joined us as the morning went on, along with a larger crowd of onlookers from the street. I directed the SOCOs to do a thorough investigation of the flat, whilst I headed outside to find out what information the officers had gleaned from the hungry horde.

The story from the crowd, most still in their pyjamas, was similar; no one really knew Miranda well. She kept to herself. A few knew that she worked night shifts at the local supermarket and drove the silver Vauxhall Corsa parked down the street, but that was the extent of their knowledge. By the time the officers and I had worked our way around the group of onlookers, my stomach was rumbling. Breakfast had passed, and I still hadn't found a single person who knew Miranda Alder well enough to be sad of her passing. They were curious, shocked or disturbed about the crime, but not sad.

As I regrouped with Harris by my car, a new arrival at the scene caused the crowd to stir. A ripple of dread crept up my neck as a familiar, sparkling-clean silver SUV rolled to a stop.

"Look busy," Harris mumbled. "Boss is here."

As Aaron got out of the car and made his way over, there were no signs of our salacious night before on his face. Fresh suit, grim-set expression. How he looked so composed after the amount of drink consumed and the antics we got up to the night before, I didn't know. I needed to know his secret.

"All right?" Aaron greeted me, his tone as casual as always.

"What are you doing here?" I asked.

He shrugged, without even the slightest hint of sheepishness or awkwardness. "I heard there had been a development in the case. And neither Chris nor Jay are in much of a state to join you this morning, so I thought I'd pop along to see if you needed any help."

Probably disappointed that I wasn't about to get a telling-off for something, Harris and the rest of my colleagues dispersed, leaving the two of us alone. Before the growing dread and embarrassment turned me into a bumbling wreck, I rounded on Aaron.

"What are you really doing here?"

Aaron crossed his arms. "I just told you."

My instinct was to call him out, to point out how unlikely it was that his appearance had nothing to do with our drunken shenanigans the night before, but I managed to refrain. This was the worst place to say it, with many of our colleagues and half of North Lynn Estate around us.

"Show me what's been found," said Aaron, but to my relief, the seriousness faded away.

He nodded in the direction of the building until I led the way. He followed me inside and I gave him a rundown of all the information that I had managed to piece together about our Catfish Girl from her home. The scene-of-crime officers had bagged and tagged the laptop, and were working on the bedroom as Aaron and I entered. Hearing my voice again, one of them poked their head out of the door.

"McArthur, we found an interesting note. I've left it on the side for you."

"Thanks."

The note consisted of a long scrap of blank receipt paper, like you would get when doing a big food shop. Haphazard lines of scrawled handwriting filled half of it. I peered at it as I pulled on a new pair of gloves and Aaron wandered around the room.

"It was inside the pocket of her work fleece jacket," the officer said, pointing to a coat hook next to the door. "Thought you might like a look before we box everything up to take back to the station."

"Good thinking," I said but the words drifted off as I read the note.

When I finished, I looked up to see Aaron across the room, giving me a curious glance.

"What does it say?"

I felt my face flush warm. "It's a love note."

"Really?" His eyes widened. "As if this woman doesn't have enough admirers online, she has people slipping her love notes at work too. What does it say?"

I held the note out. "Here, read it."

"I don't have gloves on." Aaron held his hands up. "Come on, just read it to me."

"No, Aaron, don't make me say it aloud."

He snorted at my reaction. "Dead bodies don't make you flinch, but ask you read out someone else's love letter and suddenly, you're all flustered. Come on, Anna."

"All right, fine," I said with a grumble, and I held the note up.

*I have to write this down because I'll never get the courage to say this in person – I think you are the most beautiful, amazing, wonderful and gorgeous person I have ever met. I know you probably won't feel the same way but I have to take my chance. I would love nothing more than for you to go out with me and I think we could be amazing together. You're so sexy and intelligent, you are the perfect woman. Stop giving your attention to men who don't deserve you and give me a chance. I will love you like no one else and more than anyone else. I will treat you like a princess and give you all the things you will ever want. I will kiss you so passionately that you will beg for more. Please talk to me, so I know where I stand.*

When I looked up, I could feel the heat in my cheeks turning me as red as a beetroot. Luckily Aaron didn't notice because he was too busy trying not to laugh.

"Well," he said, "that's certainly wearing your heart on your sleeve. I've never had a declaration of love like that before."

"That's what the note says," I said through gritted teeth as I placed it in an evidence bag. "Although it is pretty heavy for a love note. What's wrong with just 'you're sexy, let's grab a drink' and a phone number? You have to know someone quite well to make a declaration like this."

Aaron turned his gaze away from me, suddenly very interested in the TV stand. "Oh, an expert, are you? Who sends you love notes then?"

"I got a few when I was at school and college," I replied with a prickle. "Mostly from Sam, my ex."

"The ex-boyfriend who's in prison?"

I shot my head up, giving Aaron a glare. His amusement fell away. He knew we didn't discuss that matter. We especially didn't discuss that matter given the new, unexpected development in our own relationship.

"Of course. I haven't had any other boyfriends. I'm gonna see if the SOCOs have found anything in the bedroom."

*  *  *

After wrapping up the search of Miranda's flat, I found Aaron was still hanging around, following me like an enticing smell I couldn't get away from. He even offered to help me go door to door to Miranda's immediate neighbours. I wanted to drill him about why he was wasting his Saturday off at work with me, to make him admit he was waiting for us to discuss the night before. Unfortunately for him, we had work to do.

We took half the building each; Aaron took downstairs, and I took up. I found the upstairs tenants even less forthcoming than I expected. Mostly annoyed at being disturbed by the police, they gave nothing more than grunting answers and poorly concealed sneers. The community spirit only seemed to extend as far as the houses down the street – when it came to the police on your doorstep, the goodwill vanished.

I could never get used to the animosity some people had for the police. Some expected the world of us, whilst others would happily spit in our faces. Many had. I reminded myself it wasn't personal. It was the job, or rather the uniform in my frontline days. It had the wrong image now; constant criticism from the media, rising taxes to fund us, increasing crime rates. No wonder people didn't like the police. They thought we were all useless.

And I was starting to agree.

Despite finding an identity for our victim, by the end of the morning I was no closer to finding the person who had murdered Miranda. She was no saint – a loner and a con artist – but she still deserved justice. Her killer was still walking the streets, going about their day. Who could do something like that to someone and then just carry on as normal?

I met Aaron back outside Miranda's flat in the foul-smelling foyer, just as the SOCOs finished removing anything of interest and sealing the door with crime-scene tape. A bold-headed notice adorned the door: *POLICE LINE – DO NOT CROSS*.

"No luck?" he asked, reading my expression.

I shook my head, a little embarrassed I didn't have more to show for the morning's work. "How can people know so little about this woman? She died a week ago and none of them had even noticed she wasn't around."

"Well, not everyone is friendly with their neighbours," he said. "I don't think I know what mine are called."

"Really?" I wrinkled my nose up as I thought about my neighbours. "I know everything about mine. One of the joys of living in a flat."

"Oh yeah, thin walls," said Aaron with a knowing nod. "I don't know their names but I know the couple next door like to get frisky every Sunday night."

"You can hear that?" I felt my face burn as my eyes widened. "Does that mean…"

Icy cold prickles ran down my neck as he nodded, bemused by my embarrassment.

Thankfully, Aaron moved swiftly on. "People aren't likely to talk to us right now. We're much more likely to get lucky through an appeal for information."

"You think so?"

He gave an earnest nod. "That's been my experience in the past."

I pulled out my phone to make a note to update the appeal when I got back to the office, only to find the battery had died. I felt my pockets for my notebook, but the small rectangular lump wasn't anywhere in my clothing.

"Do you think Chris and Jay will be at the office yet?" I asked.

Aaron laughed under his breath as he watched me search myself. "I will be very surprised if you see Chris at all today. Jay might be there. He can handle his liquor better."

"I guess I'll find out when I get there." What a time to make a big breakthrough – when my team members were too hungover to help.

"Lost something?" he asked, but before I could answer, he pulled my notebook from his pocket. I hastily shoved it back where it belonged, in the back pocket of my trousers.

"Where did you find that?"

"You're a detective, you can work it out," he replied. And without so much as a smile, he turned on his heels and disappeared down the stairs. "I'll meet you back at the station."

Leaving Miranda's flat, I headed for my car, taking a slight detour to the nearest fast-food place on the way before I went back to the nick. Takeaway breakfasts were a bad habit, but I knew there would be nothing of substance back at the station and I needed something to get me through the day. I downed the bad coffee, barely worth the money I'd paid for it, and continued onwards, praying Jay or Chris had managed to drag themselves up.

Instead, I found Aaron already waiting for me in the Serious Crimes office. He'd made himself comfortable at Chris's desk. No sign of either of my teammates.

"Don't you have your own work to do?" I asked him.

He watched me cross the room to my desk, averting his gaze as mine found the fresh cup of coffee he'd left on my desk. When I looked back at him, he was admiring the whiteboard of progress.

"So, we can confirm our victim lived locally and as such, the multiple dating profiles she had online were all lies."

"Yes," I replied.

I took a long gulp of the coffee, which tasted heavenly compared to the fast-food crap I'd just downed. Since he clearly had nothing better to do than hang around with me,

I decided I would at least use Aaron as a sounding board until one of my own teammates showed up.

"I think we can safely assume the profiles were only created to con people into a 'relationship'. She could've gathered thousands of pounds in money and gifts over the years."

"A pretty safe scam if she's conning men all over the country and lying about her location," said Aaron. "They probably wouldn't know how to track her down once they realised that they'd been conned. But what about Justin?"

"What about him?"

"Well…" He gestured to the board. "Where does he live?"

I pulled out my notebook from my back pocket. "Walsoken, just outside of Wisbech."

"So, only about ten miles from Miranda?"

Although Aaron kept his face blank, I heard the infliction in his voice. He thought there was a connection; coincidences were very rarely just coincidences. How likely was it really to live ten miles away, in the next town over, and never meet? This area was sparse but it wasn't impossible.

"Justin said he never met her in real life," I pointed out. "He fully believed she lived in Blackpool or wherever she told him it was. He had no idea she lived nearby."

"Did he tell you this before or after you told him you worked for the police?"

I opened my mouth to answer but fumbled. I knew Aaron was only trying to challenge my assumptions, but I wasn't sure I had the patience to sit here and let him pick apart my reasoning. Especially not with the huge elephant sitting in the corner of the room, a bloated time bomb about to explode.

"You mean did he lie to me?" I replied with a shake of my head. "You saw his reaction to her death. Do you really think he was covering up having murdered her?"

"No," Aaron conceded. "Not necessarily. But it's hard to believe that two people could know each other and have lived in such close proximity without running into one another."

"But it wouldn't be impossible. Especially if Miranda – or Callie, or whatever we should call her – worked night shifts. I don't know everyone between here and Wisbech, and neither do you."

"A good point," he said. "But you must admit that this isn't looking good for Justin."

"His alibi checked out. He was home the whole night of her death."

"Still, he is a suspect. He knew the victim, had a motive to harm her and lived in the same area as her. We should invite him for a voluntary interview."

I cocked an eyebrow at Aaron. "We?"

"I mean, you. The team. You guys." He waved his hand around the office, but it was too late, and I'd already caught the slip. I smirked back.

"You still think you're a part of this team, don't you?"

"No." He scoffed at me. "I didn't mean it like that. But I did use to work in here. You're sitting at my old desk. It's easy to fall into old habits."

"But you have the cushy office now. You don't need to be here, at work, on a Saturday. I have it all under control."

"You do." He was quick to agree. Too quick. And for the first time I wondered if he was actually here to keep an eye on me, rather than to help. It wasn't beyond reason to think I was being shadowed; tested and observed just to make sure I was truly ready for this. Chris was certainly watching me, and Jay was keen to manage me closely. Did Aaron doubt my skills as well?

"Then why not leave me to it? Unless you think I'm not capable of handling this on my own. Are you worried I will crash the whole case if left unsupervised?"

"No, you are perfectly capable."

"But you think I'm not ready to be working independently again."

"I never said that. I don't believe that at all."

"Then why are you really here?"

"Why do you think?" he said, clipped and sharp. After a beat, he sat up, keen to catch my gaze and read my waning expression. The elephant in the room was fit to burst and I was too tired to stop it.

"You want to talk about last night?"

"I think we should," he replied.

My options were limited. I couldn't avoid Aaron forever, but I also couldn't risk distracting myself when there was a case at hand. I didn't know what he thought about the whole drunken event but I already knew his track record.

"We can't," I said, the words sounding even harsher out loud than they felt in my head. "I mean, not right now. We're still at work."

Aaron rose to his feet with a huff. "Then when? You can't avoid this forever, Anna."

"I'm not avoiding it. I just have work to do. And if I need your help, I know where to find you."

Aaron crossed his arms, a defence between the two of us. "Fine," he said, and he let himself out of the office without a further look back.

I grimaced as the door slammed closed, sounding a hundred times louder in the silent office. The swollen elephant in the corner deflated with a pathetic puff of air and I kicked myself for being so harsh. I never wanted to upset Aaron. Later, when I had had enough time to think about what I wanted to do, I would apologise to him.

I took a long sip of the warm coffee in front of me. Damn it, he really did know how I liked it.

# Chapter Sixteen

Zola was a hippy. She was also my downstairs neighbour. Those two facts didn't connect in any way, but they were always the first two things that sprang to my mind every time I saw her. Zola's age was hard to tell, as she dressed in skimpy and funky-patterned handmade clothes, which I was certain were made from old bedclothes. A magnitude of multicoloured dreadlocks and feathers crowned her head. If I had to guess, I would say she was in her mid to late fifties, and let her slap me if I was wrong.

As I dragged myself home in the early hours of the afternoon, Zola was sitting on the stairs between her flat and mine directly above.

"Look who's doing the walk of shame." She whistled as I approached, plodding wearily up the stairs, but she didn't move out of the way.

"This is not the walk of shame," I lied. "I've been at work."

"All night? That would explain why I had to feed your goddamn cat."

"Not my cat," I reminded her. For a hippy, Zola wasn't very tolerant of animals. Or perhaps it was just Poppy. The small feline was quite a tyrant when she wanted to be.

Zola and I had a mutual understanding; we were not the types to ever be natural friends. But when the occasion arose, Zola would feed and look after Poppy for me, and in return, I looked the other way every time the wafts of cannabis came through my flat from downstairs. Which was often.

"Why are you waiting out here for me?" She didn't normally tell me every time she fed Poppy.

"I let your parents in," she said with a nonchalant grin as she pointed at my flat. "Your mum gave me a vegetable lasagne in return for me telling her where you keep the spare key."

"Are you sure they were my parents and not a middle-aged pair of burglars?"

Zola shrugged with such apathy that I wondered why she was even out here at all. "Could have been. Hey, I didn't realise you'd gone back to work. Are you working again tonight?"

"I don't know." I slowed my steps. "Why?"

"I'm having some friends over. We might get a bit… loud."

The way she said 'loud' made me pause; she didn't mean it in a raving party sense. Zola was a very open, free-loving type of person. The music wouldn't be loud but the guests would be.

"Be as loud as you want," I said, hastily stepping over her. "I'll make sure I'm not in earshot."

"Thanks, pet." Zola winked at me and jumped to her feet. "I'm glad you've finally got back on the horse."

"You mean, you're glad I'm back to work?" I frowned. I was sure having a police officer for a neighbour was no fun.

"Yeah, sure." She winked again. "Whichever horse it is that keeps you out all night in the same clothes." And with one last leering wink, she vanished into her flat.

I sighed heavily, making me sound at least thirty years older than I actually was. At least that conversation was less awkward than the first time Zola had asked me about one of her parties, and then asked me if I wanted to join in. I could turn a blind eye to recreational drug use but partaking in sex parties was definitely a limit for me.

I braced myself at my door. Not only were my parents inside, uninvited, but now I only had about six hours before who knew what sort of gathering started going on under my floor. It felt like the whole day was punishing me for giving in to my desires for one night.

I found Dad camped out on the sofa, watching the football highlights, and Mum in the kitchen washing up. At least when Mum came over unannounced, she took it upon herself to do some housework.

"You shouldn't soak this pan," she said as I entered, her back to the door. "It'll ruin it."

"Noted," I replied. I slipped off my shoes and discarded my keys, but being home didn't bring any comfort or relief. The situation with Aaron still loomed at the back of my mind, threatening to drag me back down to the depths I had felt twenty-four hours before, when our case seemed impossible to close.

"Your hippy neighbour let us in."

"Yes, she told me. Why are you here?"

Mum threw the tea towel over her shoulder as she rounded on me. "I haven't heard from you in three days, and you weren't answering your phone."

"I've been busy at work. My phone died." I waved the useless device at her to prove my point.

She huffed, unimpressed with my answers. "You're always busy at work. You shouldn't even *be* at work, you're off sick."

"Good point. Why are you really here?" I asked.

Mum narrowed her gaze at me, but it didn't work, I didn't back down. She had another reason for being here. She glanced at Dad, who wasn't at all interested in our conversation.

"I need Aaron's phone number."

My heart stuttered at the mention of Aaron.

"You what? Why?" I held off letting the panic cross my face. What did she know? My mother and her friends were relentless gossips, to the point of being considered stalkers in some respects. Was it possible she knew about our night together? Had someone she'd known seen us walking home together or our awkwardness at the victim's flat?

"Because he hasn't called Liz back yet. I think a push in the right direction might be needed."

The relief was like a flood of fresh water.

"No way."

"Why not?" she demanded.

"Because I can't. Confidentiality, data protection, all that jazz." And the fact that I just didn't want her sticking her nose in where it wasn't wanted.

Mum harrumphed and returned to the washing. "Fine. I'm sure I can get it another way." She glanced at me out the corner of her eye. "Why do you look like you haven't slept all night?"

For goodness' sake. Her cunning plan foiled, now she was going to turn on me.

"I did sleep but I was called into work early," I lied.

"Anna, you are my only child. I know full well what you look like when you haven't got enough sleep." Mum looked back at me with an unusual amount of worry filling her face. "This case, whatever it is and whatever is going on, has affected you."

"If you say so."

"I'm serious, Anna. It's not healthy to be working so much, losing sleep. It's taken you months to find your feet again. You shouldn't be throwing yourself back into a serious case, dealing with murderers and rapists and who else knows what other horrible, evil people are out there." She shot me a glare, as if that might make me open up and tell her all my troubles. But it wasn't going to happen.

"Yes, Mum…"

She gave an exasperated sigh. "Oh, Anna. For once, why don't you stop to think about what you need from your life to make you happy, rather than just living from one moment to the next? Make a plan, something that will kickstart a better state of mind. It's not healthy to bottle it all up inside, you need to be able to share it with someone."

I opened my mouth to make a joke about her wanting to become a life coach, but stopped myself as I caught sight of her expression. My mum might have been meddlesome, nosy and opinionated, but she was often right. Her setting me up on a date with Charlie Sweeney was just her way of trying to make me see that I could find someone to build a life with, if only I allowed myself to do so. She worried about me, and no matter how hard I tried to protect her, she always would.

"I'll think about it, Mum," I promised. She'd given me plenty to think about.

* * *

My dear teammates, seemingly forgetting that I had picked up the slack for them the whole day, called me into work that evening.

"Good work," Chris greeted me as I arrived. Both him and Jay were waiting outside the station, takeaway coffees in hand. Jay handed me one as I approached and promptly turned me around, heading back to the car park. The growing night brought with it a cool breeze and a canvas of twinkling stars overhead, but it was calm, like the countryside had exhaled the day away.

"Thanks?" I couldn't tell if he was being sincere.

Chris continued. "I mean it, this is the best progress we've made since the victim died. Now we have a name, we can contact her next of kin, her work colleagues. It won't be long before we find any other dirty little secrets she had."

I could hardly believe my ears; he was being sincere.

"Where are we going?" I asked.

Jay paused outside his car and motioned for me to get in. "We're off to the store where Miranda worked to speak with the manager who called her in as missing."

"All three of us?"

Jumping in the car like a child with a new toy, Jay nodded. "While we're chatting with the manager, we thought it'd be a good idea for you to put your ear to the ground and see what you can get out of the rest of the colleagues. Someone there must know more about our victim than we have already gleaned about her."

I couldn't disagree with their logic so together we set off. On the south side of town, in an ever-expanding shopping and industrial estate known as the Hardwick, we parked up in the car park of the local megastore. Its illuminated sign shone like a beacon in the blueish hues of the late-evening sky. The usually jammed roads were quiet and sparse, but the big supermarket was still busy with late-night shoppers.

After a quick chat at the customer service desk, a store colleague took us to the back of the shop, away from the customers. Back there, the bustle of the shop floor vanished, but up ahead of the plain, scuffed corridor, I could hear a commotion going on. The colleague opened the door to the staff canteen, where a group of ten employees sat around a table, deep in conversation. A mix of men and women, young and old, their speculations bouncing around the room.

"This has to be about Miranda. She didn't show up for work again last night."

"Yeah, I heard Jeremy called the police."

"I was just following procedure, there's no need to be alarmed."

"We better be getting overtime for this. I'm usually in bed at this time."

Chris cleared his throat and the room fell silent. Ten pairs of eyes turned on us, each wide with either shock, awe or irritation.

"Officers," the closest person said, standing up to greet us. He was a tall, scrawny bloke, thin glasses hanging off his angled nose, about late-thirties. He shook Chris's hand. "I did as you asked, these are Miranda's colleagues from the night shift. I haven't said anything else."

Chris hummed, not particularly impressed with the weedy guy's eagerness. "Thank you. I daresay you've already guessed why we're here. I'm afraid to tell you all that Miranda Alder was found deceased a week ago. We are currently conducting inquiries into her death and would appreciate some time to talk to each of you."

A ripple ran through the group, each giving a stiff inhale or bewildered frown at us. But they stayed silent and tight-lipped.

"Of course," the man said, giving his colleagues a pointed look, but it was too weak for them to notice. "Company policy is for us to all be cooperative with any investigation."

"Miranda's dead?" a young lad asked, his voice wavering. He was the youngest of the group, with shaggy black hair which flopped over his eyes. He seemed to be the only one visibly shaken by news of Miranda's death. His hands trembled as he fiddled with his collar.

"Is this anything to do with that body found by the Red Mount last week?" a woman asked, giving the young lad a pat on the back.

"We're not at liberty to say," Jay replied. "However, we are treating Miranda's death as suspicious at this time."

A round of hushed whispers ran through the group, but most seemed eager to speculate rather than grieve. Chris coughed again, silencing the room.

"We'll speak to the manager first. Then we'll make our way round you all. Thank you for your cooperation."

## Chapter Seventeen

The weedy man turned out to be the night-shift manager, his name badge reading, *Hello, my name is Jeremy. I'm here to help!* He showed the three of us to a small office with no windows, lined with filing cabinets and a desk scattered with papers. There were only two seats, so Jay and Jeremy sat while Chris and I hovered near the door. Now that I could get a closer look at Jeremy, I could see his bottom lip tremored as he tumbled over his words.

"Should I have someone here?" he asked. "Like a solicitor. HR?"

Jay shook his head, doing his best to put the man at ease with a relaxed grin. "No, Jeremy, you're not in any trouble. We're just trying to find out some more information about Miranda to explain her death."

Jeremy swallowed hard. "She's really dead?"

"Unfortunately, yes." Jay pulled out his notebook from his jacket pocket. "It happened a week ago. Why did it take you so long to conduct a welfare check?"

"She had booked the last few days off as annual leave," Jeremy explained, speaking rapidly. "She was due back Thursday but didn't show. Two no-shows in a row, we conduct a welfare check, but when I got no answer from her at home, I thought I better call you guys."

"How long had you worked with her?"

"For as long as she's worked here, over two years." He rattled through his answers as though he was on the clock, his legs twitching. "I can't believe she's gone. Was she in her flat? Was she there this whole time and no one knew?"

"Best to let me ask the questions, Jeremy. It's still an open investigation. Did Miranda only work the night shift?"

Jeremy jerked his head. I was beginning to wonder if the man was in control of his bodily movements at all. "She's always done the night shift, 9 to 5 a.m. four days a week. She's the only peppy one at that time of the night. The customers love her. She mostly works the customer service checkout. You know, selling cigarettes, lottery, that stuff."

"Did you ever socialise outside of work?"

"Sometimes we'd go for breakfast after work as a team."

"What about your other colleagues? Was she close with anyone here?"

He shook his head so fast I thought it might spin off. "Not really. I don't think she would socialise with them out of work, but you'd have to ask them."

"Did she ever mention a boyfriend to you? Or a significant other? Did Miranda live with anyone?"

"No." Jeremy slowed his answers as he gave Jay a wary look. "Sometimes she had a date but never anything serious."

"When did you last see Miranda?" Jay didn't falter and continued to fire out questions. He was giving Jeremy little room to think before he answered.

I risked a glance at Chris, wondering if he'd noticed the sudden change in pace of Jeremy's replies. The nervousness was still there but now he spoke with less vigour.

"Last Friday night, a week ago."

"Did she mention she had any plans for the Saturday night? That she was meeting with anyone?"

"No, I don't think so."

Over by the door, Chris shuffled his weight from one foot to the other. The distraction made Jeremy jump, as though he had forgotten we were there.

"Who worked with Miranda on her last shift here?" he asked.

Jeremy pulled a piece of paper from a noticeboard on the wall, held up by a large clip labelled *graveyard shift*. "Here's the shift rota from last week. You'll see everyone who usually worked with Miranda. They work various shifts but everyone who usually works the same days as Miranda is in the canteen now. We're a… we were a good team."

Chris glanced over the list before handing it to me, a subtle hint that I should follow up with those people. I slipped out of the room. The door creaked behind me as Chris slid out too.

"What did you notice about him?" he asked, lingering in the corridor above a flickering LED light.

"Jeremy? He spoke fast, seemed quite jittery. But then he faltered when asked if Miranda had a boyfriend," I said.

I wasn't sure what else I should have noticed. Was this a test to prove if I was worthy of the Serious Crimes team?

"He did. That's always a red flag to me. Could possibly mean that he knew Miranda had a partner that we don't know about," said Chris.

"Or he could have just been nervous. We did just confirm the death of his co-worker. And in my experience, most people speak quickly when speaking to the police, especially if it's their first time. We make people nervous."

"Okay, let's test this theory then." He pointed to the staff canteen back down the corridor. "We'll take half the list each. Let's see how many are nervous when speaking to us."

\* \* \*

Miranda's colleagues were a complete bust at proving my theory. Most of them were cool, collected and not at all nervous.

The first employee on my list was Greg Hanson, a gruff young man with a shaggy gingery beard, beady eyes and shaved head, who worked in the warehouse. As he sat down opposite me in a corner of the staff canteen, his top lip curled into a sneer.

"I barely knew Miranda," he said before I could even introduce myself. "I've only worked here four weeks."

"You didn't talk with her at all?" I asked. He wasn't getting out of talking to me that easily. "From what I've heard, Miranda was a friendly, chatty person."

"Nope." Greg crossed his arms across his chest. "I work out the back."

"What about socialising outside of work? Jeremy says the team sometimes go for breakfast after shift."

"Well then, Jeremy is a bullshitter. He's never taken me for breakfast."

That conversation went nowhere fast as Greg maintained that he didn't know Miranda, had no idea about her death and, to be honest, wasn't even sure which co-worker she was. I showed him a picture from my case file. When he saw the duck face pout that she used to lure in her victims online, Greg sneered but steadfastly maintained he knew nothing of her death.

A pattern seemed to emerge as I spoke to Miranda's other colleagues. The female co-workers all had a certain idea of her; that she was boastful and exaggerated a lot. The males said that she made them uncomfortable with her flirting and over-friendliness. They all avoided her whenever they could. Not the friendliest bunch but also not emotionally invested enough to wish Miranda harm. Only one person out of the group appeared nervous to speak to me – the only one visibly upset by her death.

The younger lad hung in the corner of the canteen until it was his turn. I guessed he was probably about eighteen, fresh out of school. His badge told me his name was Nick Bellamy. The staff rota told me he was a shelf stacker – *stock replenisher.* And he more than proved my theory about speaking fast when nervous.

"Slow down, Nick," I told him once again. "I only asked if you have worked here long." I wondered if he had some form of social anxiety. He was finding it hard to look at me as I spoke to him.

"No." He shook his head. "Only three months. It's my first proper job, I haven't had one this long before."

"Did you get on with Miranda?"

"Yeah, she was really cool. I liked her. Not many people liked her but I did." His foot tapped rapidly on the floor. Many of the other night-shift colleagues had left now that their turn was over, but he eyed the remaining ones with distaste.

"Who was she closest to out of everyone here?"

"Me. And Jeremy, she laughed with Jeremy, but she talked to me. She told me everything." A smile crossed the young lad's face, souring almost as quickly as it came.

"Everything, huh? What did she tell you? Would she have told you if she was meeting up with someone for a date?" I asked.

Nick nodded.

"Did she mention that she planned to meet with someone on the night she died?"

"No, she didn't say."

"Did she tell you anything else? Did she have any friends she spoke about or people she fancied?"

"No, but she said she had a lot of admirers. She said these men were rich and they could whisk her away at any moment if she wanted them to, but the only reason she wouldn't go was because of her dad. He's in a nursing home."

"Which nursing home?"

"Dunno."

"Did she name any of these admirers or say where they were from?" I asked.

"No."

Ugh, this wasn't going far.

"Nick." I leaned forwards, causing him to jolt back. "You said Miranda told you everything. But she didn't tell you who she was meeting on the night she died?"

Nick raised his hand to his mouth and began to chew the sleeve of his shirt. He shook his head with vigour.

"So, she didn't tell you everything?"

He shrugged, actual words not forthcoming and again, his eyes darted around the canteen.

An irritated sigh escaped my lips. "All right, Nick. How about we continue this chat after your shift? At the police station."

The young lad paled. "Station?"

"You knew Miranda the best out of everyone. It might be easier to talk away from everything going on here." I waved my hand at the room around us.

Jay had entered, speaking to Chris by the door, where the pair watched my exchange with Nick. Nick gave them a wary look. After a brief pause, Nick grunted, the only indication that he agreed to the idea. Then he rose from the table and slunk away, still chewing his sleeve like a baby.

When I re-joined Jay and Chris and we exited the supermarket, Jay revealed he'd asked Jeremy to report to the station later too. Chris had obtained the store's CCTV footage for both the Friday night of Miranda's last shift and the Saturday night of her death for us to analyse.

"So," said the team leader, not looking my way to try and hide the slightly smug look on his face, "did you find many of the co-workers nervous when speaking to you at all?"

"Only one," I conceded. "The rest just acted like the whole thing was an inconvenience."

I glanced back at the superstore, highlighted by bright floodlights against the serene backdrop of the night sky. I wondered if our presence had affected any of them; if any of them, apart from Nick, would miss Miranda.

"And what does that tell you?" Chris asked.

"That Miranda wasn't very popular among her colleagues," I replied, voicing the thoughts that had grown the more I spoke to her night-shift co-workers. "Not many of them liked her. Nick was the only one willing to call her a friend. On the whole, they weren't affected by news of her death in the slightest."

As Chris and Jay reached the car, they waited for me as I lagged a few steps behind. They grimaced at each other.

"We've still got to track down her next of kin." Jay plastered a reassuring grin on his face, going too far to be genuine. "That's a new avenue we haven't explored yet."

"And we can't rule out any of the colleagues until we've checked the CCTV footage," said Chris with a curt nod. "We're finally getting somewhere. It might not feel like many of these people care about Miranda Alder's death," he waved in the direction of the store, "but we do, and we'll find who killed her."

I nodded too, more to convince myself than to convince anyone else.

# Chapter Eighteen

So much for my weekend. I was back at the station at 6 a.m. on Sunday, waiting for Miranda's colleagues to appear as they finished their night shifts. The station was peaceful at this time of the day. Only the merrymakers from the night before were about as they left the drunk tank, sheepish and very sober, facing a long walk back to the town centre.

Jay and I hovered by the front desk, waiting for Jeremy and Nick to arrive. I hoped we could get this over and done with quickly so that I could claw back some of my day. Tiredness tugged at my eyelids. Zola's shenanigans had been in full swing when I got home after visiting the megastore. Sleep was hard to achieve when trying to avoid listening in on such a loud gathering.

I stifled a yawn. "Where's Chris?"

"He'll be in later. He said we can do this without him," Jay replied. "You can lead the interview."

"He said that? Why?" Just a few days ago, Chris wanted me off the team. Maybe I was finally winning him round.

"He didn't say that exactly, but I want to see what you've got. I haven't seen you interview before."

I opened my mouth to protest and remind him that this wasn't my first day on the job. But before I could put Jay right about my abilities, Jeremy entered the station.

I showed him to the same interview room Aaron had shown me to just a week before. Jeremy glanced nervously at the observation window, looking more like a mirror from this side, but I assured him no one would be watching us. Jay remained quiet as he took a seat, watching me as much as Jeremy.

"Okay," I said to the night-shift manager as I started the recorder and stated the time and date. I went through the procedure, informing him of his right to a solicitor and all that jazz, which made Jeremy's eyes grow wider. "Please, state your name for the record."

He coughed nervously. "Jeremy Payton... This isn't a simple unexplained death, is it? Something bad happened to Miranda."

I nodded. There was no point in hiding it from him; we wouldn't get any honesty from him unless we were honest first.

"Miranda's body was discovered in The Walks by the Red Mount Chapel last Saturday night. She was stabbed multiple times. As someone who knew Miranda well and was possibly one of the last people to see her alive, we'd like your statement for our records. Are you okay for me to continue?"

Poor Jeremy paled. He pushed his glasses up his nose and took a large gulp of air, cheeks flapping like a fish snatched from the water. After a moment, he nodded at me, ready to continue although he didn't look it.

"Jeremy, when was the last time you saw Miranda Alder?" I asked.

"Friday night, a week ago, at work." Jeremy shifted his glasses to rub his eyes, tiredness growing on his face.

"That was the last shift before Miranda was going on annual leave for a few days, correct?"

"Yes," he replied.

"Did she say anything about her plans for those days? Was she planning to meet with anyone?"

"No, she didn't say."

"Nothing at all? No shopping trips or lie-ins. She said nothing?" I asked. For a woman supposedly prone to exaggeration and bragging, I found it hard to believe.

"It's not that she said nothing." Jeremy stumbled a little. "Miranda was... she liked to tell stories. She was a bit of a dreamer. It was hard to know what she was fantasising about and what was actually true. Most of the time, we just chalked it up to fantasies."

"What sort of things did she fantasise about?"

"She used to go around saying she had lots of admirers, secret lovers, that sort of thing. I don't know how true it was. She did appear to have nice gifts sometimes. She showed up with this really expensive watch one day and I knew she couldn't afford it."

"So, you think maybe there was some truth behind it?" I asked. "Maybe she did have a secret admirer?"

"No, I think she made it up. She probably bought the gifts herself."

"And where were you last Saturday night, the night of her death?"

His reply was instant. "At work. All night. You can check the logs."

Although his hands fiddled with his wedding ring, Jeremy's tone was far more assertive than before. Miranda's death had settled on him, and he realised now how easily the cloud of suspicion could fall on him.

"Are you married?" I asked.

He looked at me with a little frown. Next to me, Jay gave the slightest of hums; he approved of my shift in questions.

"Yeah, four years."

"Any kids?"

"Two. Emma is three, Logan is one."

"Sounds like you've got your hands full there. And working night shifts must be hard on family life. Do you see much of your wife and children?"

"Sundays, when the store is shut overnight. And on the odd weekend off. But it's very hard."

"Where were you the night Miranda was killed, Jeremy?"

"At work all night, I've told you."

"Talk me through that whole day, the Saturday."

"Um…" Jeremy glanced between me and Jay, confused. "I woke up at six in the evening, just in time to put the kids to bed. Then Kate and I had dinner and spent some time together. Then I went to work at 9 p.m. It was a busy night, especially with one person off. I finished at 6 a.m., did the handover, came home and got the kids up. I went to bed about ten."

"Who else was at work that night?"

"Everyone except Miranda."

"And no one left during those hours? No one could have slipped out?"

"Not without my knowledge."

"What was your relationship with Miranda like?"

"We got on well. She was a good laugh."

"Would you describe yourself as friends?"

"Yeah, I suppose."

"More than friends?"

"Umm… Well, not really. I was her boss."

"What about the other employees, did she get on with them?"

"Not particularly. Only Nick really, the others didn't have much time for her and her fantasies. She would brag about her gifts, and it pissed people off."

"But you could put up with the bragging and stories?"

He shrugged, tugging at his collar as though he was hot. "I just didn't take her at face value. These admirers she said she had; they were just stories. Some people have so much crap going on in their lives that they feel the need to make up a persona for work to hide the truth. I just assumed Miranda was like that."

"Did Miranda and Nick ever socialise outside of work?" We were interviewing Nick next, but it was still a good idea to get another person's perspective of him.

"Not that I'm aware of. Nick idolised Miranda, he was completely smitten with her, but she only gave him the time of day when it suited her."

"Really? Because he described their relationship as very close."

"It was some days. Other days she just ignored him or could be a bit nasty. I pulled her up on it a few times. But poor Nick, he never noticed, he was too in love with her. He's a bit… odd."

\* \* \*

Nick was next for interview. Jay said little as we finished up with Jeremy and fetched Nick, so I guessed I was leading this one too. I had no idea if I was succeeding in this little test, but I was sure my interview skills were rusty, and Jay's expression was harder to read than a doctor's handwriting.

Nick sat hunched in the chair opposite me, huddled inside his oversized hoodie as though he was willing it to swallow him. He glanced nervously at Jay and me, back and forth like he was watching a game of tennis.

"Nicholas Frederick Bellamy," he replied when I asked him to state his name.

"Now, Nick, you're not in any trouble here," I said to reassure him. It didn't relax him in the slightest. "I'm just going to ask you some questions about Miranda, and I need to you to answer honestly. Don't guess or speculate, just tell me what you know about her. It may help us to find who killed her."

He nodded and raised his hand to his mouth to start chewing on his hoodie sleeve.

"When did you last see Miranda?"

"In the car park. Friday night. I mean, Saturday morning. After our Friday night shift. I waved goodbye to her."

"Did she wave back?" I asked carefully. He was like a tight coil ready to snap at any second.

He nodded with a hint of a smile as he remembered.

"Did she tell you of any plans she had for that weekend?"

"No."

"Was she planning to meet with anyone? A friend perhaps?"

"I don't know."

"What can you tell me about these admirers Miranda said she had? Did you ever meet any of them?"

"No, they were all on the internet. They didn't live round here."

I tried not to let any frustration seep into my even voice. A night shift hadn't changed Nick's demeanour in the slightest, but his talkativeness had vanished along with the night. "But you knew about them? Did Miranda ever tell you their names?"

"Not really, maybe one called Mike. I don't remember, it changed quickly."

"What changed quickly?"

"The guy who was after her. There were lots of them. She was always really excited when she had one who was rich and liked buying her expensive gifts. She liked to show them to me."

"So, you knew that she lied to men online to get them to give her gifts and money? That she was a catfish?"

Nick shrugged like a moody teenager. It had been a while since I was a moody teenager myself – and I could have rivalled the worst of them – but my ability to speak their unspoken language was waning.

"Is that a yes, Nick?"

He nodded with a quiet, "S'pose."

"What gifts did she get?"

Nick hummed a moment. "There was a gold watch, earrings, a bracelet that had lots of charms on it, a necklace with a big stone in it. And a new mobile phone and a computer. Lots of clothes. There were loads of things."

"Did you get jealous of all the things Miranda had?"

"No," he answered instantly but glanced my way. "Maybe a little."

"Did you ever wish you had some of those things?"

"I didn't steal anything off her! Miranda is my friend."
Nick sat up in his chair, like a bolt of lightning had shot
through him. He glared at me, red-ringed eyes peering out
from under his mop. I didn't move or react. I'd been
squared up to enough times to know a cool response was
the best way forward.

"She was your friend," I agreed calmly.

"I don't have many friends…"

I felt a pang of sympathy for the young lad who was
desperately chewing a hole in his own jacket sleeve. He
was sad and scared, and that sometimes came out as anger.
I knew he hadn't stolen from Miranda. All the items he'd
listed were found in her flat or on her body, the only thing
missing being the mobile phone.

"Why is that, Nick?"

"I was expelled from school. I get angry sometimes, I
did some bad things. No one wanted to be friends with
me. Then Mum got me a job at night, where there
wouldn't be many people around, and Miranda was the
only person who was nice to me. She's my friend."

"Do you like your job?"

"Yeah, it's good."

"Do you like your boss, Jeremy?"

Nick finally leaned back in his chair. "A bit. He makes
fun of me."

"Does he? What does he make fun about?"

"Miranda. He says I love her. He calls me things like a
lapdog, whipped, and a stalker. I don't know what some of
that stuff means but he laughs more when I ask."

"That sounds like bullying, Nick. Have you ever told
anyone about it?"

He shook his head. "I like my job. And I try really hard
not to get angry. Mum says to ignore him because it's
childish."

"I think that's good advice," I said kindly. Maybe I was
making my assumption a little naively, but Nick wasn't a
bad kid. I believed him when he said he tried very hard to

control his emotions. "Can you tell me one more thing, Nick? Did Miranda ever mention someone called Justin?"

He shook his head again. "I don't think so. Maybe. I don't know."

"Okay, thank you."

## Chapter Nineteen

"You were good in there," said Jay after we'd finished up with Nick and shown him out of the station. We made our way upstairs to the office, the station still quiet for a Sunday morning.

"Did I pass your little test?"

"It wasn't a test. I told you, I just wanted to see you in action. So, what do you think of them?" Jay asked, acting far too innocent. His inquisitive gaze sought out the whiteboard of progress.

"I think Jeremy is a bullying wanker and Nick is a lovesick child," I replied. In the safety of the office, there was no need to hide my thoughts of them.

Jay barked a laugh. "Don't hold back. Do you think either of them have motives?"

"Not really. Jeremy doesn't, he just found her a bit annoying. Nick has anger issues. It's possible he snapped but I doubt he would harm Miranda, they were friends. I didn't get the sense that he was hiding anything and his reaction to Miranda's death was the most genuine out of the lot of them. He's the only one who actually seems sad she's dead."

Jay grimaced as he flopped into his chair. "I agree. And if we confirm that they were both working at the store at the time of Miranda's death then we're still no closer to finding who stabbed her."

I shook my head, my disappointment evident, and yawned again.

"Oh well, we have several leads to follow up on," Jay continued. "I'll look for Miranda's next of kin. You can wade through the CCTV footage from the store and corroborate the alibis of Nick and Jeremy. Let's see how far we can get by the end of tomorrow."

"You don't think we'll finish it before then?"

Jay smiled, a handsome smile that crinkled his eyes and made his face glow. His positivity was almost infectious, a stark contrast to Chris and his usual glumness. "I think you need to go home for a rest."

"Is that another order?" I felt myself grin, even as a yawn tried to warp my jaw open once more.

He gave a subtle nod. "I'm pretty sure working the DCs to exhaustion is frowned upon, so yes. Besides, the store has over thirty CCTV cameras. I don't think you'll finish watching it this week."

\* \* \*

When I finally made it home to the peace of my own flat, I could feel the tension from the whole weekend in my shoulders. I ran myself a bath, as hot as I could take it, and sank into the water to wait for it to ease my woes away. That was wishful thinking though – it would take more than some hot water in my eighties-era tub to soothe my thoughts.

My mind reeled about the case and all I had discovered about Miranda in the interim. We were closer than we had ever been before but still felt so far away from finding her killer. There were so many avenues to look down, so many leads to follow now, when before there had been none. I didn't know where to start and the ideas spun round and round, too fleeting to capture. I would have to rely on Jay and Chris for guidance on where to investigate next.

Jay was right, I needed a rest. Keen to prove myself, I was in danger of working myself too hard. But when I was so close to finding out the truth, I wasn't about to stop myself and give up just for the sake of sleep. This wasn't something I could switch off from.

When I got out of the bath, my flat was cold and empty. Poppy was nowhere to be seen; probably downstairs with Zola, her way of turning her little pink nose up at me for abandoning her the other night. Without even the small presence of the cat, the place felt hollow.

I shivered and pulled my towel around me tighter. Was this how Miranda felt? She had no one to keep her warm at night, just a string of desperate, perverted guys on the internet who didn't even know her real name. It must have been a lonely existence.

I hadn't ever felt this lonely before. I was usually quite happy on my own. But now I felt the empty air around me more than ever and crawled deeper into my self-pity, wishing it would go away.

I hadn't had a real relationship since I was eighteen. It had ended in disaster and I hadn't seen Sam since. I had dates in the years between, some lasted a few months, but the flings were never long enough to label as anything. And they nearly always ended because I was far more interested in my work than I was in the other person.

But I didn't have to be alone. A small voice in the back of my mind reminded that it didn't have to be that way. In fact, only two nights before, I had been the opposite of alone. I'd been with Aaron, and as much as I tried to ignore it, I had very much enjoyed it.

As my conscience relived our satisfying time together, my subconscious got me dressed. I found my car keys. Before I knew it, I was driving from one town to another, hair still wet from the bath and my worst casual clothes on. Hopefully it wouldn't matter.

I stopped my car outside Aaron's house, leaving it behind his SUV on the street. My conscience finally took over once again as I knocked on the door. What was I doing? I was drowning myself in my own despondency and now I was at his door again. I couldn't do this to myself. If I was lonely and wanted companionship then I was at the wrong door. This was just a short-term fix to a bigger problem.

From inside the house, I heard the thumping of footsteps. It was too late. He'd heard me knock.

I owed him an explanation at the very least. Despite my own feelings flitting between longing for him more and eagerness to push this situation far away, I still owed him an apology.

"Hey." He looked surprised to see me. A small smile crept onto his face as he took me in, amused by my presence.

"Hi," I said, the word sounding far more nervous than I'd intended. "Can we talk?"

"Of course." The smile disappeared and Aaron moved aside to let me in.

Only when I was inside – placing my keys on the same side table we had knocked over during our making out – did the dread of the conversation in front of me make itself known. It drenched me like a cold shower. What was I going to say?

This was Aaron. He didn't do relationships. And if I was honest with myself, that was what I wanted most, wasn't it? I wanted not only physical attraction, but a deeper connection, and someone who understood me, every part, and who cared.

I made myself comfortable on Aaron's pristine grey couch and he sat in the chair opposite me. He gave me a quizzical look and before I could line up the words to say, he opened his mouth.

"I'm sorry, Anna."

My eyes widened. "You are? What for?"

"For bringing up Sam yesterday," he said, his hands twisting around each other. "It just slipped out, I never meant to remind you of him. I didn't realise it was still sore subject."

"I'm not here about that," I said hastily. "I'm sorry for pushing you away."

Aaron shrugged. "I deserved it."

"You didn't."

"Still, I shouldn't have brought him up."

"You just caught me off guard," I said. "I try not to think about Sam. But I'm not upset about it, promise. He was a long time ago."

Aaron hummed as he found a piece of lint on the arm of the chair. "You know, he's up for parole soon."

I nodded. I knew that. I kept a close eye on any news concerning that particular person. "Yeah. How do you know that?"

Aaron's gaze darted away, unable to look at me. "I have a mate in the prison service who keeps an eye on his appeal for me. You only told me about him once, but it was enough to know he's not one to mess with."

"I don't even remember telling you," I admitted.

"It was a long time ago," he said.

He fell quiet, focusing on the piece of dust he rolled between his forefinger and thumb. I watched his hands and imagined those fingers were rolling over me instead. The thoughts made my mouth run dry. I could feel his touch, and I longed for it once again.

"What did you want to talk about?" he asked.

I swallowed in a useless attempt to get the saliva going again. "The other night." As if that wasn't obvious. "The... what do we call it?"

"I don't know," he replied with a fleeting smile as he remembered it too.

"One night."

"One night," Aaron repeated but he sounded unsure. "Is that all you want?"

"It's all it should be," I said. "Come on, Aaron. We both know this isn't a good idea. We're colleagues, for a start. We have to work together."

"We can be professional."

"I know that."

"It's not like we did it in the office."

"Aaron!" I laughed and felt my cheeks burn under his gaze. "There are rules about this sort of thing."

"We didn't do anything wrong, Anna. If relationships with co-workers were forbidden, then half the force would be gone. It's only a problem if it's in the chain of command."

"Which we are now."

He may have been several rungs above the ladder than me, but Aaron was now station lead. I and everyone I worked with ultimately reported to him.

Aaron considered this for a moment. "It's only frowned upon. Anyway, if it was only one night then it doesn't matter."

He rose from the chair and slid onto the sofa next to me. He was right. If it was only one night – one drunken mistake – then it didn't matter. We would just go back to how it had always been.

"Is that what you wanted to hear, Anna?"

No, it wasn't. I wasn't sure why I even came here, because although what he said was true, it was still disappointing.

Aaron touched my shoulder, catching my gaze.

"What do you want?" I asked him. In all this musing about my own feelings, I'd neglected to consider his.

"Me?" He frowned and threw one arm around the back of the sofa, brushing past my damp hair. "I want whatever makes you happy."

"That's noble but it's bullshit. What do you really want?"

He inhaled stiffly. Again, I felt that arm around my back lightly swish my hair as if he wanted to reach out and touch me. With painfully slow movements, his fingers grazed my neck, sending a shiver down my spine.

"I want more than one night."

My breath caught in my throat.

"When I was drunk, I thought this was a bad idea, but now…" Aaron's lips reached my ear, brushing tentatively over my burning hot skin. "I just can't stop thinking about you."

And just like that, I was gone. That sensible voice in my mind telling me to stick to one night vanished into thin air, replaced with the same uninhibited idiot that usually came out when I was drunk.

Just one more night wouldn't hurt me. I could do this; I could stop this liaison before I developed feelings. Aaron was happy keeping things casual and, as he kissed me hard, causing my heart to pulsate, I assured myself that I could be too.

## Chapter Twenty

This time, Zola did catch me doing the walk of shame as I skulked home in the early hours of the morning to shower and dress before heading to work. She didn't say anything, just gave me a knowing smile and an exaggerated wink as she set off for her morning jog.

Once refreshed and ready to face the day, I went back downstairs and got into my car, which gave a few worrying turnovers before spluttering to life. I breathed a sigh of relief. My bank account couldn't cope with any costly repairs and I needed the old vehicle to get to work. It wasn't the best and it definitely didn't like the potholed roads leading up to the station. Forced to take it slow and steady for fear of losing the exhaust, I heard an impatient roar build behind me. A souped-up motorbike overtook me, too frustrated to wait behind my ageing motor any longer. It ignored the traffic lights ahead and jumped through a red light, riding off into the distance as I turned left for the station.

At work, I found Jay in the office, standing by his desk with his computer off. He tapped his foot impatiently.

"Good," he greeted me. "Let's go."

"Where are we going?"

"Heacham. I found Miranda's father."

He handed me a note and disappeared from view, expecting me to follow.

*Robert Alder – South View House, Cheney Hill, Heacham.*

"I'll drive," he insisted over his shoulder.

As I traced Jay's footsteps back downstairs and out to his car, I felt a knot form in my stomach. At long last, we had found the family of the Catfish Girl. Finally, someone was about to mourn her death. Nothing about this task was exciting or fun, but the anticipation still wavered inside, giving me strength. I needed to know that Miranda Alder would be missed by someone, no matter what opinions everyone else held about her. I needed to know that she wasn't as alone as I feared she was.

Heacham was half village, half holiday park, located on the Norfolk coast, about fifteen miles from King's Lynn. It sat next to the more famous seaside resort of Hunstanton, but Heacham had its own charms and plenty of holidaymakers, especially on a bright June day like today. Travelling closer to the north Norfolk coast, fields disappeared, replaced with stretching pine forests until suddenly, the sea was in view. Today the water over the Wash was grey and dull compared to the bright blue sky above.

I found South View House easily enough, on the main road into the village. Jay followed my directions into the car park. A large purple sign hung by the front door – *South View House, Private Residential Care*. It was a nursing home. Everything was peaceful as we parked and rang the front doorbell for entry. Everything seemed peaceful by the coast. We were still too far away to hear the sea, but the salt in the air gave the whole place a nostalgic feel, reminding me of seaside caravan holidays as a child where my mum insisted on working on her tan and my dad taught me to paddleboard.

A nurse let us in, who when faced with my police ID badge and Jay's sternest expression, ushered us into an office. There, we came face to face with a plump woman with a toothy smile and very long false nails. She motioned for us to sit down.

"Hello, I'm Pat, the care home manager," she said in a slow tone. "How can I help?"

I gave Pat my best officious smile but was surprised when Jay jumped in before I could speak. "I'm Detective Sergeant Jay Fitzgerald with King's Lynn police. We need to speak to Robert Alder."

"I'm sorry," Pat said, her tight grin now reaching just a bit too far to be genuine. "All communication to Robert goes through his daughter, Miranda. I have her number if you need her urgently."

I saw Jay gulp, preparing himself. There was never an easy way to say this. "Actually, we're here about Miranda. I'm afraid she died."

The news stunned Pat, the smile finally dropping from her face. She bit her lip and frowned. "Oh dear, that poor woman…"

"Did you know Miranda very well?" I asked.

"Just vaguely, to say hello to when she visited. She usually came to see her dad once a week. Oh, how terrible."

If Pat's reaction was anything to go by, then Miranda and her father were close.

"What happened to her?"

"She was murdered," replied Jay.

"Oh, goodness."

"If you know anything about her or her father that might be relevant, it would be a great help to us," I chipped in.

"No, dear, I don't think I do." Guilt plastered Pat's face. She tapped one fake fingernail on her desk as she thought, barely needing to lift her finger to do so. "Let's see, she came to us about two years ago. Her father's care was becoming unmanageable for her, and money was getting tight, she needed to return to work. Always paid the bill in full every month; Robert doesn't receive any subsidies. That's it. Never stayed long when she came to see her dad, I think she found it difficult to talk to him after placing him in care."

"Can we speak to her father?" Jay asked keenly.

"Robert? Oh no, dear, that won't be possible."

"Why not?" I asked. Out the corner of my eye, I saw Jay shooting a look at me, equally as confused.

Pat looked around her but didn't answer.

"He needs to know about his daughter," I pressed.

"My dear, he doesn't even recognise his daughter most of the time," she said. "Robert has advanced dementia. We could go in and tell him now and he'll be devastated for a few minutes, maybe an hour, and then he'll forget it all and ask when Miranda is next coming to see him."

The frown didn't leave my face. "So, we don't tell him at all? You're going to lie to him?"

"When someone has such an aggressive and advanced disease as Robert's, it's the kindest thing to do. Here, I have all his medical documentation here, you're welcome to see. But Miranda managed everything for Robert. She wouldn't want to put her father through that distress."

I had my doubts about Pat's methods but then, she was the expert. She must have dealt with situations like this before and known that this was the best way to care for Robert. I shared a look with Jay, who chewed his lip. This was a dilemma he hadn't anticipated either and he wasn't sure how to proceed.

"Robert is a very frail and ill man. He barely speaks now," Pat said and she sucked in a breath through her teeth. "I don't think it will be long before he's with his daughter again."

Jay gave the smallest of hums as he mulled over Pat's words. He looked my way, an expectant look as though he was seeking my opinion. The knot in my stomach relented, releasing into a swell of disappointment. There was nothing more we could do. Not even Miranda's next of kin would mourn her death. Her only family wouldn't miss her. Sinner or saint, it'd done Miranda Alder no good; in the end, she was alone.

* * *

Back outside in the seaside air, I dragged my feet back to Jay's car. He had forged on ahead, keen to get out of the nursing home, his heavy footsteps crunching through the gravel.

"Well, that was an awkward visit," he said as he unlocked the car.

"Did you know that was a dementia care home?" I asked him.

Jay grimaced but didn't speak until we were inside the car, doors shut. "No. Probably should've looked that up before we left. Rookie mistake there." He flashed a boyish grin my way, which lightened my mood.

"Should we tell Chris?"

"God no! But here's a good lesson for you; we can phrase this to make it look like it was a useful visit and not a waste of time. We now know Robert Alder doesn't have much time left and Miranda had lasting power of attorney over his health and estate. He's been in that facility for two years."

"About as long as she'd been working at the supermarket," I said.

Jay pulled the car out of the car park and onto the main road out of Heacham. Bright sunlight guided our way, bouncing off the tarmac. "And she paid his care fees in full every month."

"I suppose that's where the money was going, the thousands she extorted from the gullible saps online." The gullible saps like Justin who were so wrapped up in love, they failed to see the con right before them.

"Her bank records should come through this morning, we can confirm that easy enough," said Jay. "And Chris was going to follow up with the dating websites, so we can get access to the records of who she was scamming."

"Do you think that's why she was conning the men online? Just so she could pay her father's care bills?"

Jay tapped his fingers on the steering wheel as he thought. "Even full time at the supermarket wouldn't have earned enough to pay those fees. Care is expensive. Let's hope Chris is getting somewhere."

As we travelled further from the coast, the traffic started to build the other way. I could see families with a boatload of buckets, spades and blankets. Retired couples heading to their caravan for the day. Jay revved the engine as a tractor joined the roundabout just ahead of us. Traffic was too thick to overtake.

It slowed our journey down enough to earn a disapproving growl from Chris when Jay and I finally made it back to the station. I abated him by making a round of tea and coffee, whilst Jay filled him in on our trip to Heacham, managing to carefully spin it so it looked like it'd been more helpful than it really had. On my return, Chris accepted his coffee as he explained that his attempts at hurrying up the online dating sites to provide information had been met with silence. An alarming amount of these dating sites were based overseas and as such, didn't pay much heed to requests from other countries' law enforcement.

"However," said Chris, his face filling with something akin to positivity, "we've had a stroke of luck. The tech guys at the lab were able to get into Miranda's laptop."

Jay and I perked up at our desks. "Does that mean…?"

"Yep." Chris nodded stiffly. "Just like the rest of us, Miranda had all her passwords saved onto the computer. We can finally get into her online dating accounts."

This made Jay punch the air, earning a tut from Chris. "I'll go through the sites and see how many other men fell victim to the catfish scam."

"Good start but don't get too excited. There are still too many unanswered questions in this case." Chris's gaze fell on me. "Have you heard from Justin?"

"Not recently," I replied.

"Check up on him," he said. "He should be out of the hospital by now. See how he's doing after his discharge and invite him in for a statement."

I gave a curt nod and added the action to my notebook. "Is he still a suspect? I thought we'd ruled him out."

Chris tapped his chin. "At this point, anyone is still a suspect. There's the DNA found on her body, which still hasn't come back with a match. The missing murder weapon. The fact she left her handbag at home and there's no sign of her phone. Her apathetic work colleagues. And the obvious; the carving on her chest, which tells us that whoever killed her *knew* about her scams online."

With his thirst quenched, which helped his mood a surprising amount, Chris divided out the jobs. Him and Jay would undertake the dating websites route, identifying any potential candidates out of Miranda's victims. I was set to work on the store's CCTV footage.

## Chapter Twenty-One

It didn't take me long to track down all the employees in the store on the cameras. They were easily distinguished from the few customers by their red uniforms. First, I watched Miranda's last shift, which was uneventful. She stayed at the customer service checkout by the store's front doors, serving anyone who came to her. She had a habit of tossing her long hair over her shoulder whenever serving a male customer.

Nick hung around her station, stopping for a chat every time he passed by. Given that Miranda was near the entrance and the warehouse was at the back of the store, he had no reason to go near her, but he managed to wheel his cage of stock by every twenty minutes or so.

At one point, she had a chat with Jeremy, which involved a lot of hair-tossing and exaggerated laughing. She touched Jeremy's arm, but he quickly flinched away and appeared to scold her lightly for the action.

And the others, just as they had told me, stayed away from her, preferring to stick to their own groups as they restocked the store and cleaned the aisles.

Saturday night was much the same as Friday night, except this time someone else was on the customer service checkout. Nick arrived at 8.30 p.m., disappearing out the back before emerging at 8.55 p.m. and setting to work. He seemed a little lost as he wheeled his cage trolley past Miranda's station but didn't stop to chat like the night before.

Jeremy wasn't seen much on the cameras, preferring to stick to the back. The cameras only covered the shop floor and entrance, not the warehouse or back rooms. Regardless, I caught all the colleagues as they entered the store at various points between 8.30 and 9 p.m., getting ready and starting their shift.

The disappointment rose at how easy it was to rule out Miranda's colleagues. Miranda's time of death was between nine and eleven that night. Her body was discovered just after eleven when I wandered over to the park after ditching Charlie at the wine bar. That was a short time frame for any of her colleagues to meet her, kill her, clean up and get back to work.

But without her colleagues as suspects, we were no further forward than we were before we knew her name.

Chris reappeared in the office after his lunch break, muttering curses under his breath as he slung his suit jacket on the back of his chair and handed a sandwich to Jay, who was too engrossed in unravelling Miranda's online exploits to stop for a break.

"Bloody traffic, there's some sort of motorbike rally going on. Fucking idiots are driving through town like it's a Grand Prix track."

Chris's ramblings sparked a thought in my mind as I remembered the motorbike that raced past me that morning. The spark set fire to a theory. I mulled it over for a few minutes. It wasn't perfect but it was possible, and that was all it needed to be.

"What about," I said, "if someone from the store met with Miranda on the night she died?"

Jay's gaze darted to me, leaving his computer screen for just one second. "You just told me you'd checked through the CCTV and all her colleagues were at work that night."

"I know but hear me out. There are no cameras round the back of the shop, in the warehouse or the staff car park. It's possible that one of Miranda's colleagues left the store, picked her up, stabbed her in the park and got back again within half an hour. And there was plenty of times when some of them were missing from the cameras for more than half an hour. At that time of the night, traffic is light. It's possible."

"It doesn't seem very likely," Jay said, but he threw a glance over at Chris, who scowled at his computer screen, apparently not listening. "It's much more likely that she scammed the wrong person online and they tracked her down. Ruling out her colleagues is just a formality."

"But if it's possible, then we can't rule them out," I said.

"Just because it's possible, doesn't mean one of them was the killer. Anyway, even that time of the night, you can't get from the store to her home, to The Walks and back again in half an hour."

"Of course you can."

Jay raised his eyebrows at me. "And commit a murder in the middle?"

"That's enough." Chris huffed, losing patience with us both. "The only way to find out is to test it. Off you go."

I blinked with surprise as he waved his hand in my direction. "Me?"

"It's your theory, go and test it. Time yourself."

\* \* \*

If that was what it took to be taken seriously, then I would do it. I knew I was really just trying to prove to the guys that I was competent enough to be on the Serious Crimes team – and probably prove that to myself too – but I was also keen to move this investigation forwards. Miranda's killer had been walking free for too long, whilst no one mourned their victim. So, when it got to the end of the day, rather than heading home, I set out for the supermarket.

Round the back of the megastore was a service road, where the lorries brought deliveries and the staff parked their cars. This was the best place to start. It wasn't quite the time of Miranda's death, but it was mid-evening and the rush hour traffic had relented. Now was as good a time as ever.

I was just about to set off, when my phone buzzed for my attention. It was a message.

*Meeting overran and got stuck in traffic. Your place or mine?*

I smiled to myself. He couldn't keep himself away. I typed out a quick reply to Aaron's message, well aware I had a grin on my face like a sappy teenager.

*Mine. I'll make dinner.*

As I tucked my phone away again, I remembered the promise I'd made myself. This could only go ahead if I was careful. I knew Aaron too well to expect this affair would end any other way than abruptly. As long as I stayed in control, as long as it stayed fun and just physical, it was okay.

With the promise of a good night ahead, I set off on my mission. First, I drove to Miranda's house, using the quickest route I knew through the centre of town. Next was The Walks, which was a bit trickier as there were plenty of places to stop and park at various points around the edge. I settled for the closest one to the Red Mount Chapel, a parking spot near the train station. I gave myself a ten-minute stop – enough time to do all the deeds committed, I reckoned – and then started off again, back to the service road behind the supermarket.

As I pulled up, I checked the time. Thirty-two minutes. Knew it.

I contemplated calling Jay just to rub his face in it, when a figure knocked on the window of my car door. I jumped and hit my head on the ceiling. Rubbing my crown, I composed myself and rolled down the window.

The figure started at me with an irritated tone. "You can't park here– Oh, it's you."

It was Greg, the unhelpful warehouse worker from the store.

"What are you doing here?" he asked, casting a wary eye over me and then my car. He bent down to face me, resting his hands on his knees to stoop low enough. He was very tall, I realised, far taller than I'd registered the first time we met.

"Just testing a theory," I replied. "Miranda's death is still an active investigation."

"Right… Well, you can't stop here, we have a delivery coming any minute and the lorry will need to get through."

"Ah okay." Fair enough, I was finished with my mission anyway. I started my engine to move away.

"Don't you normally work the night shift?" I wondered aloud before I moved off.

Greg hadn't moved from his position at my window, and now he fixed me with a hard stare. "I'm doing some overtime. What's it matter to you?"

"There are no cameras round the back here, are there?"

"Do you have a point?" He gave a slight shake of his head, his face filling with suspicion.

"No." I gave him a calm smile. "As I said, I was just testing a theory. I'll get out of the way now."

Greg's hand fell on my window edge, gripping the car door. "And what theory is that?"

"That it's possible for any of the workers to leave the store without being seen on the cameras."

With his hand still on my car, I couldn't move off, but something in Greg's eyes told me I shouldn't. He was analysing my actions, trying to guess my intentions.

"You think someone working here killed Miranda?" he asked carefully.

"Possibly. Would anyone working here want to harm Miranda?"

"Ordinarily, I'd say you were crazy, but since your last visit, things have gone to pot. Nick and Jeremy are at each other's throats, each thinks the other had something to do with her death. I'm dreading tonight."

"What makes them think that?"

Greg glanced around, as if this was a covert conversation instead of an impromptu talk. When he spoke, he dropped his voice to just a mumble. "Well, you know, Nick has been in love with Miranda for ages."

I nodded. I knew that from our conversation. Nick struck me as someone who experienced intense emotions. But Nick was also the most featured worker on the camera footage, constantly walking back and forth as he carted loads of stock to the shop floor. He was rarely off camera for more than twenty minutes at a time, and as my

150

experiment had just taught me, twenty minutes might not have been enough time to murder Miranda.

"And what about Jeremy? Is he cut up about her death too?"

"Not as much as Nick is," said Greg. "But he's still moping. Still, it's to be expected given that him and Miranda were having an affair."

## Chapter Twenty-Two

Jay wouldn't let me interview; he wanted a stab at the guy himself this time. He muttered something about me being too soft – that it would take a good-cop, bad-cop routine to get this case cracked wide open. I said that only worked when the good cop was also in the room, to contrast against the bad cop. So, he called in Chris to take my place, as if Chris was the obvious choice to be the good cop.

Relegated to the sidelines, I could only watch and wince at every heavy-handed comment Jay made and every subtle insinuation from Chris. They were determined to get to the truth, because if Jeremy had lied about cheating on his wife with Miranda, what else was he hiding?

In the dark broom cupboard that was also the observation room, I watched Jeremy fall to pieces under their intense interrogation. The one-way window framed his growing desperation. He was close to breaking point. Then the door opened and another person joined me to watch the show, as distracting as someone trying to squeeze past at the cinema. Aaron sighed, his gaze drifting over me before settling on the interview on the other side of the glass.

"This looks interesting."

"Sorry," I said. "Important shift in the case. I completely forgot you were coming over."

If he was disappointed in me for forgetting our plans, he didn't show it.

"Must be a significant breakthrough to get Chris and Jay so riled up." He observed them with a look of mild surprise as they continued to bombard Jeremy with questions.

I nodded, unable to contain my eagerness. "It is. We found out the bloke lied to us about having an affair with the victim."

"Oh." Aaron winced. "And has he confessed to it yet?"

"He sang like a bird the moment Chris and Jay sat down. But they aren't letting him go that easily, they want him to confess to murdering her also."

He glanced at me out the corner of his eye. "Did he?"

"I don't know yet," I said. Occasionally, a gut feeling came along with a big breakthrough, letting me know we were in the right direction. But, as I stared at Jeremy sobbing across the table from Chris and Jay, I just couldn't be sure. Miranda's death still wasn't fitting together yet, something still didn't feel right. Yes, Jeremy had lied about their relationship. But was he a killer? I didn't think so. And if he didn't believe her fantasies about multiple admirers, why carve *CATFISH* into her chest?

As Aaron shuffled next to me, I became acutely aware of his presence. His expression was passive, so it was almost impossible to tell just how annoyed he was at me for forgetting about him. Or maybe he was just as interested in the interview as his concentrated stare indicated.

There came a loud bang from the interview room as Jeremy hammered his fist on the well-used table. He stood up, his glasses hanging from his nose, and his face looking more like a puffy red balloon. He bared his teeth at Chris and Jay, who were both sitting still, one leaning on the desk and the other with his arms crossed.

"You can't tell my wife!"

"She'll want to know where you are when we remand you into custody," said Jay, with a bite to his voice that made Jeremy flinch.

"It was just sex! I never had any feelings for Miranda, there was nothing there. You tell my wife, and my marriage will be over!"

"Then you'll need to give us a bit more information, Jeremy. Like why you killed her."

"I told you, I didn't kill her! I had nothing to do with Miranda's death."

Like a popped balloon, suddenly Jeremy sat back down with a heavy exhale. His fight vanished, his shaking fists dropped to his sides and the redness drained from his face.

"Look," he said, sounding as deflated as he looked, "I'll tell you everything, where we met, how long, what contraception we used! But I didn't kill Miranda. Please. My wife can't know."

Jay and Chris shared a glance, an unspoken communication between them that they both seemed to understand. Switching positions, Chris leaned forwards and spoke with his usual calm tone.

"How long had this been going on?"

"About a year, maybe a bit more. I resisted her for quite a while, but then one day, I just… caved."

"So, she pursued you?"

"Miranda pursued everyone. Well, she flirted at least. It was like a game to her. There wasn't a guy in the store she hadn't already tried it on with."

"Where did you meet?" Chris's voice may have been calmer than Jay's, but it felt like a pressure, a heavy force weighing on Jeremy to get him to talk.

"We usually went straight after work to The Swan B & B on Gaywood Road. They don't ask questions."

"Is that where Miranda was going on the night she died?"

"No, I told you, I don't know anything about her death. We usually just went spur of the moment. We never planned it in advance. She had a few days off from work, and I hadn't planned to see her at all during that time."

I sighed, Jeremy's defeat setting off a tiredness in me too. I could guess where I'd be conducting inquiries tomorrow, Jay and Chris would send me to check out Jeremy's story at the seedy B & B. As they shared another unspoken look, I could almost read their minds as they planned it.

Beside me, Aaron groaned but it didn't quite cover up the loud rumbling of his stomach. "I'm starving."

"Sorry," I replied, offering a guilty smile. "I just got carried away with the case. You know, the job comes first."

"I wouldn't expect it any other way," he agreed, although it was not as relaxed as I'd hoped. "Still, you could've texted."

Yeah, I could have. I had no excuse there. I let the awkward silence take over, wriggling into the confined space and making my skin crawl. I needed to make this right, but I wasn't sure how.

"How about if I cook?" Aaron said, and when I took too long to reply, he held out his hand expectantly.

"At my place?" I asked with a frown.

He nodded. Slightly bewildered by his newfound familiarity, I fished out my keys from my pocket and removed the two for my flat, outside door and inner front door. He took them from my grip, his fingers lingering a little too long on mine.

I bit my lip, torn between intrigue at his actions and not wanting to miss any more of the interview. "You might want to stop by the shop, there isn't much in the fridge. And the electric is nearly out."

"I'll get a takeout." He made for the exit without so much as a glance back.

"Wait," I said, and he paused. "Be careful of the cat, she doesn't like strangers."

"Okay, I'll avoid the cat."

"And the hippy downstairs too. She doesn't mind strangers, she's just a bit… strange."

A slight laugh escaped his lips. "Don't be long," he said, as he left the observation room.

## Chapter Twenty-Three

Despite a forecast of heavy clouds, the next day somehow felt brighter and clearer, like a breath of fresh air exhaled over the land. I wasn't an expert in architecture, but the town of King's Lynn always felt like opening a time capsule to me. Just by driving along one road, you could pass Victorian terraces, crumbling seventies flats, a fifteenth-century bell tower and a modern multistorey car park. Even further along was the port. For an unassuming Norfolk town that most people in the country couldn't point to on a map, it was a fascinating place.

On one of the main roads through the town, Gaywood Road, Victorian terraces lined both sides, all with similar dark-stained bricks and archway front doors. Thanks to years of neglect and roadside pollution, these properties were grim, shadowed and worn-out. This was where I found The Swan B & B.

I entered via the front door, only to find the place deserted. On a counter separating the rest of the house from the front, I found a bell, which chimed through the house with a shrill *ding* as I rang it. As if summoned from the dead, a withered woman appeared in a dressing gown and slippers. She gave me an unimpressed glare as she sidled up to the counter, puffing heavily on a cigarette. Judging by the ashtray next to the bell, it wasn't her first of the day.

"What?" she asked in a raspy Eastern European accent.

I produced my warrant card and ignored her tensing up. "I'm Detective Constable McArthur. Have you seen these two people recently?"

I got out the two pictures I had of Miranda and Jeremy from my case file. Upon realising I wasn't there for any criminal activity relating to her, the woman's scrutinising glare relaxed a little.

"Oh yes, those two. They're here often, probably once a week. Haven't seen them lately."

"How long do they stay for?" I asked.

"Just a few hours, first thing in the morning." She shrugged, like it didn't matter. "Always pay for a full night."

"Who pays?"

"The girl does. Cash too, every time. She always has on the nicest jewellery."

"When was the last time they were here?"

"About two weeks ago, probably, I don't know. Nearly always a Monday."

"Did they ever give names?" I pressed.

"No, and I don't ask. People don't come here to be interrogated. I know what they're doing, I've seen his wedding ring. You want any more information – you bring a warrant."

I thanked her and made a hasty exit. There was no point in asking for evidence, receipts or CCTV of them arriving; this place had none of that. I doubted it even had a proper guest book.

I didn't need any of that though, as only two doors along from the B & B was a corner shop, with a perfectly placed security camera above the door. I headed inside to request the help of the shop owner, who was eager to assist and perhaps a little too friendly. I was willing to look past the numerous lecherous smiles if the camera caught anything useful. It paid off, as an hour later, I had the footage of the morning from two weeks before, where a car clearly matching Miranda's pulled up, followed by one matching Jeremy's. Two grainy figures got out and hurried inside; one tall and lanky, the other with flaming-red hair.

With Jeremy's affair confirmed, I made my way back to the station. In the office, Chris worked silently at his desk, shooting me a look for interrupting his peace.

"I've got good news and good news," he said, although his expression didn't make it look like any good news was coming.

"What is it?"

"Jay and I have tracked down three potential catfish victims from Miranda's online dating accounts. I've sent you the details to follow up. Definitely looks like Miranda had a type; middle-aged lonely businessmen."

"And the other good news?" I asked.

"Jay's talking to Jeremy Payton's wife and seeing if she knew anything about the affair Jeremy was having with Miranda. And I'm applying for a warrant to search their house."

"Is she a suspect?" I was surprised by their heavy-handed approach. When Chris and Jay thought they were on the right track, they didn't hang around. They were gunning for Jeremy.

Chris shrugged. "I suppose it's possible she could've found out and killed Miranda. Her husband definitely is."

"That wouldn't explain the carving on Miranda's chest," I said.

"We asked Jeremy about that. He was confused. He didn't believe Miranda's stories about the men online. No one at the store did."

"Except for Nick."

"Good point." Chris rubbed his chin thoughtfully. "While Jay and I dig into the night-shift manager, you look into the young lad again. See if he wrote that love note, invite him in to give a DNA sample. Sounds like the boy has a temper on him and he was the only one of Miranda's colleagues who believed her stories about the online boyfriends. We shouldn't rule him out completely just yet."

"Will do," I said, turning round to head back out. "Has Jeremy been invited to give a DNA sample?"

We still hadn't found a match for the one taken from Miranda's most recent sexual encounter right before her death, despite running it against all existing databases. Whoever it belonged to had never had their DNA taken before.

"Yes, I invited him in," said Chris, his tone indicating the conversation did not go well. "He says he will present himself, along with his solicitor. Do you want to handle that one as well?"

"Er, thanks for the offer," I replied, quickly ducking my head down behind my computer screen before I was lumbered with any other unwanted jobs, "but I'll leave that one for you. I'll look into those catfish victims and speak to Nick."

I knew, professionally, that solicitors performed a vital role in making sure everyone was dealt with fairly and properly. But after a short personal run-in with them, I was not a fan. I wasn't about to share my prejudice with Chris though.

"Suit yourself," he mumbled back.

\* \* \*

Directly across the river from King's Lynn to the west was the aptly named village of West Lynn. Apparently, it had a ferry crossing linking the two places, but if you can call a small rowboat a ferry, then you can call King's Lynn a metropolis and me an adept adult.

It was here I found Nick's home, where he lived with his parents in a small estate of crammed-in new-build homes. A moped scooter was parked out front, only a small-engine vehicle that couldn't hit 50 mph if it tried. If that was Nick's mode of transport, then my theory of the killer sneaking out of work to pick up Miranda and kill her was totally blown out of the water for him. It would take far too long for him to cruise around town on that thing;

158

he would never manage it in the time frame he was off the CCTV cameras in the store.

I rang the doorbell. A short plump woman answered, she identified herself as Nick's mother and welcomed me inside.

"Nicky!" she called up the stairs, whilst hanging onto the banister hard enough to turn her knuckles white. "The police are here!"

Heavy thuds through the thin floorboards preceded Nick as he came down the stairs. He paused on the last step, peering through his mop of hair.

"What do you want?" he asked, not helping his grungy teenage image with his tone.

His mother smacked him on the arm, and she gave me a nervous glance.

"I'd like to ask you some more questions, Nick," I replied. "Shall we sit down?"

"Would you like some tea?" Nick's mother asked, practically pushing her son into the living room. He flopped into the single armchair, and I perched on the edge of the plush sofa. The furniture barely fit inside the tiny room.

"No, thanks." Her nervous jittering was distracting, like a fly buzzing around my head. I gave her a polite smile, staring at her until she finally sat down, using the footstool by her son. "Nick, I'd like to ask you some more questions about Miranda."

"I didn't kill her," he said quickly, making his mum gasp.

"I didn't say that. It will just help our inquiries if you can give me some more information. Like, did you know that Miranda and Jeremy were having a relationship?"

Nick shrugged his shoulders, sinking down further into the chair. "Yeah. Everyone knew."

"Everyone?"

"Yeah," he said. "They both thought we didn't but it was obvious. They'd sneak out back, steal kisses where there were no cameras. But Miranda was like that with everyone."

"She kissed everyone?"

"No, she was a flirt. A tease."

"Did she ever try it with you?"

"No." Nick glanced at his mum. "She thought I was too young."

Well, I thought to myself, Nick was twenty years younger than her. Although she had no qualms about sleeping with a married man, Miranda did seem to draw the line at teenagers. I waited a moment, wondering if Nick was going to continue, but he just glared at the floor, his black hair over his eyes. I would have to push a little harder.

"Were you disappointed about that?"

He didn't answer but instead shot me a steely glare whilst his mum squirmed beside him. I reached into my bag for my case file and produced a photocopy of the love note I had found in Miranda's flat.

"Do you know who gave Miranda this?"

Although hard to tell under his sulking expression, I saw Nick gulp.

"Where did you find that?" he asked.

"In Miranda's possession. It was in the pocket of her work jacket. Did you write it?"

He nodded.

"You loved Miranda?"

"I dunno. I liked Miranda."

"This note seems to say otherwise. It's a declaration of love. Did she reject you, Nick, is that what happened?"

Nick furiously shook his head, making his mum jump. "No."

"Then what was Miranda's reaction to the note?"

"I don't know. I slipped it in her pocket as we left one day. I never saw her reaction and she never mentioned it."

"She didn't say anything?"

"No," he said, his voice turning firm and flat.

"So, just to confirm," I said, "you never had any sort of intimate relations with Miranda? No kisses, no sexual relations."

"No, all right!" This time Nick's fists shook in his lap. "I didn't and I never will. Is that what you want to hear?"

"But you wanted a relationship?"

"I loved Miranda!" Nick snapped as he rose to his feet. Now in front of me, he was an imposing presence as his fists gripped into tight balls and trembled with his rage. "I would never hurt her, so stop trying to insinuate I did! I didn't do it. I didn't kill her!"

As Nick's mother gasped at her son's reaction, I realised how close he was to going over the edge. She cowered, already accustomed to his temper, and if she was scared, then perhaps I should have been too. But, years of facing the worst our society had to offer had taught me how to keep my cool. I simply sat still and waited until Nick's fists stopped shaking and he collapsed back down in his seat, his anger getting him nowhere.

When all was quiet again and Nick and his mother melted back into their seats, I continued.

"I don't believe you would hurt Miranda, Nick," I said, kindly. Not that I didn't believe Nick was capable of violence if he snapped, but the camera footage of the store clearly showed him busy at work for the whole shift on the night of the murder. He didn't have the time to sneak out and kill Miranda. "I'm not here to catch you out, but I have to follow all lines of inquiry. So, if you have any idea who would've wanted to hurt Miranda, now is the time to tell me. I want whoever did this to face justice."

Retreating into himself, Nick shrugged. "I don't know. She had loads of guys online. Maybe it was one of them."

"Did she ever tell you who?"

He shook his head. "No, she only every called them the guy from Manchester, or the one from Tottenham. There was one from nearby at one point, Wisbech I think. I don't know. It was hard to keep track with Miranda."

"Did you believe her?" I asked.

"I don't know," Nick replied honestly. "Miranda liked to tell stories. They couldn't all be true... could they?"

Feeling a tight grimace spread across my face, I nodded to Nick to reassure him my questions were done. I got the impression that Miranda's fantasies were so wild that even Nick had learnt not to believe much of what she said. But if Nick and Jeremy, and the rest of the supermarket night-shift team didn't believe anything Miranda told them, then none of them would have had experienced the emotions needed to carve the word *CATFISH* into her chest. It didn't make any sense. The only people with the opportunity to kill Miranda didn't have the motive. The people with the motive didn't have the opportunity. So, what was I missing?

"Nick, it would help our case if you could come to the station later today and provide a DNA sample so we can rule you out," I said. I replaced the case file back into my bag and stood to leave.

Nick's mum rose also and dragged her son to his feet. "We can do that. Can't we, Nicky?"

With great reluctance, Nick nodded.

"Great." I smiled at them both. "Oh, and one more thing. Who owns the scooter out front?"

"I do," Nick said with a grumble. "I use it to get to work."

"It's all legal," his mother cut in. "It has insurance and everything. And it's limited, it won't go more than 30 mph."

At least one mystery solved, I supposed. Now I was certain Nick couldn't have killed Miranda; at least, not with the moped for transport. "I see. Thank you for your help. I'll see you at the station shortly."

## Chapter Twenty-Four

Back at the station, I had barely walked in the front door when a loud, agitated voice caught my attention from across the room.

"That's her, she's one of them!"

Before I could reach the secure-access doors and get away from the busy front reception, two people stepped in front of me. A sharply dressed woman, with a curved nose and glasses that barely hung on, and a dishevelled Jeremy Payton.

"Mr Payton," I greeted him, with my best stoic detective face. The two of them were firmly in the way between me and my office, and neither looked happy.

"Detective," the night-shift manager growled back at me. "What are you guys playing at? First you tell my wife I was having an affair and now there's half a dozen officers searching my house!"

I wracked my brain. I hadn't checked my phone since arriving at Nick's house. I was willing to bet that I had a message from Jay or Chris telling me that they had secured a search warrant and were wasting no time in getting started. I was missing out on the fun.

"Sorry, Mr Payton," I said as I tried to sidle past. "This is all part of our inquiries. Requesting a DNA sample and searching properties is normal procedure."

"But I didn't kill Miranda!"

"Then you have nothing to worry about," I replied.

Before I could get away, the woman sidestepped right into my path, blocking my attempt to get round her.

"Normal procedure or not," she said, "this sort of treatment will not be stood for. You have no evidence Mr Payton or his wife have committed a crime."

I crossed my arms as I faced the woman. It didn't take a detective to work out she was a solicitor, but the sharp tone confirmed it. I hated solicitors – always acted like they were above everyone else.

"We have evidence of a crime," I said through gritted teeth and rubbing my arm, "and a victim who Mr Payton knew intimately. I think it would be best if your client complied with our investigation if he's keen to clear his name from our suspect list. Don't you?"

The woman dropped her hand but her sneering expression only deepened.

"Who are you?" I asked.

"Melanie Georgiou. I'm representing Mr Payton. And I know who you are, Detective Constable McArthur. Rumour has it you nearly botched the Ali Burgess case and got yourself stabbed."

For the first time in several days, my shoulder ached and pain twinged up to my neck. I ignored it as I realised most of it was in my mind. I'd been so busy lately that my shoulder hadn't hurt a single bit. One mention of the incident and it started up again. I was sure a psychologist would have a few theories about that.

"Right, Miss Georgiou," I said, ready to get rid of this woman even if it meant drop-kicking her from the station myself. It took a lot of self-control not to sneer back at her. "If you're here at the station, then I guess your client is here to provide a voluntary DNA sample. If you sign in at the front desk, an officer will be along soon to collect the sample. It's a quick and painless procedure, and they will explain all the legalities to you in due course."

"I know how the process works." The solicitor stood up straight; she was several inches taller than me. I got the distinct impression she was after a fight. "My point is that this investigation has caused immense distress to Mr Payton and your evidence is minimal at best. I wish to speak to the lead detective. Not some grunt worker."

"Then" – the words stuck to my tongue as I tried my absolute hardest not to tell the woman to *fuck off* – "if you hurry, you can probably still catch him at Mr Payton's house, conducting the search. Now, if you will excuse me, I have some grunt work to do."

Taking my opportunity to escape, I stomped up the stairs to the office, making the metal clang far more than normal. I just hated solicitors. Even the duty ones, here to mop up whatever cases and clients needed them, got under my skin. I'd yet to meet one that didn't treat me like a useless doughnut-eating copper. Of course, my prejudice was mostly unfounded, so I tended to keep it to myself. They were a necessary evil I had to put up with. For justice, and all that jazz.

I didn't realise Aaron was standing in front of the office door until I walked straight into him. Mumbling an apology, I made my way to my desk and he followed me in.

"Morning," he said, even though it was almost noon and it wasn't the first time he'd seen me that morning, following the night before. "What's up with you?"

"Nothing," I lied, but he gave me a look. "Fine. I just ran into Jeremy Payton and his solicitor."

"Ah," said Aaron. "I know how much you love solicitors."

"One bad experience was enough."

He grimaced. I often wondered how much Aaron knew about my run-in with the legal system as a victim – I had to disclose it all when I joined the force. He knew I hated solicitors and about Sam, the ex-boyfriend in prison.

"They're not all bad," he said, amused.

"I'm sure that might be true, but the ones I seem to meet are arseholes."

He laughed. It was such a rare sound, it made me smile. I could forget all about bastard solicitors when he grinned at me like that. It didn't last long. The chuckle faded away as fast as it came, but my mood stayed elevated. Aaron perched himself on the edge of Chris's desk.

"How's the investigation going? Chris and Jay practically skipped out of here when the search warrant came through for Jeremy Payton's house."

"I don't know about them. I've just been to see Nick Bellamy," I said. "He has a temper on him and admitted to writing the love note, but it doesn't look like he killed Miranda. He was on the cameras too much and he didn't have the means of transport to get her to the murder site."

"Did you run a background check on him before you went?" Aaron asked.

His smile was gone and replaced with the usual passiveness, but I still wondered at his question. Of course I had. Was he worried about me going to see a quick-tempered suspect without arming myself with foreknowledge first?

"Yes," I said slowly. "Nick has a clean record. The only thing of note that came up was being permanently excluded from school at fourteen for getting in a fight."

"Temper indeed."

He glanced out the door and down the hall. We appeared to be alone and there was no sign of my colleagues. The other teams all had their doors closed.

"What is it?" I asked. There was something else on his mind.

He closed the door softly. "I just wondered if you minded me staying at yours last night."

"Not at all," I said and felt my face glow like a beacon as the memories of the night before permeated my thoughts. This was becoming quite a regular occurrence. Something I craved at the end of the day, the sweet dessert at the end of the meal. As usual, Aaron didn't give too much away, but the hint of a smile was still there. He wasn't just here to catch up about the case.

"In fact, you're welcome again tonight."

# Chapter Twenty-Five

For the rest of the day, the promising start to the morning rapidly vanished into dust. Out of the three potential victims that Chris had identified, none turned out to be the cunning killer we had hoped. The first was a divorced investment banker from London, who was unfortunately hospitalised after a heart attack the week before Miranda was killed and was still an inpatient. Another, a nightclub owner from Newcastle, was all too keen to prove he was in his club by sending CCTV of the night. And the third, a retired lawyer, got his rather confused wife to confirm that they were having a weekend away in Amsterdam when Miranda was killed. Plane tickets, credit card receipts and holiday snaps followed.

Although I could prove each man had fallen into the catfish trap, and parted with several thousand pounds in the process, I couldn't prove any one of them had managed to track Miranda down at all, let alone kill her.

Chris and Jay returned later that afternoon, equally as fed up. Their search of the Payton household had turned up nothing but Jeremy's vintage porn collection and Katie Payton's drinking problem. If their marriage wasn't on the rocks before, it certainly was now. But there was no murder weapon, no bloody clothes, no missing phone. Nothing to tie either of them to Miranda's death.

With little progress to show for our efforts, we called it a day and regrouped in the morning with a newfound vigour.

"I hope you've brought your raincoat," Chris said as I arrived in the office.

He was already working away, the phone balanced in the crook of his neck and the last dregs of coffee swilling round in his mug. Jay was busy too, his nose buried in a stack of financial records.

"What? Why?" I asked, growing suspicious.

"You need to go out and canvas the neighbourhood again."

"Why?"

"Someone responded to the public appeal for information last night. Claimed to be a neighbour who saw Miranda leaving her flat on the night she was killed at around 10 p.m. She left with a man."

I shrugged my coat back on. "Let me guess, the tip was anonymous."

"Of course it was. So go out and knock on some doors. See if you can find out who rang it in. It must be someone who lives nearby in order to see Miranda leave her property."

"What other information did they give?" I asked. I wasn't thrilled by the prospect of heading back out before I'd even sat down, but I smiled at the thought of someone finally coming forward. If the witness saw Miranda leave with a man that evening, then they must have seen what vehicle they travelled in.

"Nothing – which doesn't help much. But it's obviously playing on someone's conscience. So go on, get a move on. Maddie will help."

He gave me a pointed look, urging me to get going. As I headed out the door again, I heard Chris call after me.

"And don't be long! The forecast looks awful for later. Big storm coming."

* * *

The dark clouds grew overhead as I made my way to North Lynn, turning a worrying shade of black as they travelled south to north, following the line of the river and out to sea. Maddie was waiting for me outside the victim's flat and together we set off, dividing the street in half and knocking on doors as the air turned restless and threatening.

At most properties, I found the standard North Lynn friendliness; a sharp denial of knowing anything and a door closed in my face. I had more luck when I approached the building directly opposite Miranda's. This one was the same design as hers, four flats stacked on top of one another, housed within weathered grey bricks. The three upper flats shared the communal stairwell, but the ground-floor flat had its own front door facing out onto the road with a large window beside it. As I neared, the net curtains twitched and I saw the figure of someone passing behind them.

The door opened as I raised my hand to knock, and I came face to face with an ageing lady. Her hair was thin and wispy, and her skin lined and yellow like leather. A cloud of smoke flew out from the door, enough to make me cough.

"You the police?" she asked, eyeing me suspiciously.

I nodded, taking a step back before the stench of cigarettes got into my clothes. "I am. We're following up on an anonymous tip-off we had about the young lady who lived over the road. She was killed."

"I know," the woman said as her lips tightened. "I tipped you off. But I don't want any trouble."

Bewildered, I held my hands up. "I'm not here for trouble. Just a chat. What was it you saw?"

The lady glanced around the street behind me. "Same as usual. There's plenty of no-good 'uns here, they all come out at night. I sit in my chair and watch them, report in anything they do. Like when they stole all the pumpkins down the street last Halloween and smashed them in the road. I reported that in then but you lot didn't do anything."

"And what about the night Miranda Alder was murdered?" I said, prompting the lady back on track.

"Oh that." She gave me a withering look. "Well, I didn't think anything about it at the time, I only reported it in after my grandson mentioned it. He'd seen it on the internet, the police asking if anyone knew anything. He's always on that phone of his. He asked me if I knew the woman who was killed as she was from around here. I didn't know her, but I recognised her picture."

"Didn't you speak to the officers before? They were knocking on doors around here a few days ago."

"Of course I did," she scolded me. "They knocked right in the middle of *Saturday Kitchen*. Anyway, they asked what I knew about the lady over the road, so I told them. Red hair, make-up like a clown. Came and went at funny times of the night. They didn't say anything about her being murdered. And I didn't ask. Not really something you think to ask, is it. And besides, that nice young singer was on *Saturday Kitchen*, the one with the hair, and I wanted to watch him make an omelette with Matt."

"Okay. But what did you see the night she was killed?" Like the stormy clouds growing overhead, my patience was about to burst.

The woman hummed. She spoke rapidly but not fast enough about the information I actually wanted. "The loud group went by, they were heading into town, already pissed up. Then Colin at number twenty-three got back from work. He's a nice one, works at the chemical factory by the river. His missus just had another baby."

"About Miranda."

"Oh. There was a motorbike, black one. Turned up outside her flat about 10 p.m., just as the news started on the telly. Bloke on it, could tell by the way he stood when he got off, but he didn't take his helmet off. The redhead over the road came out, she got on the back and off they went. She looked like a giddy schoolgirl, skirt up to her cheeks."

"Did you catch a registration?" I asked, eagerly pulled my notebook from my pocket.

The woman's face turned sour. "No. Now get off my doorstep before anyone thinks I'm a tattler."

And with that, she slammed the door in my face. Now it was my turn to look bewildered as I retreated from the front door of the flat. At least I had gained some information. I pulled out my phone to call the office to let Chris and Jay know I'd found the anonymous source, but they didn't answer. Further up the street I could see Maddie, standing out with her fluorescent police jacket on, and I made my way over to her. Her radio crackled as I reached her.

"It's a big storm coming," she said, giving a frightful look skyward. "They've just called all units back to the station. Apparently, there'll be a storm surge and they're going to close the floodgates in town."

"Yikes," I replied. In all my years on the beat, I had never known the floodgates to be closed. The town sat next to the murky River Great Ouse, which, although tidal, was usually calm and muddy. "Well, I've found the source of the tip now so we can head back."

Maddie nodded but paused before heading away. Under her thick eyelashes, she gave me a scrutinising stare. "Are you all right?"

"Me? Of course, I am. Why wouldn't I be?"

"Did you give Kyle a call? The guy whose number I gave you."

I shrugged under her attention. I was surprised she even remembered our conversation given how drunk she'd been.

"No. I told you, Maddie, I'm not here to be your latest bit of gossip."

"All right, all right… I'm sorry. It's just when I last saw you, you were miserable."

"I'm fine," I said again. "I feel better now than I did before. I've been talking about the case and getting things off my chest. It feels better."

"Oh good." She waggled her eyebrows. "So, you're finally getting some?"

"Some wha–? Oh, for goodness' sake, Maddie. You're embarrassing, do you know that?"

"What?" She laughed heartily as she wandered by my side towards our cars. "Come on, we all need a release sometimes. Meeting people is hard in this job, the least you can do is have a good shag once in a while to de-stress."

"Not everyone needs casual sex to feel more fulfilled, Maddie."

"I know that," she said. "So, what's making you feel more fulfilled then?"

I knew the answer deep in my gut before my brain caught up. It wasn't the casual sex making me happier. It wasn't the release of pent-up emotions and stress, but rather it was a deep yearning inside. A feeling I'd never had before. And after one small taste of it, I was craving more.

*Goddamn it, Anna.*

It was Aaron.

Maddie headed off, smug with herself for sending me into a tailspin of unexpected emotions, and I made my way to the station. I couldn't get my head in gear as my mind spun round and round with the same unwanted and unwelcome thought.

After just a few days, I was developing feelings for Aaron. God, I was a sap.

But it wasn't just a few days, my rational brain told me as I made my way to my desk. I'd known Aaron for years; fought with him and laughed with him many times over. I knew his likes and dislikes, what football team he supported and how rare his smiles could be. I was a fool for thinking I could go into this and not come out the other side hurt and rejected when all I'd really wanted was someone like him to be there for me.

I didn't like being alone. And now that I wasn't, I wanted more.

* * *

After reporting my findings back to Chris and spending a few hours trying to track down the motorbike, Chris decided it was best if we all headed home. Most of the non-essential personnel at the station had emptied out, eager to get away before the storm hit and the weather turned nasty. Everyone else was gearing themselves up for a busy night. The sky looked feral when I arrived at my flat, an unnatural shade of dark grey with crimson undertones peeking through, as if behind the clouds, the sky was on fire. The echoes of thunder rumbled in the distance.

My heart wrenched inside my chest when a silver SUV pulled up next to my car. Aaron got out, giving me a grin as we made our way inside.

"I got something to eat," he said. He rustled the bag in his hand.

We ate in silence as I struggled to get a grip on my thoughts. Like the hands of a clock, my emotions went round and round, covering the same ground, never ending.

I cleared away the plates and Aaron came up behind me, putting his arms around my waist and reaching down to kiss my neck. I could tell from his touch that he'd been dying to do it all day. It was familiar, comforting and electrifying all at the same time. I reached up and ran my hand along the back of his neck, something that always made him shiver.

The fact I was starting to anticipate his movements was a bad sign. I was in too deep, already desperately trying to keep my head above the water before I fully went under. I wasn't even treading water; I was drowning. I had let my guard down too much and my only hope of saving myself was to end it now.

I pulled away. He noticed the torn look in my eyes.

"What's wrong?"

"Nothing," I lied quickly, but lying quickly never worked on a police officer. I untangled myself from his arms and made my way to the sofa, falling with an ungraceful thud. The cat hissed at me for the intrusion and made off to wind herself around Aaron's legs. She liked him, one of the only people in the world she hadn't attempted to scratch yet.

"What is this?" I asked. When I risked a glance at Aaron, standing in the doorway of the kitchen with a thoroughly confused expression, my heart skipped a beat.

"What do you mean?"

"This." I waved my arms between us. "Us. What are we doing?"

He frowned as he reached down to tickle the cat behind her ear. "I don't know what this is. I thought we were just seeing what would happen. Why… What do you want it to be?"

Oh boy, he shouldn't have asked me that question. Now I had no choice but to tell him. I suspected our fling would be short-lived and that he would push me away eventually, but I didn't think I would scare him off this quickly.

I dropped my head into my hands. I could feel the dread in my stomach working its way up as I formed the words. They were tumbling out of my mouth with no permission from my brain and there wasn't anything I could do to stop them. This was going to ruin everything.

"I want you," I said. "I want to be with you. I never feel as happy as I do when I'm with you. I want that all the time. I want more."

"I… Anna, I…"

Aaron gazed back at me, completely stunned. In fact, I had never seen him so speechless. Normally I would be poking fun at him, but I had just bared my soul and I knew exactly what he was going to say. I felt the crush of his words before he had even thought of them.

"Anna, I don't think that's a good idea. I don't think… We can't be together."

"I knew you'd say that," I said, unable to keep the sting out of my voice.

"Why?" he asked, bewildered. "Why do you want me? Or is it that you want something more serious?"

"I want both."

He shook his head, probably from disbelief.

I continued, "I want you to come home every night and look at me that way you did just now, like you're happy to see me. Not just happy to get your end over."

A flicker of offence crossed his stunned face. "I... I was happy to see you."

"But you don't want to be with me?"

"It's not that, it's just... if you want to get married and have kids and all that, then it shouldn't be with me. It can't be with me."

"Why not?" I asked. I demanded.

"Because there are so many people out there who can give you that stuff. They can make you happy. I don't think I can."

"You don't know that." My voice broke with emotion. I took a deep breath to steady my racing heart, but it made no difference. It thundered like a galloping horse inside my chest. "You always push other people away when they get too close, you've never tried it."

"I'm not the right person, Anna. You can have all that with any other person."

"But I don't want any other person, Aaron. I want you."

Slowly, he shook his head, controlled and measured. His expression told me he knew the pain it caused me inside. He could see what his rejection was doing.

"I'm sorry, Anna."

I sank down and buried my face in my hands, as though it would help this humiliation. I wasn't going to cry; I had some dignity left still.

A quick peek showed me he was still floundering by the kitchen door, unable to respond with anything other than taken-aback babble.

"It's fine, Aaron." I sighed, using the last of my strength before I broke down. "I know I'm being unreasonable here, asking this of you. We should stop, we shouldn't carry this on anymore."

"Really?"

"Look at me. If this is what a few days together does to me, imagine what would happen if we carried on for weeks, months."

"But what's caused this, Anna? Why bring this up now?"

The bewilderment was clear in Aaron's eyes. He didn't understand and he probably never would. I just didn't know how to tell him that this was the happiest I had felt in months. That I was finally starting to feel whole again, back at work, keeping busy, and sharing my free time with someone who understood me.

When I didn't reply, I saw Aaron nod a little out of the corner of my eye. Eventually, after what felt like an age, he cleared his throat.

"Okay, then." And he left.


## Chapter Twenty-Six


That night, the storm raged outside my windows, lashing the building with rain and hail like the relentless beat of a drum, drilling into my bones. I closed the curtains, but that only helped to block out the flashes of lightning and not the continuous crashing of thunder. Even without the storm, I knew I wouldn't get any sleep, so I simply laid in bed, mulling over my life choices and wondering what I should have done differently.

I considered getting up and doing something, even catching up on a soap opera I had missed for the week. The scripted, terribly acted drama might give my life a little perspective. I dragged my duvet to the sofa in the living room and bundled myself in. Poppy appeared from her hiding spot, tail fluffed up from fear of the storm, and plopped herself down on my lap. She liked watching late-night TV with me.

The soap had a long-winded storyline going about an interracial affair. It was picking and choosing which cultural stigmas it was addressing and which it was ignoring. I found myself shaking my head at the fact that the characters were fretting about the differences between them – their age, race, religion – all the while ignoring the fact that they were both lying to their partners. I had no problem with love in whatever shape or form it came in; I had a big problem with liars though.

*I* was the liar. I had told myself I wouldn't develop feelings for Aaron, that I would be careful, and I could cope with just keeping it casual. It was all rubbish.

In some small ways, I was glad I'd bit the bullet and told Aaron what I wanted now rather than several weeks or months down the line. If I had waited until then, it would have been harder to get him out of my life. Now, it was painful, but I would go back to how things were without him – my lonely little life with just me and the cat. Maybe I needed to give in to my mother's matchmaking and embrace finding someone else. Maybe I needed to give Charlie Sweeney another chance… Was I that desperate?

When morning broke and cleared the last remnants of the raging weather, I got ready for work and went outside to survey the damage. An eerie calm graced the town. The ground was saturated, large puddles covering every inch as the drains bubbled at the edge of the road. On the horizon, a couple of trees were missing from the skyline. Downham, and the rest of West Norfolk, was known for its relative flatness, so I wondered if the rest of the area looked the same since my view didn't extend very far.

A few pieces of a fence panel lay in the driveway. I moved them out of the way and tried to start my car. I almost burst into tears when the engine revved once and died with a splutter.

"No, please start. Please!" I begged the old banger. I knew she was nearing the end of her life, but I needed her today. There would be no trains and minimal bus service after all the storm damage. I needed the car to get to work.

Again, the engine rolled over once and then no more. I tried and tried but my trusty old girl was having none of it.

I hit the steering wheel out of frustration, sending shockwaves up my arms. Now what would I do?

I could call Chris, but he lived out on the other side of Wisbech, several miles in the wrong direction to pick me up. I tried calling Jay who lived a little closer, but the line was engaged. I contemplated calling my parents, but Mum would only chastise me for waking her up so early and Dad would scold me for not getting rid of my old car sooner, like he'd been telling me to do for years. I couldn't take their judgements today.

In the end, I had only one person. I called him and in only a few words, he swiftly agreed to pick me up.

When the silver SUV pulled up half an hour later, I hopped in without a word to the driver. Instead, I focused on the devastation around the town as we headed for the police station. Everywhere I looked, there were trees down and people working to get the larger branches off the road. Some roads were still flooded. Fence panels, garden ornaments and the odd trampoline lay at the roadside after a jolly adventure out of their home.

We made it nearly all the way to the station before Aaron finally spoke. "It'll be a busy day with all storm damage to clear up."

I only murmured in agreement. Aaron responded with a hefty sigh.

"Anna, we need to talk about last night."

"No, we don't," I replied, and I was right. There was nothing more to talk about.

"Yes, we do," he said, more forcefully than I expected. "Why do you want to end this? Just a few days ago… I don't understand, Anna."

"I just… I just think it's better this way. You wouldn't understand."

"Then help me understand," he insisted.

I inhaled a deep breath, the air fresh from the storm. "One day, I will want more commitment. And I know you won't – can't – do that. I want a serious relationship. I want someone to come home to every day. Marriage, children, grow old together. All of it."

"But anyone can give you that," Aaron snapped. "Why not anyone else?"

We hit a pothole disguised as a puddle and he swore under his breath, his knuckles tightening around the steering wheel.

"I don't want anyone else."

"Why not?"

"Because I like you."

"*Like* me?"

"Oh my God, Aaron." I groaned. This was getting painful. "Yes, I like you. I care for you. More than I did before, more than I do other people. I don't know how else to say it. I have feelings for you."

He fell quiet until we pulled into the station car park and Aaron silenced the car. For another full minute, he simply stared ahead, and I wondered if he was so dazed that he might not notice me sneaking out. His hands gripped the steering wheel, as if holding on for dear life.

"Feelings?" he eventually muttered.

I nodded. "Yeah. Feelings that I know will only grow further and deeper the more time I spend with you. Have you never felt like that before?"

Hollowly, he shook his head. "No."

"Then how can you expect to understand? If I let this continue, then it will only go the same way as all your other relationships. You won't want the same things I will, and it'll just end in heartbreak. I've seen you do it time and time again. The moment anything gets too serious, you push the person away. I just thought... that I'd save you the time. That's why I'm ending this now. I'm saving us the bother."

Aaron's eyebrows knitted together into a frown. "That's not fair, Anna. You just assumed I would—"

"Say no to something more? But you did."

Aaron opened his mouth to argue again but he was interrupted by the shrill ring of my mobile phone. Jay was calling me.

"Where are you?" he demanded down the line, before I could get a hello out.

"I'm arriving now, my car wouldn't start," I snapped back. Today was not a day to mess with me.

"Fine," he said with a huff. "Hurry up. We have a body found along the river to look at."

I shut the phone off. With a deep breath, I exhaled my frustration, pushing all unhelpful emotions away to the recesses of my mind. I had to focus on the task at hand.

"Are we finished?" I asked Aaron, but as I did, I was already hopping out of the car. I'd explained myself and my reasons for calling our fling off. There wasn't anything else to give.

Aaron jumped out of the car and caught up with me at the back of the vehicle. "No, we're not finished."

"What then?"

He stood still and firm, as though the words were on the tip of his tongue, ready to cut me down. But at the last second, he floundered. Whatever it was he was about to say, it vanished.

In the end, he sighed. "I don't want to finish."

He meant us, not our conversation.

"I don't either," I confessed. "But it's better this way."

"Better for who?"

"For me," I said. "Because I don't want to fall hopelessly in love with a man who can't love me back. I like what we have, Aaron, I do. But I can't let that happen."

"Anna," Aaron said, but once again the words failed him.

"I've got to get to work," I said with a mutter and pushed my way past him to the station.

\* \* \*

I hadn't made it far when something stopped me in my tracks. Standing by the entrance to the station, hidden from my view by a large police van parked next to the custody suite, was Maddie. I faltered as our eyes met. She appeared to be hovering, either about to start a shift or waiting for someone. But I knew the moment her gaze flicked away from mine what she was waiting for.

She'd heard Aaron and I talking.

I couldn't stand the thought of being the latest rumour through the mill, so without a word I hurried into the station and started to stomp up the stairs. To my dismay, she followed.

"Are you all right?" she asked as she caught me up at the top. Considering how restrictive those stab vests were, I was surprised at her spriteliness. I ignored her and carried on.

"Anna!" she hissed and caught my arm.

I spun round on my heels. "What is it, Maddie?"

"What was that about? You and Aaron?"

"Nothing," I said, but when Maddie crossed her arms, I knew I had to come clean. "How much did you hear?"

She grimaced, her gaze flicking to the floor as though she couldn't bear to look at my embarrassment. "I heard right from the part about how you don't want to fall hopelessly in love with a man who can't love you back."

"Well, that seems pretty self-explanatory then," I replied, and turned back to enter the office. Inside, I could hear Chris and Jay rattling around the room with agitation. They were growing impatient waiting for me.

Maddie caught my arm again. "Anna... Did you mean Aaron?"

"Maddie, it really doesn't matter."

"It does," she insisted. "You're upset, I can see that. And so was he. How long have you been in a relationship?"

"We're not. It wasn't even that. It was just a few nights."

"And you think you're falling in love with him?" Maddie frowned.

"No. I'm just... trying to stop anything before it goes wrong. It doesn't matter, Maddie. I ended it. It's over now. There's nothing to discuss because nothing happened in the first place."

"But you didn't want to end it?"

"Maddie!" I threw my hands into the air with exasperation. My life was not a soap opera, I was not here for her entertainment. "This isn't some juicy gossip, or even anything to do with you! I'd just appreciate it if you kept what you heard to yourself."

Although she gave a small nod at my request, Maddie opened her mouth again, new questions all ready to spill out. Before she had a chance to interrogate me, the door to the office opened.

"There you are!" Jay called, spotting me by the stairs and heading off, dragging me along with him. "I told you, we have a body. We need to go to the scene."

Chris was following close behind and, before I had a chance to protest, Jay hustled me back down the stairs, all the way out to his car. I got into the passenger seat and closed my eyes, wondering if there was a way of convincing Maddie to keep quiet and prevent her from sharing the latest gossip with the whole station.


# Chapter Twenty-Seven


The River Great Ouse is a tidal river, rising up and down by a significant amount with the sea. Last night's storm had coincided with high tide, resulting in flooding as the river burst its banks in places. The town of King's Lynn hadn't suffered too badly as they had shut the floodgates along the quay, containing the water. The smaller villages further along were not so lucky.

Jay drove us just a few miles from the station to a patch of countryside north of a village called Wiggenhall St Germans. Unsurprisingly, the village was known by locals as just St Germans. As we parked in a field entrance and trudged through to a path along the riverbank, I could see the bridge crossing the river to the south. Next to it sat a lovely pub, but today was a dismal kind of day, as though an illustrator had run out of colours and used only grey. The sun was trying to break through the clouds, peeking through in patches but it wasn't enough to warm up the day yet.

I followed Jay's footsteps along the path to the scene ahead, where the riverbank dipped as a small ditch joined it. The bank was thick with dark mud washed in by the storm, and it caked my shoes and the hems of my trousers. I wished I'd dressed better for the occasion, but I supposed one of the joys of the job was never knowing where the day was going to take you. It could be a seedy B & B, a mega supermarket, or a riverbank.

Jay slowed ahead of me as we arrived at the scene. A host of police were present on the edge of the river, installing a scene cordon as best they could in the boggy surroundings, and SOCOs clad half in white and half covered in mud. Everyone looked drowsy and haggard, having probably already worked through the night to help people in the storm. On the other side of the riverbank, the water had retreated back to its usual level, leaving a trail of silt and debris behind. The team were focused on a large pile of mud trapped in a crevice carved by the water between the field and bank. It was easy to overlook, but as we got closer, I could see shoes, the outline of an arm thrown up at an odd angle and a flap of clothing.

Jay was quiet as we approached, taking in the surroundings with care. I appreciated the silence as I was not in a mood to talk to anyone. As we surveyed the scene, Chris appeared behind us.

"Any ideas yet?" he asked.

Jay shook his head. "From what the control room told me, a dog walker called in to say they stumbled across a body this morning whilst out walking along the riverbank. I guess that's her over there." He pointed to a middle-aged lady talking to an officer further along the bank from us, with a bouncy black dog.

Chris hummed as he gazed around. "Well, it looks like the body was washed up by the storm last night. Judging by the mud across the field, the river breached its bank all the way up to there." He gestured to the far end of the field, where the mudline abruptly stopped. "I'll talk to the SOCOs, see what they've found out about the body so far. The storm brought a lot of missing-person reports so the quicker we identify them, the better."

"All right, I'll go find out who owns this piece of land. We're going to be on it for a while, I think." Jay thrust his hands into his pockets, eager to get moving.

They both turned to me, waiting for my input.

"I'll talk to the dog walker," I decided, which earned nods from both of them. "I'll get her statement and details."

"Good plan," Chris agreed and we all set to work.

The dog walker's name was Christine Bond-Willsby and she lived in a cottage at the edge of the village. She said she walked Thisbe, the excitable Scottish terrier, by the river every day, but had never seen anything washed up before. She warned me Thisbe may have licked or bitten the body – she was quite a naughty dog – but Christine had pulled her away the moment she realised what the lump of mud was, and called the police.

I thanked her for her time and offered to get an officer to drop her off home. The poor woman was holding it together well but as more and more officers arrived, along with the coroners in their ominous black van, her complexion started to pale. Even I could tell something important was happening as more people gathered around the body, and eventually Aaron turned up at the scene. He made his way to Chris and Jay without a glance at me.

"This isn't just some poor soul who died in the storm, is it?" Christine asked me, as I directed her back to the field entrance, where a police car was waiting.

"We will have to investigate it further," I replied. There wasn't much more I could say other than that, as I didn't know myself. But I was eager to find out, especially if it was serious enough to call Aaron out.

With Christine's details in my notebook in hand, I headed back to Chris, Jay and Aaron, gathered a few feet away from where the coroners and SOCOs were attempting to get the mass of mud onto a gurney. There was a pressure over the scene to get finished; another high tide on its way, threatening to spill over and wash away crucial evidence. The guys were in deep discussion, tension holding them together. As they spotted me approach, they all jumped.

"Anna!" Jay was the quickest, reaching me in two steps and steering me firmly in the opposite direction.

Aaron and Chris were close behind and none of them stopped until they'd marched me far from the scene and almost back to the car.

"What are you doing?" I shrugged Jay away and came to a stop.

"Anna, look…" Jay said. He gave a glance at Aaron and Chris, who both bore tight grimaces.

"What is it?" I could feel an urgency rising within my gut. They knew something.

"Let's go back to the station first," Jay offered, trying to steer me away again. "Get a good cup of tea before I fill you in."

I slapped his hand away. "No. What's wrong? Don't try and hide it from me, it has something to do with that body over there. Tell me."

One by one, I looked them over; first Jay, who couldn't keep still nor look me in the eye, then Chris, who could face me with a stoic expression. And then Aaron, who briefly met my gaze, but gave nothing away.

Chris finally relented and took a deep breath. "The coroner reckons the deceased died sometime in the last couple of days, before the storm washed them up. It's hard to identify them. Cause of death is not clear at this point."

He said *hard to identify* – not impossible. They already knew who it was.

"Who is it?" I asked. My blunt question made Jay flinch.

"Anna, this isn't anything–"

"It's someone I know, isn't it? You wouldn't be trying to get me out of here if it wasn't. How did you identify them?"

"A wallet was found on the body," Chris confirmed with a nod.

I noticed Aaron and Jay shoot him a look. Chris must have been in favour of telling me the truth, whilst Aaron and Jay wanted to keep me in the dark.

"Great. So, who is it?"

"It's Justin Carter."

The world spun around me for a moment, twisting my vision whilst I remained fixed in place. How could this be? It couldn't be Justin. I had saved him; Justin was safe and doing well. He was recovering. If he was dead, then my actions had been for nothing, saving him on the bridge was for nothing. He still died. *How?*

Aaron, Chris and Jay gave me a moment, staying silent whilst I processed the news. As the world corrected itself and settled the right way up, my ability to form logical questions returned with it.

"Are you sure?"

"We won't be sure until he's back in the morgue and cleaned up," said Jay with a solemn shake of his head, "but he had his driver's licence on him. And, from what little I can tell, I think it looks like him."

"Me too," Aaron said quietly.

"What happened to him?" I asked.

"It's too early to tell yet," said Chris.

"Well, the hospital can tell us," I replied. "They were treating him. Even if he wasn't an inpatient anymore, he still would have been under the care of the mental health team. They'll know whether it's actually him or not. We need to speak to them – I can go do that now."

I thought back to the formidable matron and doctor who accosted me in Justin's ward. They could confirm if Justin was discharged, if he posed a danger to himself or if he was really lying dead a hundred yards in front of me.

I turned back to the car, ready to go and do something, *anything*, but a hand caught me on the arm. It lingered too long, and I spun round to meet the unwavering gaze of Aaron.

"You'll have to go back to the station, Anna," he said, as deadpan and calm as always. "You can't help out with this case."

"What? Why not?"

His gaze didn't falter once. "You knew Justin in more than just a professional capacity."

"Barely!"

"You saved his life," Aaron replied, his voice deep enough to shake through my bones.

"Come on, Anna," Jay called to me. He was already at the driver's side of his car. "I'll take you back."

"But…" I babbled. I couldn't give in this easily. The urge to help Justin was only increasing. "I can help. I can be objective. You can't take me off the case."

"I can," came Aaron's indifferent reply.

I turned to him, the fire inside growing into anger and resentment. He was sidelining me.

"Is this because of…?" I let the question die off but he knew what I meant; *because of last night.* As angry as I was, I didn't want to open that can of worms in front of Jay and Chris, not after Maddie had already found out.

Aaron's gaze narrowed at me. "Absolutely not."

I opened my mouth again, ready to argue back, but abruptly, the fire went out. My anger dissipated into feeble spits, no longer spurring me on to find justice for Justin, and only leaving me with the begrudging realisation that he was right.

"Fine," I said. Without another word nor a look at any of them, I got into Jay's car and let him drive me back to the station.

## Chapter Twenty-Eight

Later that evening, there was a knock at my door. I expected my mother, since I hadn't replied to any of her texts in several days, but she knew where my spare key was now. Whoever it was had managed to wrangle their way in the front door, so I had no other option but to answer the tentative knock or pretend that I wasn't home.

Maddie stood on the other side. She was out of her uniform, but her hair was still tied in a tight bun, a sign that she had just gotten off shift. When she saw me, she gave a thin, unsure smile and held up two bottles of red wine, one in each hand.

"Apology drink?"

I frowned back. "What for?"

"It's my way of saying sorry for overhearing a clearly private conversation," she said, "and also offering a friend to talk to after what looked like an uncomfortable break-up."

"You can't break up if you never have a relationship in the first place."

She surveyed me. "And yet, here you are, going through a break-up."

She had me there. I was wearing my scruffiest, most comfortable pyjamas and ploughing my way through a family-sized bar of chocolate whilst watching a crappy romcom on the TV. Poppy the cat was asleep on the chair, not even stirring at Maddie's intrusion into our evening. I was revelling in my post-break-up bad mood, which had only grown worse after the events of the day.

Stepping aside, I let Maddie in and fetched two glasses from the kitchen as she settled on the sofa and opened the first bottle. The cork escaped with a satisfying *pop!*

"How did you get in, anyway?" I asked. Maybe the ground-floor neighbour, Mrs Roach, had left the front door open again. She was going a bit senile in her old age.

Maddie poured my glass to the top. "Your neighbour was leaving as I approached. The hippy one with the crazy hair."

Ah, Zola. She really didn't care about us getting burgled.

"I think I know her," Maddie continued. "I think I arrested her at an anti-hunting protest in town last year. She was… well, she was attracting a lot of attention with her methods."

"Why? What was she doing?"

"She was stark naked."

I nearly spat my wine all over the sofa. Zola never ceased to surprise me. I pushed the mental image as far out of my mind as I could.

Once recovered, I took another sip and turned to Maddie. "So, why are you really here? You know you have nothing to apologise for. You did nothing wrong."

For the first time in the several years I'd known her, Maddie appeared a little sheepish. "I just thought you could use a friend tonight. I heard about the bloke you saved off the bridge too."

"Ah," I said. "Yeah, it's been a difficult day. Where is Cass tonight?"

"She's out with some friends, they've gone to a concert. She doesn't even bother inviting me anymore, she knows that most of the time I'll get called to work and will miss it."

"That's shit."

Maddie shrugged as she sipped her wine. "That's the nature of the beast. Neither of us got into this job because of the good work-life balance, did we?"

"That's true." I gave up on sips in favour of hearty gulps. I preferred rosé, but when a day turns as bad as mine had done, red would do. Anything to help me forget.

"What happened with the jumper?" Maddie asked, still watching me carefully. "Do you think he killed himself?"

"I don't know," I replied. Which was true, I had no idea. The guys had kept out of my way all day, so I couldn't ask them. "I hope not." A deep well of guilt churned away in the pit of my stomach, throwing out questions such as: *Why didn't I check in on Justin more? Would he have attempted suicide again? How could I have stopped him?*

Maddie sensed my tenseness and she set her free hand on mine. "It wasn't your fault, Anna. You know that, right?"

"I know." I nodded, not even convincing myself. "But I'm always going to wonder what I could have done differently."

"We all wonder that when a difficult case goes pear-shaped. I've got a few more years on you, and I still find it hard to digest those jobs that hit harder than you expect. That's what I like about working in uniform – you never get much of a chance to dwell on things before the next job comes along. I could never understand why you left."

"I like working in CID, I like being a detective," I replied. "But sometimes I do think maybe I should go back to uniform. This case has bogged me down, it's got into my head. I might need a change."

"Maybe." Maddie hummed. "Or you might need someone to talk to. Like I have Cass."

I almost rolled my eyes at her. I wasn't going to have this conversation yet again. I had taken her advice; I'd found someone so that my life wasn't quite so lonely anymore. It hadn't worked.

"How did you meet Cass?" I asked. If I wasn't going to go down this road again, then I needed to distract her. The best way to distract someone was to get them talking about themselves.

Maddie shuffled on the sofa beside me, adjusting her position. A wistful smile crossed her face. "You've met Cass, actually."

"I have? When?"

"Five years ago. We were on a late shift, we were double-crewed after one of the response cars was out of action for repairs. You insisted we stop and get a coffee from the services on the A47 by the Pullover Roundabout. But you wanted to go in, not through the drive-thru."

I felt my face flood with heat as I remembered the incident she was talking about. Yes, the coffee chain store at the services between King's Lynn and Wisbech. I knew exactly what she was talking about.

Maddie continued. "You remember it now, don't you? We walked right into a robbery in action. The poor girl on the till was shaking like a leaf, she dropped coffee all over the floor. The guy gave up as soon as he saw our tasers. Whilst you handcuffed him, the girl slipped on the coffee on the floor and–"

"Almost knocked herself out," I finished. Once the assailant was under arrest, Maddie had called for backup and checked over the coffee shop girl. They'd talked for a long time. "That's how you met Cass. She worked there."

She nodded with a lax smile. "She still does, she's the manager now. We got a commendation for that arrest but I got a much better prize. And all because you insisted that we went inside for our coffee, for whatever reason."

Well, it wasn't an unknown reason, more of a hunch. As we'd arrived at the services, I'd spotted the shifty-looking customer as he entered the building. It had already been a disappointing day and I was looking for some sort of distraction. At the time, Maddie had grumbled over being dragged into another 'Crazy McArthur bullshit job', but now, she was staring into space with a wistful smile.

"What about Aaron?" she asked.

The way she so bluntly said his name made me flinch. I retreated into my oversized, scruffy pyjamas. "I told you, it was just a few nights."

But Maddie was shaking her head. As she poured another glassful for each of us, she hummed.

"You know that you still have to work together?"

"It will be fine." I said this with confidence, but inside I wasn't so sure.

"Will it?"

I nodded again but my voice wavered. "It has to. Things will go back to normal. I'll get over him."

Maddie raised her glass to her lips but I caught her grimace and saw the unconvinced look in her eyes.

"I hope so," she said.

"Why are you really here, Maddie?" My voice came out sounding as tired and drained as I felt. "You were Aaron's friend long before you were mine, we've never even done this before." I waved at us side by side on my sofa, wine glasses almost empty. "What do you want me to say?"

"Nothing," she replied stiffly. "I wasn't lying, I am here as a friend. You forget that we're a small force, we all know each other. And we were all there the night you were stabbed. Aaron, Chris, Jay, me; we were all there, we all heard the aftermath over the radio, those horrible words, *officer injured*. Ambulance sirens screaming. And I meant what I said about being lonely because before all that happened, you weren't. You had us. You'd trade gossip with me, jeer Pres whenever Norwich lost a match or avoid Harris like the plague. *You* were the one who pushed everyone away afterwards, and we let you. I hoped you'd have some time off sick and come back, just like your old self. But you didn't. Nothing has changed, Anna, only you."

Her words niggled into my mind, a woodworm burrowing in. Had I really pushed everyone away?

"I'm here because I want the old Anna back. Despite how much we all moaned about Crazy McArthur, we missed you. We're a team. And when one of us stumbles, we pick each other up."

Silence fell over us, filled only by the cat's rhythmic purrs as she gently breathed in and out. Maddie lay her hand on my arm, her warming touch almost enough to make me smile. Her words settled on me, uncomfortably true.

"And Aaron?" I asked.

Maddie smiled back. "We'll pick him up too. It's what we do."

## Chapter Twenty-Nine

The next morning, with a wine-induced headache still clinging to the corners of my mind, I wondered what the day ahead would bring. I felt lighter after my chat with Maddie, but it didn't take long before the rosiness waned away and the deep pit of despair reopened. I called my dad to beg for his help to get my old car going again. He must have sensed the frustration in my voice as he didn't chastise me once and came right over.

By mid-morning, I was back on the road and arrived at the station to find Jay alone in the Serious Crimes office. The case of Justin Carter had taken over every inch of space, including my desk.

"Sorry," Jay said as he hastily swiped a file from my keyboard. "I didn't expect you to be in today."

"Why not? We still have to find the killer of Miranda Alder," I said.

I handed him a cup of fresh coffee and left another on the desk for Chris – a pick-me-up Jay sorely needed, by the looks of him. He hunched over his computer, staring with long blinks at the screen.

"Any leads on Justin?" I asked.

He gave me a pointed look. "You know I can't talk to you about it."

"No, Aaron only said I couldn't help on the case. Not that you couldn't tell me about it."

Jay threw a sceptical look at me and hummed, "I'm still not sure."

"I could just look up the case notes myself if I really wanted to know," I said with an exasperated sigh as I gestured to my computer. "So, you might as well tell me now and save me the time."

"Okay, okay." He huffed and pushed himself away from his desk. "Fine. Justin was found about twenty-four hours after he was killed. He had a large blunt-force trauma wound to the head."

"So, he didn't kill himself?"

Jay shook his head. "It doesn't look that way. It looks more like he was hit over the head with a heavy object. We're not ruling out the possibility that his death could be linked to Miranda's."

"Really?" That wasn't an angle that had crossed my mind, but anything was possible now that suicide was ruled out. It was highly unlikely to have two suspicious deaths so close together, especially between victims who knew each other.

"Actually, I'm glad you're here," Jay continued, picking up his case file. "We've been having some trouble tracking down where Justin was staying. Turns out the address he gave the hospital on discharge was wrong. Didn't he tell you when you went to see him in hospital?"

Spurred on by the thought that I could be helpful, I dived into my bag for my notebook. "He did, he said he was staying with a friend, an apprentice who used to work for him. I wrote it down… Here. It's an address in town."

I handed over the scrap of newspaper from my notebook, Justin's shaking writing just about legible, and Jay scanned it.

"Not too far away from Miranda."

"Same estate." I nodded.

Before we could speculate further, Jay was already searching the address into the police database. He gave a disappointed growl. "No records for council tax, looks like the property's owner recently died. I guess I'll have to take a visit."

"Can I come?" I asked eagerly.

Jay glanced around the room. Wherever Chris was, he was nearby and I could sense Jay's reluctance to let me help.

"No, you better stay here. Search up on the previous owner for me. See if you can track down their next of kin, whoever would have ownership of the house now. At least if we have a name, we have somewhere to start."

It wasn't exactly exciting, but at least he was letting me help.

Jay grabbed his car keys and made for the door. "Tell Chris where I've gone when he gets back from his briefing with Aaron. I'll be back soon."

And so, I was on my own again.

I tried my best to focus and not let the misery rumbling deep inside start to spill over again. I did as Jay asked and attempted to track down the previous owner of the property. With the last registered owner deceased, I contacted the bank handling her estate and requested they give me the name of the executor of the will and the new owner of the house at 121 Alice Fisher Crescent, North Lynn. The bank deferred my request to their legal team, who wanted everything dotted and crossed and signed by the chief constable himself. In the end, I managed to wrangle a promise from them to forward a copy of the will as soon as the paperwork was approved.

Jay returned a couple of hours later, grumbling at his unfruitful visit. The house appeared uninhabited. The neighbours all reported they didn't know who owned the property now that the old lady had died. They rarely saw anyone come and go. The curtains were always shut.

As the day slipped away, I felt the same empty feeling creeping back in, the same reminder that not only was Miranda not mourned, but now Justin wasn't missed either. I needed to find justice for these two people. Their lives may not have been perfect, but they deserved peace and their killers deserved prison. Yet it all seemed so hard when the threads led nowhere but dead end after dead end.

With more bottles of wine calling my name at home, I called it a day as late evening descended on the station. The idea of spending yet another night alone was unappealing but there wasn't anything I could do about that. I had brought the loneliness on myself; now I just had to live with the emptiness. The wine would help.

Downstairs from the office, at the front desk, I found a commotion in the almost empty foyer. A riled-up member of the public was arguing with the desk officer, who remained calm and firm in the face of the distressed man. As I neared, wondering if I'd be able to sneak out without being dragged into it, a stench hit me. Strong alcohol and several-day-old clothes; the smell of someone who'd hit rock bottom. I realised it was Jeremy Payton.

"Mr Payton," I greeted him, loudly. I succeeded in drawing him away from his argument with the desk officer and he rounded on me. His eyes were bleary and red, his face flushed.

"You." He sneered at me, obviously forgetting my name. "Tell him I want my stuff back!" He jabbed in the direction of the desk officer, who rolled his eyes and gave an irritated huff.

"McArthur, please tell Mr Payton that I have no control over the items that were seized from his house during the search. It's you and your team that need to release them."

It took a moment before the penny dropped. During the search of his house, Jeremy's phone and computer were seized as evidence. They'd be returned if he was cleared of any suspicion.

"He's right," I said to Jeremy, trying my best to look understanding. My presence had stalled Jeremy's anger and he floundered now, unsure what to do. "We can't give the items back yet, not until they've been analysed. What is it that you want?"

"My phone," Jeremy said, along with a hiccup. "I want to call my kids."

"Why do you need to call your kids?"

"Why do you think? Katie kicked me out!" After saying the words out loud, Jeremy's fight evaporated, leaving him swaying on the spot. He was still a little drunk but his distress was waning, along with his energy.

"Your wife kicked you out?" My stomach twisted. It wasn't really a surprise – he had been cheating on her after all – but seeing the demise of a marriage was never nice. A family torn apart.

Despite the fact that Jeremy had brought this on himself with his infidelity, I still felt an overwhelming amount of sympathy for the man. Maybe Jeremy Payton just needed a sympathetic ear, like Maddie had given to me.

I gestured for him to join me on some seating away from the desk and Jeremy reluctantly followed. He threw clumsy glares at the desk officer as he went before collapsing into a chair.

"What's happened, Jeremy? You're very worked up."

"Well, it's all gone to shit," he replied, throwing me a dirty look too. "Ever since you guys showed up and told me about Miranda, it's all fallen apart. Katie chucked me out. I can't contact my children. I can't go to work."

"You can't go to work?"

He shook his head, the motion making him sway with dizziness. "No, they've suspended me until you lot find who killed Miranda. So, I'm just... stuck. In limbo until I can clear my name and get my life back."

I sucked in a deep breath. It was a shit situation to be in. Whether he killed Miranda or not, Jeremy's life was in the gutter. The best I could do was offer some reassuring words.

"It may seem unfair but it's just our jobs, Jeremy. These are the processes we have to go through. Don't you want the person who killed Miranda to pay?"

"But I didn't do it!"

"We will find who did," I said carefully. "Miranda deserves as much."

Jeremy snorted back. "I don't care about your investigation. This is all your fault. This isn't fair. None of this would've happened if it weren't for you lot..."

I sighed, releasing the breath I held. Even drunk and with his life in tatters, Jeremy didn't care about Miranda. He didn't care who killed her. He only wanted his life back, not hers. Pushing the nagging feeling of loneliness away, I rose to my feet. Someone needed to care about Miranda Alder and care about her death. If it wasn't the people in her life, then I guess it would have to be me. Same as Justin, someone needed to bring justice to those who had murdered them. It would have to be me.

\* \* \*

That night, I dragged myself home, weighed down by the lack of progress on our cases. Poppy the cat was happy to see me, desperate for food. At least someone was pleased by my presence.

I called my mum, who gave me a rundown of her thrilling day tidying up the garden after the storm. She asked me about work – she always did – but like always, I couldn't tell her. I just spun an answer to make her believe my life was fine and dandy and left it at that. She probably knew I was lying. She couldn't do anything about it though.

After a shower, I switched on the ten o'clock news, waiting for it to end so I could watch something a bit less depressing. It had taken so long to calm down Jeremy and convince him to leave peacefully that evening had merged into night. I could feel the tiredness deep in my aching bones but sleep wasn't going to come so easily. I fired up my laptop, wondering where best to start. We were still waiting on the DNA results for Jeremy, to see if they matched the sample taken from Miranda's body, and the details of the property where Justin was staying. I decided to focus on Justin, doing a quick search for his name which brought me to the website of his company, Carter Coach Hire. Despite going under, the company's website was still active, adorned with a grainy photo of two large coaches face to face, and a group of people standing in front of them, all giving a thumbs up. Justin was front and centre, beaming at the camera.

The website's information was sparce but the little there was, was interesting. At its height, Justin's company had fifteen coaches, a host of drivers, a workshop with a full-time mechanic and a booking office. They ran excursions to the beach, day trips to Norwich and Cambridge, and even holiday tours to Europe. He'd been successful, which made his turn of fortune and his death feel all the more unfair.

One photo caught my eye. It featured a smiling young man holding a wrench under the title *Apprenticeships available*. He looked familiar – beady eyes, clean-cut and smooth face and curly ginger hair. He was young, barely school-leaving age.

My laptop pinged, signalling the arrival of an email. I realised I was scowling at the young man's photo, so I switched tabs to my work emails, where evidently someone else was also working late. It was from the bank.

I opened the attachment.

*The deceased leaves her property, 121 Alice Fisher Crescent, King's Lynn, Norfolk, to her nephew and only living relative, Gregory Hanson.*

The young man...

I scrambled up and to the bedroom, finding my work trousers in the same place I had thrown them on the floor. My notebook was inside and I flicked the pages until I found the scrap of paper Justin had written for me, the same one I had shown Jay.

*Gregory – 121 Alice Fisher, N Lynn.*

I snapped it shut. That was it.
I knew who killed Miranda Alder.

# Chapter Thirty

The bright lights and white ceiling of the megastore shocked in contrast to the night outside. Guttural grunts bounced off the walls, an odd soundtrack to the show the crowd had gathered around. Two people scuffled across the tiled floor, insults and inept punches thrown back and forth. It was Nick in his store uniform, and Jeremy, still very drunk.

"You lied to me – you said there was nothing going on with Miranda!" Nick shouted.

Jeremy was unsteady on his feet, even more so than when I'd seen him in the station a short while before. The smell of booze was strong surrounding him, and I wondered if he'd been drinking some more. How he was able to stand up and throw insults back at Nick, I didn't know.

"It doesn't matter, Nick! She's dead now! She wouldn't have gone anywhere near you anyway!"

"Miranda was my friend!" Nick landed a right hook to Jeremy's chin, twisting his face into an agonising expression.

Jeremy reeled but he staggered back to his feet. "She used you, Nick, just like she used me for a quick shag! She was a superficial bitch!"

"You take that back! I cared for her!"

"She didn't care for you!"

Nick's anger reverberated through him like an electric shock, making his fists tremble as he threw punch after punch. There was hatred in his eyes, grief, and a longing to hurt Jeremy. He launched forward, but Jeremy was too impaired to jump out of the way. Pained screams filled the air. Around the rumble, the rest of Miranda's co-workers simply watched. No one was keen to step in and break the pair apart. More than a few held their phones out, filming the action.

It was up to me to stop the two men before one of them got seriously hurt.

"Stop!" I barked the order as I approached Nick and Jeremy. "Stop it!"

My interference did nothing and the two men continued to belt each other. Nick was wild with rage. He punched Jeremy to the floor, waited for him to get up, then went for it again. Jeremy was poorly balanced and poorly aimed. This was a fight that would be over in no time unless I stepped in. If no one intervened, one of them would end up killing the other.

"*Stop!*"

This time, my harsh shout worked and the two of them paused and looked to me. Now I could see the blood pouring from Jeremy's nose, the grazing on Nick's knuckles. The pause lasted only seconds before Jeremy let out a feral cry and tackled Nick to the ground. I dived in after them and managed to pull Jeremy to his feet.

"Stop this now or I'll arrest you both," I warned them. They ignored me. I dodged out the way as Nick threw himself at Jeremy once again. He was rabid, calling Jeremy every swear word known to mankind as he hit with no restraint. Jeremy pulled his body inwards but swung his fists, hoping blindly to meet his target.

One of Jeremy's ill-aimed punches caught me on the arm, knocking me out of their path. But just as I prepared to wade into the fight again, a customer strode into the store and straight into the madness. A towering bloke dressed all in black, he must have been a nightclub bouncer or a security guard on his way to work. He strode confidently over to the fight and picked up Nick by the scruff of his clothes with ease. With Nick no longer attacking him, Jeremy sunk down to the floor.

"You!" I pointed to the closest person from the crowd and gestured to Jeremy. "Check he's okay."

They did as they were told and rushed to Jeremy's side but I ignored them and turned my attention to Nick, still struggling but now restrained and gasping for air.

"What the hell is this?" the bouncer asked, holding Nick like he was nothing more than a wriggling puppy.

I helped to hustle him back, away from centre stage. Behind me, I heard Jeremy whimpering, which reassured me he wasn't hurt too badly.

"Nick, can you explain?"

"He started it!" Nick roared, fighting against the unrelenting grip on his collar. "He turned up here, off his face, saying how Miranda liked him more than me. How they…" For the first time since my arrival, Nick's blinding rage relented enough for him to recognise me, and his face burned red. "He was trying to rub it in my face. Trying to get me to confess to killing her because I was jealous!"

"That's no excuse to attack each other," I said.

"Did you do it?" Nick ignored me and pulled against his restraint, aiming for Jeremy. "Did you kill her?"

"No," cried Jeremy. "I wouldn't."

"Well, someone did! Someone took her to that park and killed her!"

"Yeah, you!"

"Shut it!" I warned Jeremy as Nick let out another tortured cry. I wasn't here for this. I had a much more pressing matter. A glance over the crowd showed me most of Nick's colleagues had now dispersed, but the one I wanted still remained. He was helping to calm Jeremy. Greg, the warehouse worker.

"Nick," I said, and placed myself between him and Jeremy, firmly in his view. "I know this is tough and you're still hurting over Miranda's death. But beating Jeremy to an inch of his life isn't going to bring her back."

"She was my friend," he said again.

His fight ebbed away with a good distance between him and Jeremy. Tears formed at the corner of his eyes, but with a shake of his head, his hair flopped back over his face, hiding them from view. Sensing his energy wane, the man lowered Nick to the ground, hand still hovering by his shoulder. Nick sank down to his knees. I crouched down with him.

"She was my friend." His voice broke, no more the furious roar but the meek meow of a broken boy. "She was the only one here who was nice to me."

"Nice to your face," Jeremy mumbled, his head still buried in the ball.

"Can you call the police?" I asked the bouncer.

He pulled a face at me, edging away from Nick like he was a dangerous animal, but Nick wasn't baying for blood anymore. The young lad sniffed as he inspected his sore knuckles, pulled the sleeve over his hand and started to chew.

The man nodded at me and pulled out his phone.

I waited a few moments, just to see if either Nick or Jeremy would make any other moves, but the two of them were done, too exhausted and distraught to bother with each other. Satisfied they were no longer a threat to anyone, I rose to my feet and pulled my own phone from my pocket. A shadow moved out the corner of my eye. Greg shifted, trying to keep Jeremy still.

"Do you need any help?" I asked him, keeping my tone firm. He was the one I was here for, but I couldn't let him see that.

"I think I've got him," he replied.

Jeremy rocked back and forth on his side, too drunk to notice that Greg was trying to help him. He swatted the man like he was a fly buzzing around his face. Nick was sobbing quietly into his sleeve behind me.

Admitting defeat, Greg rose to his feet. He cleared his throat. "That was some good timing, you showing up then."

I smiled to myself. "I have a knack for being in the right place at the right time when things go a bit crazy."

I had to keep Greg talking and make sure he wasn't suspicious of me. At first glance, that ginger-haired young lad from the photo didn't look anything like the man in front of me now and I wondered if I could be wrong. But the harder I looked, the more I saw the youth in him. He may have shaved his head but his eyes were the same, as was his nervous-looking grin. Greg had known Justin. He'd been the one to take Justin in after his suicide attempt.

*Gregory – 121 Alice Fisher, N Lynn.*

"You said you've worked here a few weeks? What happened to your last job?" I asked.

"The company went bust," Greg replied. He watched me now, eyes fixed on my expression. "It was the only place I ever worked, started there as an apprentice."

"What did you do?"

"Mechanic. For a coach company."

"You worked with Justin Carter?"

The pieces slotted into place and the puzzle was finally complete. He was the connection between the two.

"How do you…"

When I looked up, Greg was already backing away. In his eyes I saw a spooked man, but I didn't have long to look. I took a step forward, bridging the gap between us, and that was enough for Greg to realise my intentions.

He spun round and gave me a forceful shove, sending me flying across the tiled floor. When I picked myself back up again, he had vanished.

"Where's he gone?" I asked the few remaining colleagues, hovering next to the customer service desk.

They pointed to the back of the store, to the warehouse. I sprinted that way, leaving the remnants of the fight behind me.

Out the back of the store, the warehouse was almost pitch black. It was only the light from the loading bay outside, stretching in from the open doors at the far end, that gave me any light to go by. Long shadows were cast by the stacks of wooden pallets lining the room, a delivery not yet unpacked. Garden furniture, I realised, ready for summer barbecues and days at the beach. The plastic wrappers, half unwrapped, flapped in the slight breeze from the bay door.

If Greg had any brains, he would have run straight out that door and be halfway across town by now.

To my left, I heard a scuffle.

"Greg?" I called out to the dark. "It's Detective McArthur. You should really come out. We need to talk."

The scuffle could have been a rat. But it moved again, definitely a man-sized shape creeping along between the boxes, pallets and cage trolleys. I heard a crackling, a series of pops that I couldn't place.

With one foot in front of another, I made my way closer. He could still run for it. He was young, tall and twice my size; I would have never caught up with him. Plus, I was already out of breath from wading into the fight. I could hear Greg just a few feet away, rustling frantically and trying to avoid me as I neared.

What was he doing?

With a groan like a dying animal, the sound of creaking mechanisms filled the void around me. Darkness descended as the moonlight from outside was swallowed steadily when the bay door began to close. The crackling and popping continued, unrelated, coming from somewhere within the pallets. Soon, I found myself in darkness, only the weak emergency lighting above the closed doors offering any relief.

He wasn't running. Which meant he was going to fight.

Out of nowhere, a dead weight dropped on me from a stack of pallets to my left and crushed me to the ground. There came a primal scream as I gained my bearings. Greg was pinning me down. I moved quickly to the side as his shadow lunged, a punch aimed at my head. He hit the concrete floor.

"She was a monster!" he shrieked. "That woman destroyed Justin's life!"

I leaned the other way, dodging another strike but Greg corrected himself and caught me on the jaw. His dead weight sat on my legs. I bucked my hips, jolting him enough to give me the leverage to hit him hard in the gut. The force knocked him back and we both scrambled to our feet. I backed away from him, putting enough distance between us to catch my breath.

"So what?" I asked between pants. "You killed Miranda after you realised that she was the one conning Justin. You recognised her. Why not just tell him the truth?"

"Because the stupid man was still in love with her!"

Greg staggered forwards as I grabbed the nearest object, a broom, to defend myself. I swung it outwards in the hope it would deter him. In the gloom, a gleam of sweat shined off his head. His eyes darted around, desperately looking for options. The crackling noise grew beside us, turning into a steady roar. An acrid stench filled the space.

"Did you kill Justin as well?"

"It was an accident!" Greg tried to snatch the broom, but I jumped out of his reach. "I didn't mean to kill him. I thought if I told him the truth about Miranda and what I'd done, then he'd stop moping about her. It didn't work. He was mad."

Another swing and Greg managed to grab my broom with one hand. He snatched it and threw it away. I dodged his steps as he advanced on me. The light danced off his panicked face and blood slowly trickled from his lip. I must have caught him with my broom. But above him the room seemed to grow darker, and I realised what the crackling roar was. Auburn fire was lapping at the piles of pallets, rising with ferocity until it was already as tall as me.

Greg didn't intend for us to get out of here.

"I didn't mean to hurt Justin, I would never hurt him," he said, his chest heaving, "but killing Miranda was so satisfying. You have no idea of the trouble she caused. I lost my job because of her. We lost the company! And then here she was, showing off the gold watch that Justin had bought her on my very first day here! That woman deserved to die."

A chill ran through me. I was close to the door now, ready to make an escape back to the shop floor. Quick as a flash, Greg tripped me up. I threw out my arm to break my fall, hearing a concerning crunch as it crumpled beneath my weight.

"I don't want to go to jail," said Greg. He jumped up and down on the spot, but he was looking less and less worried about me being a threat. He paced several steps around me, not bothered by the flames or smoke as they grew in the delivery, eating away at the pallets. The taste of burning plastic seared on my tongue.

"It's a bit late for that," I mumbled back as I climbed to my feet. I was no match for this guy and we both knew it. He was fit and strong. I could fight dirty but there was no point when I could barely get a chance. He would just overpower me.

We surveyed each other for a moment. My arm throbbed painfully. Greg's body shook. He was filthy from rolling around on the floor; blood starting to mix in with dust and dirt, sweat leaving sooty trails on his skin.

"What would happen to me? If I gave up," he asked. For the first time, a look of fear crossed his face as he paced between me and the door. I wondered if he was contemplating an escape, exiting while we still could before the flames grew high enough to seal our way out. The smoke hung heavy above us.

"You'll be arrested," I said, surprising myself at the calmness I could manage whilst struggling for breath. The air was growing thicker.

"Prison?" he asked, completely petrified.

"Most likely." But of course he'd go to prison. He was a murderer.

"I don't want to go."

"There's no other way out now, Greg."

I watched him tensely as he thought this through. His shaking hands flexed but his face was still terrified at the thought of arrest. He was beginning to realise that this was the end as the warehouse burned around us. I hoped if the store had any sort of sprinkler system, it would kick in soon.

"Come with me, Greg," I said. "There's no point in fighting, it'll just make things worse."

He considered this. Then he shook his head fiercely.

"No. If I'm going down, I'm not going alone."

And he ran at me. His intention was to tackle me to the ground again where I'd be helpless, but I was one step ahead. I jumped out of his way, getting far too close to the flaming pallets for my liking. I felt the fire lick my skin. Greg corrected himself too late and I aimed a well-placed kick into his abdomen. It stopped him dead in his tracks and dazed him for a much needed second. I kicked him twice more, once in the chest, once in the stomach, and he went down, giving me a chance to pull away from the fire trying to suck me in.

Greg fell to the floor like a sack of potatoes, gasping desperately for air and greeted only by smoke. He stayed down, long enough for me to draw in my own smoke-filled lungful of air. It offered no relief. I waited and braced myself, ready for him to jump up again. Something would need to give because with each passing second, the fire was spreading and the smoke thickening.

But he didn't move. Greg didn't get up, not to take another shot at me nor to finally make an escape. He just lay there, barely visible anymore in amongst the raging flames, as the room darkened around us.

I spun round on the spot. Any light the flames offered was swallowed just as fast by the thick, plastic-ladened smoke. I couldn't see the exit anymore, the emergency light just a tiny dot carefully concealed by the licks and spits of fire. One way led to the bay doors and the other to the shop floor, but I couldn't be sure which was which. Another deep breath only made my head spin.

I needed to get out.

Heading further into the smoke, I held my hands out in front of me like I was blind. I felt the red-hot fire tug at me from the right so I headed left. One of my hands felt duller than the other and I wondered if I was actually holding it out at all. Something took a hold of my ankle and I tripped, landing hard on the floor.

It was Greg, crawling his way to me. I kicked out at him, scuffling back until I hit solid and cool. The wall.

Greg's hands appeared from the thick smoke, like a nightmarish ghoul seeking me out. I kicked at him as I scrambled to my feet and to my relief, I felt something on the wall. A button. I pressed it. I didn't care what it did.

The groaning noise replied in response, almost defeated by the roar of the flames. Cool air rushed in as the bay door opened at the far end of the warehouse, sucking the smoke out. In seconds, the atmosphere was clear enough to reveal Greg scrambling around by my feet.

At the same moment as the smoke took its escape, a siren rang out loud and clear throughout the warehouse. It drilled into my skull, enough to knock me sideways. From the ceiling rained spits of water, at first not enough against the flames, and then plentiful, and far colder than it had any right to be.

I spotted the door as the room cleared, the sprinklers dampening down the towering flames. As Greg reached out once again for me, I snatched his wrist and dragged him across the slick floor to the entrance to the shop, where I was met by the blessed sight of two uniformed constables on their way in.

Backup. And not a moment too late.

## Chapter Thirty-One

I used to be quite quick on my feet. When I was in uniform, I kept fit; I jogged in my spare time, even took the odd martial art class when it coincided with my shift pattern. Now that I was a detective, I had let my fitness dwindle and ten months on sick leave hadn't helped. I was regretting it right this moment. My shoulder ached, which was weird as that was the one part of my body that I was sure I hadn't hurt in my scuffle with Greg.

I sat on the back steps of one of the ambulances, watching the world go by and cursing myself for my aching muscles. Two paramedics had checked me over before abandoning me to go and help their colleagues, who were attempting to bundle Jeremy in another wagon. In his drunk, confused and probably concussed state, he still thought he was being attacked.

The pretty blue lights of the emergency vehicles lit up the supermarket car park, flashing with entrancing rhythms. Fire engines worked around the back of the store but they had put out the fire with relative ease. Now, only pitiful grey smoke drifted behind the street lights from the bay door of the warehouse.

A police car set off from the car park with Nick inside, taking him to the hospital for a thorough check-up. He'd be fine, I heard some of the paramedics say, just a precaution before he was handed over to be processed for the fight.

Greg was in a nearby police van, which was ready to set off and take him to the nick. Chris and Jay waved to the driver, giving the signal to go, before they made their way over to me. I jumped to my feet. Adrenalin was a hell of a hormone and I still had plenty of it coursing through my body.

"So, who gets to interview him?" I asked, as they both gave me a withering look until my excitement drained away. "What?"

"You're not interviewing. You're getting into that ambulance," said Jay, pointing to the hulking yellow vehicle. "Let's see; unable to move right arm, that's broken. Nice cut on the chin, that will probably need stitches. You've probably inhaled more smoke than a sixty-year-old smoker."

"Don't forget the adrenalin shakes," said Chris. And sure enough, my good hand, the one that I could move, was shaking uncontrollably.

"You need medical attention now," Jay concluded. "We will drag you to the hospital if we have to."

"All right, fine," I said, huffing as I gave in.

I wasn't in any state to argue with them, that was for sure, and from their irritability, it would only hurt my case if I did. However, there was something else there, something that wasn't quite the fury I deserved. Chris's face was set in his usual frown but he also bit his lower lip. Jay chewed his thumbnail so hard it was almost gone. I'd never seen them that way before but if I had to put my finger on it, I would say they were worried about me.

"How did you end up in all this mess?" Chris asked.

Rather than the adrenalin helping me come up with a good enough explanation, I floundered. I didn't want to ruin whatever tentative trust I had built up with them over the last few weeks. But there wasn't an explanation forthcoming that could explain my actions.

"I didn't expect this," I said earnestly. "I didn't expect the fight, I didn't expect the will to come through and name Greg. I definitely didn't expect him to set fire to the warehouse. I just found myself in the right place at the right time and things went a bit… crazy."

Jay and Chris nodded, passing between them one of their looks. I couldn't tell whether they believed me.

"Yep, crazy is right," Chris agreed.

For an awfully long moment, no one spoke as we watched the scene around us, dozens of people trying to repair the mess left behind by a few. I wasn't sure how I could repair the chaos that I'd caused to the supermarket. Customers were being turned away at the door. The night-shift workers huddled in small groups and threw suspicious looks at everyone around them. A murderer had walked among them, fooling everyone.

Would they miss Miranda now? Would any of them be sad about what had happened, at how many lives had been ruined or taken?

"Come on," Jay said, pulling me from my daze. "Let's get you to the hospital."

"Then what?"

"Chris and I will get Greg Hanson processed. Let's get to the bottom of why he killed Miranda Alder."

* * *

As I waited at the hospital, the adrenalin spike slowly faded away, taking the shakes and my energy with it. Pain grew throughout my body, like it wanted to remind me indefinitely of how lucky I'd been. I didn't have the strength to assure anyone that I was fine anymore, and neither did I believe it. My wrist ached sharply as I cradled it in my sleeve. My head spun, reliving the events. My clothes smelled like I'd wandered through a bonfire and my favourite hoody was singed beyond repair. I wanted nothing more than to crawl into bed and sleep off the whole ordeal.

I was ushered to the X-ray department and seated in a darkened corner of the waiting area. I think I almost fell asleep while I waited for my turn and listened to the gentle talking of the technicians just along the corridor from me.

Then someone abruptly entered the waiting room and interrupted my dozing. The doors flew open, clattering loudly against the wall. Sterile white light flooded into the dim area, casting a long shadow as the figure scanned the room.

Without a word, Aaron took the seat next to me. With his lips pressed tightly together, his face gave nothing away. I waited for him to say something because I knew exactly what was coming, but for several excruciating minutes, he didn't speak.

Eventually, I couldn't take the silence anymore. "How did you find me?"

"Jay told me, of course," he said, an uncomfortable edge to his voice. He was teetering on the verge of yelling at me. "Said he insisted you went to the hospital, and you actually agreed with him, so I knew it must be bad."

"It's not bad, I'm fine." I gave a tiny cough, the raspy sound showing a hint of all the smoke I'd inhaled. "Go on then. Get it over and done with. Shout at me and tell me how stupid I was, how reckless."

At my prompting, Aaron snapped. "It's always you! Why is it always you, Anna? Whenever something like this happens, I just know it's you in the middle of it. And never even mind the fact you went there without backup!"

"I didn't intend this to happen," I replied, my own exhaustion meaning I couldn't quite match Aaron's anger. "I didn't expect the fight or to confront him or the fire. I didn't expect this." I gestured to my lifeless arm hanging in my lap. The pain was waning, replaced by a grogginess I couldn't fight off.

Aaron gritted his teeth together. "You didn't expect it because you didn't think before you acted! You never do, you throw yourself into a situation without any regard to your own safety. Do you have a death wish, Anna? Is that it?"

"No."

"Then why do you do this? I don't understand."

"Neither do I," I said, as I cradled my arm across my chest, like a defence. "Why are you here, Aaron? Did you come here just to scold me?"

"No." He released a deep, achingly fragile sigh. "It's because it's you. It's always you."

Before I could ask him what that meant, a nurse appeared at the door to the X-ray suite. She peered into the dark waiting room, spotting the figures of Aaron and me.

"Miss McArthur?"

I stood up and to my surprise, so did Aaron. When I gave him a questioning look, he simply nodded towards the nurse, urging me on, and followed behind. It appeared he wasn't going to be leaving any time soon.

The X-ray was quick and painless. Diagnosed with a nice, clean fracture, I was patched up and sent on my way with some good painkillers and strict instructions to rest. They issued me with the necessary paperwork for work, clearing me for light duties only, which was underlined. I trudged my way to the exit in silence, the strength seeping out of me with every step. Aaron walked beside me the entire way.

In the cool night outside the hospital, I took a moment to catch my breath. The air awakened me and I realised just how close I had come to doing something truly reckless. I had confronted a killer on my own; one who outmatched me in strength, weight, height. No wonder Aaron was mad at me. I was lucky to only have a broken wrist and a slight cough for my troubles.

Aaron didn't wait and immediately set off for the car park, down a slight incline from the hospital entrance. I could still smell smoke, but maybe that was just my imagination, or the remnants of the blaze etched into my clothes and skin. When we reached the car, Aaron paused.

"Get in," he said, no emotion in his voice.

I obeyed and climbed in the passenger seat. Aaron got in the driver's. He made no other move. A street lamp cast light down through the windscreen, creating shadows across his face. He no longer looked mad – just defeated.

"It's always you," he muttered to himself. "Always you, Anna."

I growled back; I was too tired for this fight again. Yes, it was always me, Crazy McArthur, always in trouble. We both knew the spiel. I opened my mouth to tell him to spare the oncoming lecture but his dazed words beat me to it.

"I'm… just trying to figure out why."

"Why it's always me?" I snapped back. "Okay, I get it, we always have this conversation. I need to be more careful. It's always me in trouble, always me in the middle of it. I don't just attract trouble – I go looking for it. I get it! I know!"

"No." Aaron shook his head. "No, that's not what I meant."

"Then what?"

"I meant why... why do I always worry about you? You're like the cat with nine lives. Every time something like this happens, I find you in the middle of it, mostly battered and bruised but okay. But I still worry. Every time I hear there's an incident, an officer hurt, I worry it's you and I come looking for you because I have to see for myself that you're all right. Why? I knew you were okay tonight, Jay told me you just needed patching up. But here I am!"

"You're wondering why you're here?" I questioned. "It's your job."

"It's not my job. I don't do it for anyone else."

"Then it's because you care."

"I do care about you. That's the problem."

"How is that a problem?"

"Because I care too much."

I snorted, growing frustrated. I wanted nothing more than to crawl into bed. "There's no such thing as caring too much."

"You broke up with me because you were developing feelings for me. You cared for me too much."

"I broke up with you because I knew you didn't feel the same way," I said.

"What if I do?"

I stared at the man, totally bewildered. He hid it well, but anxiety and worry were tearing at him. He was scared for me, and even now, after seeing I was okay, he was worrying. Maybe he did care more than he realised.

Aaron started the car, the noise jolting me. "Come on, I have to get back to the station."

"Hang on, we need to talk about this."

"We will," he said with an earnest nod. "Just give me… just give me a bit of time to get my head around it."

## Chapter Thirty-Two

"Gregory Hanson. My name is Detective Inspector Chris Hamill and this is my colleague Detective Sergeant Jay Fitzgerald. We're here to interview you in relation to the deaths of Miranda Alder and Justin Carter, for which you have been arrested. Do you understand?"

Greg nodded, slow and controlled. Now seated in the interview room, he was less frantic and panicked than before. He regarded Chris and Jay with suspicion. He even threw side glances at the duty solicitor.

I made myself comfortable in the observation room, sliding some of the old recording equipment to the side so I had room to sit on the desk and watch the proceedings. With my arm in a sling and some hefty painkillers in my bloodstream, I was as comfortable as I was going to be. Tiredness still tugged at me, making my eyes heavy, but I wasn't going to miss this. I needed to know why.

They started with all the formalities, informing Greg that he was also under arrest for the assault of a police officer and informing him of his rights. He nodded along, his head hanging low, defeated. It surprised me; just a couple of hours before, Greg had been so anxious to get away, so determined.

There was still work that I could be doing. If Greg had killed Miranda, then there would be evidence to collate. The CCTV footage from the store on the night of Miranda's death would be the first port of call, checking to see when Greg was off camera and for how long, and whether that matched up to the time of Miranda's death. But I just couldn't will myself to move. There was no more urgency to find the killer since he now sat on the other side of the glass to me. So I leaned back against the wall and watched the interview unfurl as a sense of finality fell over me.

Chris continued. "You confessed to our colleague that you killed Miranda Alder. Do you stand by that statement?"

Greg nodded once again. "I do. She deserved it."

"Why did she deserve it?" Jay asked.

"She was a fleecer. A con artist. She'd had Justin under her spell for so long that I couldn't do anything but watch as his life crumbled around him. He lost the company because of her. I lost my job – one I'd been in since I was a lad. And then, when I started my new job, she was there. Bold as brass, showing off the gold watch I'd watched Justin send her a few months before. She lied to him. God knows how many others she lied to."

"You thought there were others like Justin?"

"I knew there was. Every shift, I would come in and hear her telling Nick tales about a different man online, one who paid her rent or bought her flowers. I knew Justin wasn't the only one."

"So, you planned to kill her?"

Greg flinched, the questions landing like heavy punches. "I didn't start off planning it that way. I wanted to give her a taste of her own medicine."

"How did you plan to do that?"

"My plan was to fleece her like she'd done Justin. Take her for everything she had. I started talking to her, charming her, gaining her trust. It was so easy. We grew friendly and swapped numbers, she started texting. She carried on lying all the time, telling me stories as if that was impressing me, as if I didn't already know the bullshit that she spun Justin. She'd give anything for a bit of attention. I realised she wasn't going to change; I couldn't teach her a lesson. Even if I took everything she owned, she wouldn't change her ways. She lived for the thrill, for the attention and the money she swindled. I had to stop her another way."

"Tell us about the night she died," said Chris.

A flicker of a conceited smile crossed Greg's face. "I told her I'd booked the day off, that I wanted to spend the night with her. Take her out. I knew that even if she asked Jeremy if I had, he wouldn't tell her. Stick up his arse, that one. I snuck out of the warehouse and picked her up on my bike. She had to hold onto me, so she left her purse at home. We went to The Walks, and I rode my bike right along the paths." A brief laugh escaped his lips, as if reliving a pleasant memory rather than a brutal murder.

Jay winced at Greg's laughter. "Then what happened?"

"I'm sure you know," said Greg as he leaned back in his seat. "We had sex."

"In the park?"

"What can I say? The bitch was a freak."

Chris caught Jay's gaze out the corner of his eye. "So, it will be your DNA we recovered from Miranda's body then?"

The man opposite nodded his head. "Probably."

"How did you kill her?" Jay asked.

"I stabbed her." Greg sighed, as if a weight had been lifted. "Five, ten times. I lost count. Then, I carved into her chest what she was."

"What was that?"

"A catfish. A liar. A lying bitch."

An unsettling silence engulfed the interview room, the occupants acting as though the air was as thick as it had been in the burning warehouse. Greg's chest heaved.

"Why?"

"I wanted the world to know. I wanted to make you think that one of the dozens of men she'd scorned online had finally caught up with her. I knew Justin wasn't the first or the last."

Chris and Jay gave each other a look, an unspoken glance which seemed to speak volumes to them. Chris leaned forwards on the desk, making the solicitor give a wary shuffle.

"Are you pleased with yourself, Greg?"

Greg faced Chris, his steady gaze unwavering as he nodded and rolled his shoulders. "I never had anyone when I was growing up, apart from that old bat of an aunt who left me her house. Justin gave me a chance. He gave me a job, some skills, a life. And I just had to sit by and watch as Callie, or Miranda or whatever the fuck her name was, took that all away. I knew the first moment I met her in the store that she had to pay. She deserved it."

Jay bent across the table too. I wished I knew what they were thinking, but I could only guess. They were just a bit too rigid to be completely at ease when sitting across the table from a killer, but they hid it well as Jay ploughed on to the next question.

"If Justin gave you such a chance in life, then why did you kill him?"

For the first time since he'd sat down, I saw Greg falter. His breath hitched and his gaze fell away, darting over to the solicitor, who too watched him with expectant eyes. When he returned to Chris and Jay, they hadn't moved, their body language pressing him for an answer.

"I didn't mean to," he replied, his voice a husk of what it had been. "It was an accident."

"That sort of blunt-force trauma isn't an accident."

"It was!" Greg flared up like the flames in the warehouse before settling back in his seat. "We fought. The first night he stayed with me, at the old place my aunt left me, he was miserable. All he could talk about was Miranda, how she'd lied to him, how much he missed her despite knowing what she'd done. I couldn't take it. I told him the truth, that I was the one who'd got rid of her after finding out what she was."

"And what was his reaction to that?"

Greg nodded and bit his lip. "He was furious. We fought. Next thing I know, he's on the floor in a pile of blood. I realised it was too late and that I couldn't save him. I guess I panicked. I loaded him on the bike, got to the first bridge I could find and chucked him over. He deserved better. But by the time the storm came, I couldn't fix what I'd done."

An unearthly silence fell over the interview room and for a moment I wondered whether my hearing had gone. No one dared to breathe. Regret chewed away at Greg, and he sank down into his seat as though the ground was trying to swallow him. He looked at Chris, then Jay, then back again, waiting for one of them to say something.

"You could've called for help for him," Jay said, unafraid to break the silence.

"And have you lot crawling all over my place, finding my DNA and linking it to Miranda?" Greg fired back. "I'm not stupid. I regret fighting with Justin. He was a good man, he helped me."

"And Miranda Alder?"

The man sneered at her name. "Hell no. She deserved everything she got. I only wish I'd done it sooner."

## Chapter Thirty-Three

After a few hours' sleep, I felt like a new person. I wandered through the station, marvelling at how little activity there was. My colleagues were nowhere to be seen, but then they had spent half the night here, interviewing Greg Hanson. I guessed they deserved some rest too.

Upstairs, the Serious Crimes office was empty and I fiddled with the door handle, trying to figure out how to open it with a coffee mug in one hand and a plaster cast restricting my fingers on the other. It was not an easy task.

From nowhere, a hand reached forwards and took the door handle for me, opening the door with a slight click. I looked up to thank my saviour, expecting a random colleague who would make a Crazy McArthur joke, but I was greeted by an unknown face. It was a man in black uniform, with military-cut silver hair and a clean-shaven face. He gestured to the open door, his hazel eyes surveying me up and down.

"Thanks," I said as I made my way inside. The coffee was hot, and I needed to set it down on my desk. The stranger followed me into the room.

On second inspection, I noticed unusual epaulettes on his shoulders and a police lanyard around his neck. The ID badge hung outwards but too far away for me to read. He gave a polite smile, one that appeared almost friendly, but it set me on edge. I knew everyone in the station by now and I knew nearly every officer in our area. I didn't know this man.

"Detective Constable McArthur," he greeted me. His eyes finally left me and surveyed the room, settling on the whiteboard.

"Sir," I said, hedging my bets. Whoever this man was, he was senior to me.

"Please," the man said, settling himself into Chris's desk chair, "don't feel you need to be formal just on my account. I know DCI Burns runs things a little more informally here than I do at head office."

I almost kicked myself. The man was Chief Constable Ian Price, the head of the whole of Norfolk Constabulary. My heart stuttered inside my chest.

"Quite the catch last night, detaining Gregory Hanson," Price said, still gazing over the whiteboard.

I nodded and plastered an officious grimace on my face to hide my growing suspicion. "It was impromptu, but it all worked out in the end."

"Indeed… I heard he confessed to premeditated murder. What about the second victim?" Price motioned to Justin Carter, who was on the board as a victim of the Catfish Girl, a suspect and a murder victim, all at once. He knew a lot about the case already, far more than I expected.

"He still maintains that he didn't mean to kill Justin, that it was an accident during an altercation they had. DI Hamill and DS Fitzgerald were going to question him further about it today." The chief constable gave me an expectant look, urging me to carry on. "They had to stop the interview when the solicitor said it was getting late. The detained has the right to be interviewed at a reasonable time, and all that," I explained.

Price hummed, unsatisfied. "Indeed. And of course, the most pertinent question – what are you doing here?"

Cold fingers of dread worked their way up the back of my neck.

"Sorry, sir?"

Price rolled his eyes at my ignorance. "Not only are you here, in Serious Crimes, a team well above your station, but you're back on active duty without completing the necessary evaluations."

I struggled for a response. I'd been so caught up in the case over the last couple of weeks that I'd forgotten what Aaron had suggested; that we'd keep my assistance quiet. I wasn't supposed to be here.

Price turned his gaze on me, his expression unaffected by my wavering and stutters. He simply watched me flounder.

With no immediate response coming, he continued, "And why did you think it was necessary to visit Gregory Hanson at his place of work yesterday, rather than tell your team of your findings? Hoping for a prominent collar to cement your return to work?"

"That wasn't why I went there," I managed to spit out. "I was just following a hunch."

"Yes, it's better to maintain that story. You had the same excuse during the incident with the Ali Burgess case, did you not? You were posted in a strategic spot, keeping watch over the area. But you left your post against orders to track down some ghostly scream in the night and found the assailant following another potential victim. You were damn lucky to escape with only a knife in the shoulder that time. You have an extraordinary habit of being in the wrong place at the wrong time."

My mouth ran dry as I felt a familiar ache rear up in my shoulder. There was only a thin scar now, but the pain ran deeper. It was the constant reminder that sometimes I wasn't as lucky as I thought I was. That night, I hadn't heard a scream in the night and gone chasing it. I'd simply got fed up with watching over my designated post and decided to take matters into my own hands. I'd gone searching the local area. I'd stumbled on a lone woman walking home in the dead of night being accosted by the killer of Ali Burgess, hunting down another victim. I didn't stop to think before I jumped in to save her.

"Between you and me," Price continued, "I know coppers like you. You think you're indestructible. Above the law and the rules, you operate how you think is best, not how officers with seniority and more experience tell you to. I've looked back at your service record and this wasn't the first time your actions could be described as rogue. For your sake, I hope this is the last."

As his words echoed in my mind, disrupting any of my own thoughts, I heard the telltale clinks of someone heading up the stairs.

A few seconds later, Aaron appeared in the doorway. Confusion creased his face.

"Sir. What are you doing here? I wasn't expecting you for another hour."

Price rose to his feet and greeted Aaron with a sharp nod. "Traffic was better than I thought. I decided to use the time to have a quick informal chat with DC McArthur."

"About what?" His gaze narrowed on Price.

"About the incident last night, of course. I take it personally when an officer of this force is injured in the line of duty."

"McArthur is fine," Aaron replied. He glanced at me and I nodded quickly, backing him up.

"So it appears," said Price. "But still, it is unfortunate that a good result was tainted by something so preventable. Maybe next time, McArthur will be more considerate of herself."

Price looked to me, once again seeing right through me.

Under his glare, I found myself nodding again, anything to get him to look away. "Of course, sir. It won't happen again."

Price smiled, like the unsettling toothy grin of a shark. "Good to hear. I would hate to have to come back for a second chat."

With that, he motioned to Aaron, who stepped aside and directed Price down the corridor to his own office. Aaron hung back a step, using the pause to meet my gaze, but there was nothing we could say to each other. All I could do was offer a weak smile back and hope he could handle himself better when faced with Chief Constable Price.

* * *

"Oh boy," Jay said as he entered the office later that morning. He stifled a yawn, his face contorting with the effort. "Have you seen whose car is downstairs?"

Chris, already slumped at his desk, hummed back in acknowledgment. "Yep, the chief constable's. I'd know that poncy Jag anywhere. Anna said he stopped by for a cryptic chat with her this morning."

Jay turned to me, eyes wide. "He did? What did he say?"

"Basically, don't fuck up again," I replied. "Only he said it a bit more diplomatically than that." The slight anxiety left behind by Price's words still churned away inside, although I kept it firmly hidden from the guys.

"Oh." Jay almost looked disappointed with this. "You got off easy then."

Price was one of those men whose reputation preceded him. He was known as a tyrant at HQ, intolerant and unapologetic. I was always quite glad that he'd never taken much interest in our quiet corner of the county.

"Are you ready for round two?" Jay asked, practically bouncing with excitement as he looked to Chris, who didn't match his enthusiasm in the slightest.

They were due to re-interview Greg this morning. Today would be the tricky subject of Justin's death. I didn't plan on watching this one; instead, the pair of them had left me plenty of paperwork to get through. My punishment for letting the crazy side out again.

"I suppose, although I can think of better ways of spending my day," Chris answered with a grumble. "Best get going before Price reappears. I don't want to get caught in the crosshairs."

"What do you think he's talking to Aaron about?" Jay whispered, as inconspicuous as a pantomime character.

Chris rose to his feet, snatching a case file up from his desk. "Not a clue. Maybe he's finally going to promote him."

Jay snorted. "Yeah, that'll be the day."

I gave a confused glance between the guys. "What do you mean?"

"Did you not hear about what happened when Superintendent Russell retired?" asked Jay.

I shook my head. I'd been out of the loop a few months, so whatever the rumours were from that time had bypassed me.

"Price is a bully," said Chris simply, giving us both a derisive look at the sidetrack away from our work. "He clawed his way to the top and beats down anyone who doesn't agree with his leadership style. And he's never seen eye to eye with Aaron."

"Why not?" I asked.

Jay took over the story with a level of eagerness that was usually reserved for only the best gossip. "A few years back, Price offered Aaron the job of superintendent over at Yarmouth."

I raised my eyebrows. Great Yarmouth was a popular seaside town on the other side of Norfolk – a busy patch, but it was the furthest possible point in the county from here, ninety minutes each way on a good day. Even so, it was a great career opportunity for him.

"Aaron turned it down. He said he didn't want to leave his home patch. He liked being DCI here and he'd rather wait for the superintendent job to come up for this side of the county. So, when Russell retired, we all expected him to take over." Jay grimaced and gave a nervous glance at the office door. "It was Price's way of getting his own back on Aaron for turning down the Yarmouth job. Instead of giving him the job, Price made the role of superintendent temporarily redundant here and essentially made Aaron take on the job without any of the benefits or pay. Aaron's been doing the role of acting superintendent for the sake of keeping this station running."

"That's extremely petty."

Chris shrugged. "That's Price. You don't like his way, tough. He can make life hell until you bend to his will."

"Then what is he talking to Aaron about now?" I asked.

Both Chris and Jay shrugged but neither held an expression of ease at the thought.

"I'm sure it's nothing to worry about," Chris said, but his reassuring words missed their mark. "Aaron knows exactly what Price is like. He does everything he can to keep this station running smoothly and out of Price's interest. He can play him at his own game."

Before Chris could elaborate, a noise from down the corridor silenced us all. Two sets of footsteps walked past the office, heading for the stairs, but only one set of metal clangs signalled someone leaving.

After a few moments, the office door creaked open and Aaron let himself in. He looked none the worse for his meeting with the chief constable, but there were some subtle hints that things had not gone well. His jaw was clenched and he ran a hand over his face, rubbing his eyes.

"What happened?" Jay asked, alert and on guard.

Aaron sighed and waved his hand at him, calming him down. "Nothing. Nothing to worry about."

"You're lying," said Chris.

"It's never just nothing when that tosser shows up," Jay chipped in.

Aaron grimaced at the team. He weighed up a few responses, before settling on one that didn't appear easy to say. "Fine. He's given us six months."

"Six months?" I asked with a frown. "What does that mean?"

"Six months to close the Ali Burgess case," Aaron explained. "Find the killer, no more excuses."

Jay gave a frustrated groan. "Does he even know how impossible that is? What happens after six months?"

I could imagine several possibilities, the most likely being that the case would be given to another team. Chris and Jay would fight tooth and nail for that not to happen. But from their desperate expressions, that couldn't be just it. Losing a case wasn't the end of the world, only a dent to the pride. There was something more.

Aaron inhaled a deep breath. "If the Burgess case isn't closed within six months, Price will disband the Serious Crimes team. You'll all be posted off to different corners of the county. Including me."

## Chapter Thirty-Four

I was fidgeting worse than a guilty man stood before a judge. My cast was making my arm itch and there was no way I could reach it to scratch. The seat was too warm.

The air was too cool. I felt a breeze by my ear, as though someone was breathing down my neck.

"Dear God," Jay said through gritted teeth, "if you don't stop moving, I will kill you."

I froze in place. It must have been really distracting if he was threatening to kill me in a police station.

Across the room, leaning by the door as she sipped a steaming mug of coffee, Maddie laughed at Jay's threat. Chris ignored it all, pretending that everyone's presence was just an inconvenience. I knew why they were all hanging around the office today, dragging their feet rather than getting on with work, and if anything, it made me even more nervous.

In an attempt to distract himself, Jay turned to Maddie. "Have you seen Aaron this morning?"

"No," she said with a frown as she blew across the top of her mug. "Why?"

"There's something different about him," Jay mused. Chris glanced at him, his interest piqued. "He was all laid-back and smiley this morning, despite Price's visit from last week. I wondered if you'd heard anything. Any gossip to explain his good mood."

Maddie put her fingertips to her mouth, hiding her sly grin, and she shot a look across the room at me. "I haven't heard anything but I'll keep an ear out. Maybe there's a new woman on the scene."

Jay's disappointment caused him to sag back into his seat. "Maybe. I thought you were the Queen of Gossip. You notice these things before the rest of us."

"I have limits to my gossiping," said Maddie. "I don't dig into places friends don't want me to dig."

Chris shot her a glare over his shoulder. "Bullshit. You told everyone I was turning fifty, even when I told you not to. Including telling Jay."

Maddie shrugged and gave a devious smirk. "It's a new policy I'm now starting."

The gang was silenced by the sound of footsteps approaching and the door to the office flew open, revealing Aaron in the doorway. In an instance, their light-hearted banter vanished and I remembered why I was edgy.

"Ready for you now," he said, a tight grimace on his face, not quite able to meet my gaze.

I stood up on shaky legs. I purposely hadn't turned my computer on, hadn't made myself comfortable at my desk. I didn't want to tempt fate and have to face the humiliation of potentially having to pack up my belongings and walk shamefully back out the door. With no words of encouragement coming from my teammates or Aaron, I exited the room and made my way down the corridor to his office. I let myself in.

The chairs in the room were rearranged into a cosy formation, facing each other. A woman sat in one, middle-aged with a long face but kind eyes. She tucked her bobbed hair behind her ears as she watched me enter.

"Hi Anna," she said with a soothing voice like a cat's purr. "I'm Gemma, I'm a clinical psychologist. Do you know why we're here today?"

I sat down in the free chair. The sunlight poured through the wide windows, hitting just right to fill me with a warm sensation. I bent my head to shield my eyes from its glare and nodded.

"Psych eval," I said.

Gemma giggled to herself. "You lot always call it that. It's not that rigid. It's just a chat about the recent events, to see how you are after your period off work. A chance to talk through any concerns you have about returning to duty. There might be some adjustments needed or some recommendations I can make to help ease things along. How does that sound?"

I nodded again but clamped my mouth shut, words failing me. I didn't want to be here and my jittery gaze probably told Gemma that.

"So, Anna, let's start with the obvious. How are you?"

"I'm fine, getting there," I said as I shuffled in my seat. I took a pause, weighing up the words. 'Fine, getting there' didn't feel so accurate anymore.

"Actually, I'm good."

An hour later, I left Aaron's office only to find him, Chris, Jay and Maddie all hanging out the door down the corridor, waiting for my return. They hastily dived back inside the room but it was a poor attempt at espionage. I clutched in my hand a piece of paper; not any sort of official report but something I'd persuaded Gemma to write after talking to her for a while. She was amused as she jotted the note down for me.

Inside the Serious Crimes office, the four of them were failing at acting inconspicuously. Jay and Chris were seated again, Aaron had taken my desk. Maddie was back near the door, her coffee mug still in hand but cold and empty. Their heads shot up, searching my face for any hint of how things went. I gave little away, instead pulled my mouth into a tight, grim look and waited for someone to break the silence.

"Well," Jay asked first, unable to help himself. "How did it go? Are you officially back on duty again?"

I held up my prized note, unfolding it slowly in front of me, and turned the paper so the loopy handwriting faced them.

*Anna McArthur is not crazy.*

The End

If you enjoyed this book, please let others know by leaving a quick review on Amazon. Also, if you spot anything untoward in the paperback, get in touch. We strive for the best quality and appreciate reader feedback.

editor@thebookfolks.com

www.thebookfolks.com

## More books in this series

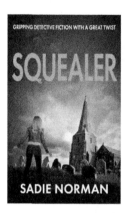

**SQUEALER**
**(book 2)**

Hot on the heels of the ex-husband of a murdered woman, rookie Norfolk detective Ann "Crazy" McArthur must penetrate the wall of a close-knit, churchgoing community to find the truth about the crime. If she does, she might win the respect of her colleagues. But can she keep a cool head, and her complicated love life under wraps?

*FREE with Kindle Unlimited and available in paperback!*

**Other titles of interest**

**WE WERE SEEN**
**by Mark West**

A professional woman who is opposing the development of a golf course on a local nature site finds her life falling into turmoil when someone begins to blackmail her with compromising photographs. Will she succumb to their demands or can she deliver the extorter into the arms of the law?

*FREE with Kindle Unlimited and available in paperback!*

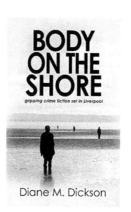

**BODY ON THE SHORE**
**by Diane M. Dickson**

When police retrieve a body from the flat sands of a popular beach, DI Jordan Carr is presented with his first murder case. The victim is a woman, but they know little more about her. Tracing the events that led to her death will take the detective on an uncomfortable journey into the dark side of Liverpool.

*FREE with Kindle Unlimited and available in paperback!*

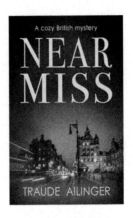

**NEAR MISS**
**by Traude Ailinger**

Almost hit by a car, fashion journalist Amy Thornton visits the driver who ends up in hospital after evading her. She soon becomes convinced she's unveiled a murder plot. But it won't be easy to persuade grumpy Scottish detective DI Russell McCord who is not happy about a young woman telling him how to do his job. Even if she seems better at it!

*FREE with Kindle Unlimited and available in paperback!*

*Sign up to our mailing list to find out about new releases
and special offers!*

**www.thebookfolks.com**